# PREVAIL

## Book 2 of The Pike Chronicles

# G.P. Hudson

### © 2015

ISBN-13: 978-1542904797
ISBN-10: 154290479X

Cover art by Justin Adams

# Also By G.P. Hudson

To join my email list
and be notified of new releases go to

**http://gphudson.com**

Subscribers get lower prices on new releases
no spam

# Chapter 1

"He's a bit of a mystery, our passenger, don't you think?" said Milo, Captain Seiben's nephew. "He just sits in that life pod of his all day long, never saying more than two words to anyone. What do you think he's up to?"

"I don't know and I don't care," said Captain Seiben, tiring of his nephew's questions. "His affairs are his own business. Soon as we get to the station he'll be off this ship and it'll be the last we'll hear from him. Mr. Jansen can figure it out."

"What do you think he'll do?"

"Mr. Jansen?"

"Yeah."

"Not sure. I don't involve myself in his affairs, and I suggest you don't either. I'll tell you what, he's always got a plan that man."

"What do you think his plan will be for our passenger?"

"Not my concern."

"What do you think he's hiding in that life pod?"

"You sure ask a lot of damn questions."

"He won't let anybody go in there. Must be something important. Maybe something valuable." Milo's eyes were full of urgency, like he saw some master plan unfolding before him.

"Maybe you need to concentrate more on your duties and less on the stranger."

Captain Seiben brought both hands to his face and rubbed his eyes. He just wanted to focus on his job and forget the stranger, but his nephew was making it impossible. What would Mr. Jansen say about the whole thing anyway? He was only supposed to carry freight, not pick up passengers. If this angered Mr. Jansen he might give the long hauls to someone else.

"And he eats a lot. He's always taking extra food. Do you think he's got someone else in there?"

"Can you just focus on your job? When was the last time you checked your scans?"

Milo nodded and looked at his console, focusing on one of the displays.

"Uncle..."

"That's Captain to you."

"Sorry, Captain, I am picking something up on my scans."

"I don't care about any more space garbage. We're not picking anything else up."

"It isn't space garbage. It's a ship and it's on an intercept course with us."

"Goddammit. Can you identify them?"

"Oh no..."

"Nephew?"

"They're raiders, uncle. Raiders!"

"Raiders? How far are they? Can we outrun them?"

"No, Sir. They're too fast. Even if we try to run at our top speed, they'll still catch us."

# Chapter 2

"Contact picked up through freighter's scans, Captain," said the AI.

"Can you identify?" said Jon Pike, studying the screen.

When Jon first came on board the freighter, he had the AI hack into its systems so that there wouldn't be any surprises. That gave him access to all the ship's data. The AI could monitor their scans and sensors, as well as communications.

"Yes, Captain. They are being referred to as raiders, and are considered hostile."

"Do these people have any hope of escaping?"

"Unlikely, Captain. The contact is a much faster design and will eventually catch the freighter, even if they run. Extrapolating from this information, they will likely board and seize the freighter along with its cargo."

"Does the crew have any means of defending themselves?"

"No, Captain. This is a merchant vessel with limited defense capabilities."

Jon sighed. He couldn't allow these raiders to take control of the ship. He had to get involved. He just didn't want to.

"Thank you AI. Please feed updates on the situation to my comm."

"Yes, Captain."

Jon stood from his pilot's chair, holstered his rail gun, and left the lifeboat.

# Chapter 3

A loud clanging sound echoed throughout the freighter as the raider ship attempted to dock. Captain Seiben clenched his armrests, his anxiety increasing with every sound. With any luck they would get through this unharmed. He hoped Mr. Jansen would pay the ransom. That's all these raiders wanted anyway. A quick score and then they'd be on their way. Sure they could take the freighter, but they would need to find a way to move its cargo. It could be done, but a ransom is always the easier, less bloody option.

His nephew looked at him with nervous eyes. He could tell the kid was trying to hold it together. It was his first long haul run, and he had never had to deal with raiders before.

"It's okay," said Seiben. "Just don't cause any trouble and we'll be okay."

"Are you sure?"

"All they're interested in is profit." He tried to sound reassuring. "Do you think there is any profit in killing us?

"But I've heard stories of them slaughtering entire freighter crews." Milo looked like he would fall apart at any moment.

"Look," said Seiben, his voice stern. "Those people tried to be heroes and that's what got them killed. If you just stand aside and don't challenge them they'll leave us alone. Once Mr. Jansen pays their ransom they'll leave."

"What if he doesn't pay?"

"He'll pay. The cargo and the freighter are worth more than the ransom. The raiders don't want to take the ship. They just want to be paid to leave us alone. That's all. Mr. Jansen knows this. It's just a cost of doing business."

The kid didn't look convinced, but he hoped he would hold on long enough for them to get through this.

The clanging stopped and he knew they were through. It wouldn't be long until they reached the bridge. He wished his ship had more sophisticated internal sensors so that he could monitor their movements, but he knew it wouldn't change the outcome either way. The rest of the crew was experienced enough that they should know how to behave. Still, he had to be sure. He tapped his console a few times and a grizzled face appeared.

"Rutger," said Seiben. "The raiders are on board."

"Yeah, that's what it sounds like."

"You and the twins know not to cause any trouble?"

"I'm not ready to leave this life just yet, Captain."

"The twins?"

"I'll bust their heads open if they try anything."

Seiben smiled. He believed the old engineer could do it too. "Good. We'll get past this in no time."

Rutger nodded and his face disappeared from the console.

"What if our passenger makes trouble?" said Milo.

"What?"

"Our passenger. He doesn't look like the type that stands by and lets things happen."

Seiben glared at his nephew. He hadn't considered their mysterious passenger in all this. For once, he was afraid his nephew was right. He was obviously a military man, and he was armed.

"Do you think he'll make trouble, uncle?"

Seiben looked back at Milo, trying to keep the worry off his face. "I don't think so, nephew," he lied.

Seiben heard the door slide open behind him and swiveled his chair around to see several weapons pointed at him. He counted five disheveled looking men. They all wore pieces of body armor, some on their torsos, some on their arms, others on their legs. Only one had what looked like full body armor on, including helmet and visor. Seiben assumed he must be the leader. The man stood his ground while the rest of his men fanned out, flanking Seiben and Milo on both sides.

Seiben didn't want there to be any misunderstanding and slowly raised his hands. Milo followed his uncle's lead.

The leader stepped up to Seiben, his weapon still pointed at him.

"Are you the Captain of this vessel?" said the leader.

"Y-yes," said Seiben.

"Not anymore. This is my ship now."

Seiben nodded in agreement, trying to keep himself from trembling. Looking into that black visor he could see his reflection, and the fear on his face. Fear was good, he thought. It wasn't a challenge. The worst thing he could do right now was challenge this man.

"You will communicate with your employer and tell him that this ship has been taken. You will then instruct him to transfer one million credits to a designated account. If your employer does so, you will have your ship, and your lives. Fail and you forfeit both. Understood?"

"Yes, understood."

# Chapter 4

Despite its massive proportions, there wasn't much usable space inside the freighter, as cargo took up most of the ship's capacity. Jon knew the bandits would search the ship, so he decided to wait in the hangar bay until the first ones showed up. He sat perched on an upper level catwalk, giving him a clear view of everything below, including the lifeboat.

He didn't have to wait long. Two bandits appeared on the lower level, walking through the doors with their weapons ready. They scanned the large room, pointing their weapons left and right, then looked up at the catwalks. They scanned slowly and carefully, but didn't see Jon.

He sat and waited for them to become confident enough to enter the cavernous room. Soon they let their guards down and started to explore, walking around more freely, inspecting everything to see if there was anything of use or value.

Jon continued to watch from above. They were undisciplined. Simple criminals with no military training. They probably didn't need much training to prey on these merchant freighters. What made it worse was that they were also human. It disgusted Jon to think of humans preying on each other like this. Still, he felt a pang of regret about what he knew he had to do. When one of the bandits approached the lifeboat, any second thoughts were gone.

Jon fired one shot. The bandit's head blew apart, his blood speckling the side of the lifeboat. The second bandit wheeled around in response, but had no chance. Before he could pull the trigger on his weapon Jon let loose a second shot, which pierced the top of his head. The force of the bullet drove the man into the ground. He lay there on his back, eyes open, and for a moment Jon almost swore the man looked right at him.

He knew he didn't have long so he rushed down to the main level. The men seemed relatively young, probably in their mid-twenties. They looked like they hadn't changed their clothes in weeks. They also didn't seem to care for personal grooming. Each had a full beard and long matted hair.

He picked up one of the weapons and examined it. He hadn't seen the design before but could tell that it was an energy weapon. He checked their clothes for anything useful, but found nothing.

He took each bandit and moved their bodies away from the lifeboat and behind some heavy machinery. Walking back he eyed the pool of blood on the floor. There wasn't much he could do about it. He had to move. He knew that most of the activity would be on the bridge, so he needed to head in that direction.

Jon had downloaded and studied the ship's schematics, and committed its plans to memory. Accessing that knowledge, he walked down the corridor looking for an access panel. He found one quickly, opened the metal door, and climbed into an engineering conduit. A maze of conduits crisscrossed the ship, but Jon knew the direction to the bridge. The confines of the conduit, however, forced him down onto the cold hard floor. He had to crawl on his forearms and knees to make any progress.

It was clear the freighter was an aging ship by the state of disrepair. He kept ducking his head and twisting sideways to avoid hanging wires. Electrocution wasn't part of the plan. A rancid chemical smell filled the conduit. Stale dusty air clung to his throat. He held back the urge to cough, afraid that an echo might alert the bandits. It was warmer than the rest of the ship. Beads of sweat dripped off his brow into his eyes. He ignored the annoyance and steadily pulled himself through the tunnel.

He would exit just outside the entrance to the bridge. How many more raiders were there? He hoped the element of surprise would give him enough of an edge to take all the raiders out before they killed any of the crew. The last thing he wanted was more innocent blood on his hands.

When Jon reached the exit he listened first, trying to determine if anyone stood in the corridor before opening the panel. When he didn't hear anything, he opened the panel and quietly dropped to the floor of the corridor. The bridge was just around the corner directly in front of him.

Jon inched closer, careful not to make a sound, one foot stepping carefully after another. He brought his forearm up to his head and wiped the sweat off his brow onto his sleeve. He had nearly made it to the corner, when a bandit came around and almost bumped into him. The bandit's eyes widened and his hands moved fast, raising his weapon to fire point blank at Jon.

Jon was faster. He let off a single round which made a hole the size of a pebble going into the man's forehead, and the size of a fist coming out the back. The gunshot might as well have been an explosion, breaking the silence and any hope Jon had of surprise.

# Chapter 5

The sound of the gunshot was unmistakable. Seiben instantly knew who pulled the trigger. None of his crew would risk firing on the raiders. It had to be their passenger. He quietly cursed his nephew for convincing him to bring the lifeboat on board.

The raider leader stood close and moved without hesitation. He seized Seiben by the throat and rammed his weapon into his cheek. The force of the impact made Seiben's head snap back violently. The raider held him there, his head pushed all the way back, sending spikes of pain down the back of his neck.

"Do you want to die?" said the leader in a low voice that was almost a growl.

"No," said Seiben, hearing the fear in his own voice.

"Who's out there?"

"It's not one of my men. I swear it."

"Then who?"

"I don't know who he is. We found a life pod and brought it on board. He was in it."

"Just him?"

"I think so."

The raider increased the pressure on Seiben's throat, making him gag.

"I don't know. He won't let anyone in the life pod."

The leader studied Seiben, his expression hidden behind the helmet's visor. Then he tapped his communicator and spoke to one of his men.

"Go to the hangar bay. There's a life pod there. Take a good look and make sure nobody is hiding inside."

The leader turned his attention to the doorway. Two of his men were flanking it, weapons drawn. The fourth raider pointed his weapon at Seiben's nephew.

The leader shouted at the doorway. "You're outnumbered. We know you're out there. You have no chance. Give yourself up and we won't kill you."

No answer.

"We have hostages. We will kill them."

Still no answer.

Seiben trembled. He tried to control himself, but the fear was too powerful. He knew the raider wasn't bluffing. They would think nothing of killing the entire crew. Even if the stranger gave himself up they would likely kill everybody anyway, just to set an example.

An instant later Seiben had doubled over, his hands clenching his ears. The leader had let go of his throat and raised his hand to his helmet. If anything was said, Seiben couldn't hear it. He couldn't hear anything.

The stranger streaked onto the bridge. His movements were a blur, but Seiben could see his weapon firing, even if he couldn't hear the shots. He saw the men on either side of the doorway drop. A split second later the leader hit the floor, a hole in the center of his visor. Seiben turned to look for his nephew and saw Milo and the raider on the floor amidst a growing pool of blood. Had Milo been shot? But Milo was moving, clenching his hands to his ears. The blood belonged to the raider.

He turned to see the stranger approach him. He was saying something, but Seiben couldn't hear it. The stranger pointed to his ears and gestured with his hands in a way that seemed to say his hearing would come back. Seiben wanted to shout at the man, to tell him how stupid he was to put all their lives at risk. He held back, though, deciding he'd rather hear himself do it.

# Chapter 6

The raider entered the hangar bay, weapon at the ready, finger on the trigger. The life pod sat at the far end. There was a pool of blood on the floor, and blood on the side of the vessel. His heart beat faster, pounding against his ribs. He scanned the room looking for threats, but found nothing. He advanced slowly on the life pod.

The raider covered half the distance to the life pod without incident. He stopped when he reached the pool of blood. Someone had been shot here. The thought made him feel very exposed. He looked up to the catwalks, pointing his weapon and visually sweeping the upper levels. If he wanted to ambush someone that was where he would wait.

Again he didn't see anyone. He looked back down at the pool of blood. Whoever had been killed here was careless. He had a feeling that it was his men. Two had been sent in this direction. They likely stood like idiots out in the open, when they should have taken the upper levels first and made sure there were no snipers.

He knew that made him an idiot as well, but the boss said the life pod was the threat, so that was the priority. Besides, if someone had still been up there, they would have taken him out already.

He moved forward again, still scanning the catwalks, weapon ready to fire on anything that moved up there. By the time he reached the life pod he felt satisfied that he was alone. Only one question remained, was there anybody inside the vessel?

The design was unfamiliar. He had never seen the markings before. It looked to be a military craft. But who's military? It certainly did not belong to this region of space.

He stepped up to the hatch. It was closed, but had obviously been forced open. He stood to the side of the hatch, reached out and pulled. The door swung open with a moan, but nothing else. No weapon fire. No sound of any kind.

He inched closer to the opening and peeked from the side, careful not to expose himself. Still nothing. Inside was total darkness. He gripped his weapon tighter and took several deep breaths to calm his nerves. He had to get inside. There was only one way to do it, fast and hard. He would rush in and shoot anything that moved.

He prepared to charge, took a few more breaths and nodded to himself. He would go in on the count of three.

One.

Two.

Three.

He pushed off and bolted into the dark opening.

The bullet hit just below his collar bone, spinning him around and backwards. He landed on his stomach, just outside the life pod. His entire right side on fire. He heard footsteps behind him and groped for his weapon, but he had lost it when he fell. He used his last bit of strength and struggled to push himself onto his back.

He looked up and saw a dark haired woman standing over him. She had a cold, deadly look in her eyes and held a weapon in her hands. Without a word she raised the weapon, pointed it at his head, and fired.

# Chapter 7

Chief Engineer Rajneesh Singh ran through the Hermes corridors, desperate to reach the bridge. The abandon ship announcement mingled with the furious sound of firefights. Everything was falling apart.

He pushed against throngs of crewmembers heading the other way, trying to get to the lifeboats. Lynda had not responded to any of his messages since her last comm. The last thing she had said to him was, "I'm sorry." Then the Hermes crash landed. The violent landing had thrown him several meters. He could only imagine what had happened to Lynda on the bridge.

He kept repeating her last words in his head. What was she sorry about? He had never heard that tone in her voice before. The words were spoken with a profound sadness that made his chest tighten.

It had angered him when she volunteered to serve on the Hermes. He had tried to break their relationship off, but knew he wasn't strong enough to stay away. The Hermes assignment was supposed to solve that problem. Yet she insisted on following him there. Her belief that they belonged together was unshakable, despite his weakness.

In truth he was afraid of his feelings for her. He didn't understand it. Now that she was all he could think about, he didn't know why he ever tried to end things. He couldn't imagine a life without her.

When he first reached the bridge, he didn't see her. The room was completely abandoned and he thought, with some relief, that she had left with everyone else. Then he saw her broken body wrapped around a console.

"Lynda!" he cried, and ran to her. He felt her neck for a pulse. Nothing. He moved his fingers around, in case he made a mistake. Still no pulse. She was dead. The realization overwhelmed him. His legs gave way. He collapsed onto her lifeless body and wept.

"I'm sorry," he said. "I'm so sorry." He looked deep into her empty blue eyes and said, "I'm going to fix this. I'm going to make it right. You'll see." He lifted her into his arms and stroked her hair.

"Why would they leave you here? Why didn't anyone help you? It doesn't matter. I'm here now. I'll save you."

He looked around frantically, not sure what he hoped to find. He spotted the open weapons locker, as the abandon ship announcement repeated over the speakers.

"I'm going to get you out of here, Lynda. We're going to get through this."

He picked up her dead body and threw her over his shoulder in a fireman carry. He turned and headed for the exit, but first stopped at the weapons locker and picked up a railgun.

He needed to make it to the lifeboats, and he didn't have any time to spare. Carrying Lynda slowed him down considerably. She felt much heavier than he expected and he whispered, "Lynda, I know you're hurt, but you have to help me a little so we can make it to the lifeboats in time." Lynda's corpse didn't answer. "Never mind. You just rest and get your strength. I'll get us there."

Turning a corner he came upon two Kemmar soldiers who immediately opened fire. He ducked back behind the corner. He stood there for a moment, breathing heavily, unsure of what to do. His mind cleared and he knew he had no other option. He had no time to spare.

Lunging out from his hiding spot he charged the Kemmar, firing his railgun at both of them. They fired back, but Singh's resolve was too powerful. He sprayed both with railgun fire as he charged. For a moment the soldiers seemed confused by his fearlessness. That was all the hesitation he needed. Several rounds shattered the visor of one Kemmar, then the other. Both dropped at Singh's feet. He stepped over them without a second look and continued for the lifeboats.

When he arrived at the hangar, the rest of the crew had already boarded. Every one of them was safe, even while Lynda, their XO, lay dying on the bridge. All they cared about was their own safety. It disgusted him. He searched for a lifeboat, but each one seemed full. No extra room. Sorry.

He was about to lose all hope when the last lifeboat was empty. He rushed inside and set Lynda down. His hand felt wet. He looked down to see it was covered in blood. Had he been shot? No, he had no wounds. His stomach dropped as the realization struck him. Bending down he pulled Lynda foreword so he could examine her. There was a large wound in the center of her back. She had been shot by the Kemmar.

Singh carefully set Lynda on the floor and seized the first aid kit. He poured a gelatinous substance onto her wound and it spread out, filling every crevice.

At that moment the lifeboat launched with all the others. Singh didn't need to look at the instruments to know that an FTL bubble had formed around the vessel. He heard the faint hum. But he had no interest. He stared at Lynda's dead body, tears filling his eyes.

"You keep getting hurt. None of this should have happened to you. It's all their fault. I don't know why they left you, but they will pay. You'll see."

It was then that he made a solemn vow.

"I swear to you, Lynda, all those who left you to die will pay. Captain Pike will pay. Space Force will pay."

# Chapter 8

The Kemmar warship had no way of capturing all the lifeboats. It focused on one and gave chase. Even at FTL speeds it had no trouble keeping up. As it bridged the gap between them, the Kemmar ship fired an ion cannon, disabling the smaller craft's FTL bubble.

When both ships came to a stop, several smaller vessels sped out of the large warship and raced towards the tiny pod. Once in range the Kemmar vessels fired grappling arms at the lifeboat, seized it, and returned to the warship with it in tow.

When the tiny craft was secured, Kemmar soldiers quickly surrounded it, energy weapons at the ready. A large bot rolled up to the lifeboat. It had arms with large claw shaped instrument on the ends. The bot went to work on the hatch and ripped it open with little effort. Several soldiers rushed in and found two occupants, a male holding a clearly dead female in his arms. The male stroked the female's hair as he whispered into her ear.

The Kemmar soldiers seized the male, hoisting him up by his arms. As they dragged him away he yelled, "Don't hurt her. She needs a doctor. She needs a doctor!"

"It's ok Raj"

Singh couldn't believe his ears. His head spun around and there, walking beside him, was Lynda. He looked back at her body lying on the floor of the lifeboat and then looked beside him. Still there.

"How can this be?" he asked the apparition.

"Don't worry, Raj," said Wolfe. "I'm here now. That's all that matters."

"I thought I lost you."

"I'll never leave you, Raj."

"They all left you on the bridge to die. None of them helped you."

"Yes they did. And they're going to pay, Raj. Together we're going to make them pay."

# Chapter 9

Security Chief Kevin St. Clair stared at the Kemmar interrogator. They had pumped him full of drugs and questioned him relentlessly for days. He wasn't sure how many. They took shifts, making sure he didn't get any sleep. The counter agents in his blood stream did their job for the most part, and mitigated the effects of the Kemmar drugs. But the sleep deprivation was getting to him. His eyes felt like stone curtains, his arms and legs like cement. The fatigue wore on his mind, too. He earned repeated blows from the interrogator for losing focus, not hearing questions, forgetting what was said.

They had tortured him, preferring electric shock to tender parts of his body. The voltage seared through his body like burning lava coursing through his veins. The stench of his own burning flesh made him retch causing terrible stomach cramps. Each time he thought he would break. Each time he thought he couldn't take it anymore. But he could, and he did. They couldn't break him. He was too stubborn. He was pretty sure they knew it, too.

Despite the grogginess, Kevin sensed that there was something different today. Now that he saw the Kemmar more regularly, and without their combat suits, he hoped he had a better read on them.

They were nasty looking creatures. Their bodies were covered with thick orange hair, like fur. The same thick hair covered their big round heads, including their faces. It made it difficult to see their eyes, which were nothing more than slits. The small nose seemed out of place on the massive head. It twitched constantly. How strong was their sense of smell? Below the nose was a savage looking mouth which revealed rows of razor sharp teeth every time they spoke.

Today his interrogator bared his teeth at Kevin. He had seen them show their teeth before and deduced that it was a sign of dominance, maybe even aggression. But even then it was only for a few moments, after which they would close their mouths. Today the interrogator bared his teeth and left them that way, giving Kevin a real good look. There were three rows of teeth on the top and three rows on the bottom. Vicious looking things. Each tooth was narrow and pointy, and looked like it could tear the toughest material into tatters. He couldn't count them but thought there must be hundreds of those things in its mouth.

"You smiling at me?" said Kevin. "Want to be friends now?"

The interrogator looked back at him without responding, teeth still on display.

"Keep smiling you ugly fuck. One day soon I'm gonna fix that smile for you."

The interrogator spoke in a low growling tone. They used a translator that had quickly analyzed Kevin's speech and language, facilitating communication.

The interrogator said, "You believe you have power, even now when all is lost. You make threats with no hope of fulfilling them. Do they help you endure?"

"Sure. I know your time is coming. You just wait and see."

"Unfortunately for you, that time is not today. I have something special planned instead."

"You hitting on me now? I knew you were weird but this is messed up, even for you, don't you think?"

The interrogator barked a command and a door opened. Two Kemmar soldiers escorted one of the Marines, Private Denney, into the room. Denney was naked. He had restraints on his wrists and ankles, forcing him to shuffle along rather than walk. They pulled him hard causing him to trip, and when he did they beat him with batons. He had been hit by those things before and knew they carried an electric shock with each blow. Denney dropped and writhed on the ground. The guards kicked him a couple of times and lifted him to his feet again. The shuffling continued. When they reached the middle of the room a cable dropped from the ceiling. The two Kemmar attached it to Denney's wrist restraints and it retracted, pulling his arms up over his head and then his whole body until his feet no longer touched the ground.

"Chief, what the fuck are they doing?" said Denney, clearly starting to panic. They could take the beatings. That was simple. Sooner or later the beating would end, or you would be dead. Either way it would be over. The anticipation of torture was another matter entirely. Stringing up Denney like that, making him wonder what was coming next, was the worst part. That was when your fear spiked. The unknown was the worst torture of all.

"They're just trying to scare you," said Kevin. "Remember your training."

"His training will not help him," said the interrogator. "The only thing that will help him is you. Tell me about your ship. How does it travel such great distances?"

"Don't tell him anything, Chief," said Denney. "Don't worry about me."

The interrogator turned to Denney and said, "Your Chief will worry about you. He will worry a great deal."

"Let him go you piece of shit," said Kevin.

"You do not wish to answer my questions?"

"Go fuck yourself."

"That is an unfortunate response," said the interrogator, baring his rows of sharp teeth again. He then turned and prowled up to Denney, growling.

"Get the fuck away from me," said Denney, kicking out with both feet at the interrogator, who sidestepped the blow.

Kevin strained against his own restraints, trying desperately to get to him. His muscles burned with the effort and the restraints dug into his wrists, but he couldn't break free.

Denney kicked again. This time the interrogator caught his legs and bit down on Denney's left thigh, ripping off a chunk of flesh and muscle. He let go of Denney's legs and they swung back, hanging uselessly from his hips. The bite had left a large, hideous wound in Denney's thigh. Blood gushed out of it in heaving spasms. Worse than the wound was Denney's screams, their effect more fearsome than any torture. The interrogator turned, blood dripping off the hairs on his face, and let Kevin watch as he chewed and swallowed.

"You sick bastard," said Kevin, unable to watch the horrific display any longer.

"Will you answer my questions now, or will I finish my meal?"

Kevin clenched his teeth and remained silent, looking away from the gruesome sight. "I'm sorry," he whispered to Denney, tears streaking down his cheeks.

"Good. I prefer it this way," said the interrogator.

He turned and bit down again, tearing another chunk out of Denney's thigh. Denney continued to scream in terror while the interrogator chewed. The interrogator took one more bite, then looked at the two Kemmar guards and nodded. The two fell upon Denney with snarls, tearing off fresh slabs of flesh with their teeth.

Denney eventually stopped screaming. Kevin hoped that he was dead. Hoped that he wouldn't have to endure anymore pain. But he couldn't look at the horrid scene to confirm it. He couldn't block out their grunts and growls though. Nor could he block the slapping sound of their chewing, and gulping. All along he continued to beg Denney for forgiveness.

The Kemmar took their time with the body, eating their fill. Every once in a while he heard the snapping sound of breaking bone, followed by slurping as the marrow was sucked out. When they were done they let Kevin sit alone for a few hours, with Private Denney's mutilated body lying at his feet. He had thought that the anticipation of torture was the worst, but he was wrong. There was nothing worse than this. As the shock of what had happened faded, Kevin focused on only one thought.

Escape.

His mind cleared and he focused on getting his men out of this nightmare. He thought about the interrogator and the guards. None wore combat suits. They were large creatures, and they looked strong, but Kevin didn't think they could hold up against a Marine in hand to hand combat. Their only real advantage was their teeth, and those shouldn't be too hard to evade.

The Kemmar hadn't realized that Space Force had pumped each Marine full of counter agents to offset the effect of drugs an enemy might use, which was an advantage. If they thought the Marines were drugged up they would lower their guard some more, like they did with the combat suits. They needed to be ready to take advantage of any opportunity. Time was running out.

# Chapter 10

Kevin inched his way down the long hallway, a guard just a step behind him. The restraints on his ankles made walking almost impossible. On both sides of him were prison cells, Marines in all of them. He hadn't seen any sign of the Reivers. Were any still alive?

Relief washed over him when he saw Sergeant Henderson. During the attack on the prison, he thought Henderson and his men had been killed. The Kemmar had captured Kevin with an EMP weapon. They must have captured Henderson's team the same way.

Henderson stood when he saw Kevin and walked up to the bars. He looked healthy enough. Still strong. His eyes fierce. He was like a caged tiger. The two made eye contact and Kevin said two words, "Be ready."

That was more than enough to get a reaction from the guard. He punched Kevin in the back of the head making him fall onto the cold, hard floor. He tried to get up, but the guard hit him with his baton. Like the other batons, this one carried a powerful electric charge. Kevin collapsed.

"Chief? You ok?" said Henderson, concern and anger mixing in his voice.

"I'm ok," Kevin gasped. He tried to move but the guard clubbed him again sending voltage through his body like a burning pitchfork. He fell back down onto the floor, his teeth clenched together, body convulsing.

"Leave him alone, you son of a bitch," yelled Henderson, his powerful hands gripping the bars of his cell.

The guard swung at Henderson, but Henderson pulled his hands back and the baton harmlessly hit the cell's bars. He growled at Henderson, baring his teeth. He looked down at Kevin and said, "Get up."

Kevin lay on the floor trying to catch his breath, but was winded and could barely move. The guard swung a powerful kick into his ribs.

"Get up," the guard snarled.

This time Kevin moved his arms quicker, trying to avoid another heavy boot to the ribs. He pushed himself to get up until he stood at his full height. He looked down at the guard who threatened to hit him with the baton again, and wondered how much pressure he would need to snap his neck.

He resumed shuffling along until he reached his cell. The guard touched his belt and the door opened. He shoved Kevin from behind causing him to fall to the floor again. He hit the ground hard, the restraints preventing him from getting his hands up to break his fall. He did manage to turn his face and avoided losing any teeth, or breaking his nose again. Closing the door, the guard touched his belt and the restraints slackened, allowing Kevin to free his arms and legs. Kevin forced himself to stand up, walked to the bars and watched the guard as he left. He rubbed his wrists and reminded himself to be patient. The right opportunity would present itself soon enough.

# Chapter 11

Kevin was actually allowed to sleep for the first time in days. It wasn't a full night's sleep, but it was something. When he finally woke he went over the previous day in his mind. The Kemmar weren't going to stop until they got what they wanted. They were changing tactics. He feared he would have to endure the slaughter of another of his men.

The guard showed up again that morning with another Kemmar who Kevin started referring to as the doctor. He would pump Kevin full of drugs every morning. If he was a smart doctor he would've realized his drugs weren't having any effect on Kevin. But he was clearly complacent and just assumed that they worked. Kevin was human, just like the Reivers, and the drugs worked on them without a problem. Same species, same results. Only the Reivers didn't have a bloodstream full of Space Force counter agents.

Kevin played the role of the drugged prisoner convincingly enough. That was part of the trick. The counter agents allowed him to feel enough of the drug's effects to modify his behavior appropriately. He played the role, and the Kemmar bought the act.

The guard escorted him back to the interrogation room. Walking down the hall he made eye contact with each Marine as he passed their cell. They all nodded at him, letting him know that they were ready to follow his lead. When they reached the end of the hall the guard touched his belt and the door opened. Kevin wondered how many doors that belt opened.

They arrived at the interrogation room, and the door opened. As they walked in, Kevin noticed the interrogator first, but what he saw next stopped him in his tracks. Sitting in a chair in front of the interrogator was Chief Engineer Singh.

The interrogator looked at Kevin and bared his teeth in a way that Kevin recognized. He was happy. The interrogator said, "The most remarkable thing has happened since we spoke yesterday. One of our ships arrived and delivered a surprising visitor." The interrogator turned to Singh. "What is your rank and name?"

"Chief Engineer Rajneesh Singh."

"What is the name of your ship?"

"The Hermes."

"And where is the Hermes now?"

"The Hermes was destroyed."

Destroyed? The word hit Kevin like a kick to the stomach. How could that be possible?

"Where are the rest of your crew?"

"I don't know. The lifeboats all scattered in different directions."

So the crew might still be alive. But they could be anywhere.

"How did the Hermes travel such enormous distances?"

"It used an experimental propulsion system that allowed it to fold space."

"Singh!" said Kevin. The guard hit him with his baton and Kevin went down. The guard bludgeoned him two more times. Kevin convulsed as the electricity surged through him.

Singh stared back at him, expressionless. He showed no sign of empathy whatsoever. What happened to him?

"What planet are you from?" said the interrogator.

"Earth," said Singh.

"Will you show us where this Earth is?"

"Yes."

"And will you show us how to build this propulsion system?"

"Yes."

"Why?"

"Because they must pay. They all must pay."

# Chapter 12

"Are you crazy?" said Seiben, the vein in his temple bulging so much Jon thought the man might have a stroke. "Do you have any idea who these people are? They could've killed all of us without a second thought."

"They didn't," said Jon, wishing his translator was malfunctioning.

"They could have," yelled Seiben. "You're a stranger here. You don't know anything about us. All the raiders wanted was their ransom. Once they got it they would have let us go."

"Well, I saved you some money."

"You didn't save me anything. I wasn't going to pay their ransom, Mr. Jansen was. The only thing I could've lost was my life."

Jon glanced over at the twins who were cleaning up the blood in the hangar bay. "Who is this Mr. Jansen?"

"Mr. Jansen owns this ship."

"So you all work for him?" said Jon.

"Most people work for him. He would've paid the ransom, so you risked our lives for nothing."

"The raiders were an unacceptable threat," said Jon, looking at Breeah who stood silently behind him.

"Yes, of course. And when were you going to tell me that you weren't alone?"

"It wasn't your concern." Seiben's tone was starting grate on Jon's nerve.

"This is my ship!"

"This is Mr. Jansen's ship. You said so yourself."

Seiben glared at Jon. "I should never have rescued your vessel. Is there anybody else with you?"

Jon looked at Breeah again who nodded yes. "There is a little girl with us. Breeah's daughter."

Seiben's face softened. "You have a child with you?"

"Yes."

"Is that all? No pets I should know about?"

"Funny." At least sarcasm was an improvement.

Seiben sighed and some of the tension in his shoulders eased.

"Why wouldn't you tell me you had a child on board?"

"Again, not your concern."

"That vessel is no place for a child. Hell, this freighter is no place for a child. But until we get to the station it's all we have, so you might as well let the girl out. Let her run around a bit."

Jon frowned at Seiben, but didn't respond.

"Look, I'm not going to condemn someone for protecting a child. You should've been honest with us."

"I don't know you."

"Of course. I understand. But really, you should let the child come out of that tiny vessel. There's lots of room here in the hangar bay and even the rest of the ship."

Seiben seemed to be sincere. Regardless, he wasn't a threat. He was also right. Anki did need to get out of the lifeboat and get some exercise.

"You're right. Just remember, Breeah and I are very protective when it comes to the child."

"I don't think anybody will question that here."

Jon gestured to Breeah and she called her daughter. Anki stepped out of the lifeboat and came to Breeah's side. Instantly a smile spread across Seiben's face.

"Hello little one," said Seiben. "What's your name?"

"Anki."

"That's a pretty name. How old are you, Anki?"

"Seven."

"Seven! You're a big girl, aren't you?"

Anki nodded yes.

Seiben let out a loud belly laugh. "I bet you want to stretch out and have some fun. There's lots of room in here to play. Just don't touch any of the equipment."

Anki looked up at Breeah, silently asking her if she could explore the hanger bay. Breeah nodded yes. Anki took off like a tornado.

Seiben looked back at Jon and Breeah, still smiling, and said, "She's ok to play in here. She can even explore the ship if she likes. Some areas will have to be off limits, but most of the ship is safe enough." Seiben's eyes moistened as he watched Anki playing. "I have two girls myself, one the same age as Anki. I can't wait to see them again."

Jon thought of his own two little girls. One had been Anki's age when they died. Ancient, buried pain tried to surface, but Jon caught it in time and suppressed it.

"It must be hard to leave them for such long periods of time," said Breeah.

"It is," said Seiben. He looked at Jon and said, "I don't know what you people have been through, and it looks like a lot. But you're lucky that you are all together. There's nothing more important than family."

Jon nodded but wanted to change the subject. "Tell me more about this station you are taking us to."

"Ah yes, the station. For us the station is home."

"You live in a space station?"

"Yes, we all do. There are close to a million people living there."

"So this station is more of a city than a space station."

"Yes, that's right. Why? What did you think it was?"

"I assumed it was some sort of commercial facility."

"Oh, it's that too. The station is a major trading hub for this sector."

Jon nodded slowly, "It sounds like an interesting place."

"That's one way of describing it." Seiben looked back at Anki playing, "She's having fun. She'll like it at the station. There are lots of things for her to do there."

# Chapter 13

"Do you think these are the lost colonies your people have been looking for?" said Breeah. She wanted to understand where they were and what would happen next.

"I don't know. Most of the information we had on the colonies was lost during the Juttari occupation. Up until I was assigned to the Hermes, I thought it was all just a legend. Something you told children when they were scared." Jon's eyes took on a faraway look, like he was lost in some distant memory. "The idea that there were humans somewhere in the galaxy who weren't subject to alien rule was a great bedtime story."

"What did the legend say?"

Her question seemed to pull him back to the present. He looked back at her, his dark eyes calm. "There were many versions of the legend," he said. "The most popular described a powerful human empire that would come back to Earth one day and liberate humanity."

She liked the idea of a human empire. After what the Kemmar had done to her people, she wanted to believe that there was a human empire capable of righting the wrongs committed against humankind. "Do you think there is any truth to the legend?"

Jon shrugged. "I'm not sure. I can see how the stories developed. The Earth was in ruins. People needed something to believe in. Whether there was any truth to it? I don't know. My guess is we're dealing with more of a diaspora of human colonies, rather than one central power."

"Why do you think that?"

"Just a hunch, really. While we don't have much data left about the colonies, I would think that the central authority would have been Sol. When the Juttari invaded Sol and the colonies shut down their gate, there would have been no central power left. While the different colonies might have created a central government to replace Sol, I think it was more likely that each colony just looked after their own affairs."

"You don't think the colonies would have united?"

Jon smirked. "They might have. If they had enough shared interests for it to make sense it could've happened. It's more likely that they traded with each other, but stayed independent." Jon paused, his face serious again. "What's curious is I haven't heard any talk of authorities, even after the incident with the raiders."

"Maybe they don't want the authorities involved? They might be carrying contraband."

"Could be."

"But you don't think so." It had taken some time, but she was starting to read his expressions.

"It's the way the Captain talks about this Mr. Jansen."

"His employer?"

"Yes, although I get the impression he is more than an employer."

"Do you think he is some sort of governor?"

"I don't know. There's more to this Mr. Jansen than we've been told."

Breeah looked over at Anki who hadn't stopped running and dancing since they set her free in the hangar bay. Anki's resilience always amazed her. She looked back at Jon who smiled as he watched Anki dance. "What do you think about this station?" said Breeah.

"It sounds interesting. I've seen space stations like this before. Some even bigger, with several million people living there. All were alien though. I've never seen a human station that size. I think it'll be a good opportunity to get our bearings. Find out where we are and what's next."

"Ok, just promise me you will try not to kill anybody," she said playfully.

Jon laughed. "I promise."

# Chapter 14

The long, dimly lit corridor stretched out ahead like a long winding snake. Doorways and dark nooks flanked it on both sides. Hostile aliens could be hiding behind any one of them. She needed to be cautious, and quiet. If she didn't make a sound she might be able to pass without being noticed. If the lights were brighter she could better see where they were hiding. But then they might see her too. That wouldn't be good. Anki decided that she liked the dim lighting after all and stayed close to the walls, moving slowly, silently.

The ship had an awful smell. A chemical smell. It wasn't familiar, and she hoped she wouldn't have to smell it again. She was sure it had clung to her by now. Her mom would have to send her for another shower to get rid of the stink. It was great to finally have a shower after all that time in the lifeboat. How long were they in the lifeboat? She had lost count of the days, but knew it was several weeks at least.

Weeks with no shower and no real food on a tiny ship. They had to eat some ridiculous paste every day. Jon had told her that it was filled with nutrients and that they could live on a little bit a day for years if they had to. The thought horrified her. Years in that cramped space with no shower and only some gross paste for food. The food on the freighter was nothing special, but at least it was real food. She never thought that she would miss chewing her meal so much.

The paste had no taste. None. She thought they must have made it that way on purpose, so that anyone could eat it without saying they didn't like the flavor. The food on the freighter was simple, but it actually tasted like something. When she first bit into it the sensation had surprised her. Her taste buds came alive and sent waves of pleasure through her. Her mother had to tell her to slow down and not eat so fast. But she couldn't help herself. Then Captain Seiben brought her some cookies. He said his wife had made them and that his little girls ate them all the time. She understood why. They were so sweet they made her want to spin and dance. Her mother didn't have to tell her to slow down then. She savored every wonderful crumb.

Anki continued to creep down the corridor, stealthily peaking around each bulkhead. A consistent hum reverberated throughout the ship, but otherwise there was total silence. It struck her how little actually happened on the freighter. On the Hermes there was always something going on. You couldn't walk down a corridor like this without passing an endless stream of people. She missed it.

Her mother explained that they had to leave the Hermes because of the Kemmar. That Jon had tried to rescue their people from the Kemmar, but in the end the aliens were too powerful. She told her that Jon was a good man. That anybody else would have left their people to their fate. She didn't understand it all, but she liked Jon. She felt safe around him. She saw how other people were afraid of him, but he didn't scare her. He showed the world his hard side, like her mother did, but deep inside they were both soft, like Captain Seiben's cookies, and that is the side they showed her. She did miss the Hermes, but so long as her mother and Jon were with her she knew she could deal with any hardship.

Suddenly there was a sound up ahead. An alien. It came from just around the corner in front of her. She heard it again. Her pulse quickened and the tiny muscles in her arm flexed. Don't be afraid, she thought. Her mother wouldn't be afraid. Neither would Jon. She had to be brave, like them. Jon told her to believe in herself. So she did. She believed in her ability to deal with whatever creature lurked around that corner. She crouched as low as she could and stepped forward, slowly advancing on the noise. She stayed close to the wall and raised her weapon. As she drew closer she held her breath. Could she really do it? Could she beat an alien? She had to believe in herself. She had to move. There was no turning back. She decided to go on the count of three. She took a deep breath, calmed herself and counted.

One.

Two.

Three.

She jumped out of her hiding spot like a panther striking at its prey. Her hand came up and she pointed her fingers and yelled, "Zap, zap, zap, zap."

"Hello," said the man standing there. "Off fighting raiders, are you?"

"You're an alien! And I shot you."

The man put a hand to his heart and groaned. "You got me. I'm a goner."

Anki fired again, "Zap, zap, zap!"

The man stumbled backward, his hand still clutching at his heart. He fell onto the floor and lay there with his eyes closed. Anki stared at him, worried. "Are you dead?"

The man opened one eye and smiled. "No, I'm okay." He sat up and said, "My name's Milo. What's your name?"

Anki smiled back, relieved that she hadn't killed the man. "I'm Anki."

"Hello, Anki. I'm happy to meet you."

"What are you doing here?" said Anki.

"Me? I was just heading down to the galley. I'm a little hungry."

"I know what that feels like."

"I bet you do. Have you been eating well since you came on board?"

"Oh yes, although my mother says I should slow down when I eat."

Milo nodded knowingly. "My mother used to say the same thing to me. I always ate my food too fast. But it was only because it tasted so good."

"That's what I say to my mother."

Milo nodded. "Does she listen?"

"No."

"Neither did mine."

"You should be careful, there are plenty of places for aliens to hide here."

Milo became serious and nodded. "I'll be careful. But what about you? Aren't you afraid?"

Anki threw her shoulders back and said, "I'm not afraid of aliens. They're afraid of me."

"I bet they are. You're a brave girl."

Anki beamed and said, "I'm seven."

"Wow, you're big."

Anki nodded.

"Well I feel much safer now that you're on board. Wait, did you hear that?" said Milo.

Anki looked around. "No. What was it?"

Milo smiled. "My stomach. I'm starving. I've got to get something to eat. Will you make sure no aliens come after me?"

"Don't worry, Milo. I'll make sure you're safe."

"Thanks, Anki. See you later."

"Bye."

Milo turned and walked down the corridor. Anki liked him. She knew the aliens were watching them, though. She had to make sure he escaped unharmed, so she turned and crept down the hallway, back to the serious business of stalking her prey.

# Chapter 15

Jon slowly walked down the long corridor, head down, shoulders slumped, deep in thought. He headed for the galley, hoping a hot meal might lift his spirits. He had lots of time in the lifeboat to think. Weeks of thinking. None of it did him any good. He didn't want to think anymore.

He analyzed things over and over. How did things go so terribly wrong? Should he have listened to the Diakans? To Breeah? Should he have left the Reivers to their fates? Turned a blind eye to their imprisonment? To their torture and enslavement?

Tactically that is what he should have done. That would have ensured the survival of the Hermes. But then why were they out here? What was the point of looking for humans if they weren't prepared to defend them? They were too far from Sol to wait for reinforcements. If they didn't act, nobody would.

His whole life had been spent fighting for humanity. He joined the resistance when he was a kid, just like his father and his grandfather. Killed his first Juttari when he was thirteen years old. He had taken his time. Picked his target. Stalked it. Timed his move. Killed. Prey transformed into predator. The alien never even saw him coming.

His grandfather said he had left childhood behind. Proven himself. Became a man.

For the first time in his life he had felt powerful. These aliens, who had oppressed humanity for centuries, could be killed. He didn't fear them anymore.

Before that moment he had been afraid. Always worried they would come, kill his family, and take him away. Turn him into a Chaanisar. They had tried once. When he was five years old they came for him. Apparently he showed promise. Men came in the night. The Governor's men. Not Juttari. Not Chaanisar. Humans. Selfish humans who cared nothing about the suffering their actions caused. Traitors to their own species. They came and took him from his mother. He could still hear her screams. She sounded like someone had thrust a knife into her heart. Like life itself was over.

But it wasn't. Not for her. Not for him. His grandfather and his father came for him, and they brought the fury of the resistance with them. Those men learned the meaning of hell that night. It was a time of reckoning, and blood ran through the streets like a river. All collaborators in the region were slaughtered. No one had been spared. Not even the Governor. Until then, no one knew his family were members of the resistance. All that changed.

His family had to leave their home. They fled to the mountains. The Rockies had been a base of operations for the resistance for generations. Now those same mountains became their home. Living that rugged lifestyle made him strong and tough. His grandfather and his father trained him daily in the ways of guerilla warfare. They taught him how to survive. But he was still afraid. Night after night he woke up in a cold sweat, panicked and thrashing about, thinking that he was being taken again. He would scream for help, half awake, and his mother would come and soothe him. Night after night she stayed with him until he fell back asleep. The poor woman. How much sleep had she lost in those years? Nonetheless, the terror of being taken to the Chaanisar stayed. It haunted him until he was thirteen. Until he killed his first Juttari.

No more.

He realized that he had power. That he could defend himself, and defend others. His grandfather taught him that it was his duty to fight, not just for himself, not just for his family, but for humanity. What followed was a lifetime of hunting. Humanity would not be enslaved by aliens again. Not while he breathed.

Why should the Reivers be any different? How could he stand by and let an entire human colony be slaughtered and enslaved? Should he have listened to the Diakans and left? The Diakans were just another alien race playing with human lives. They would think nothing of sacrificing a colony if the act benefited them somehow.

Perhaps they shouldn't have given him command of the Hermes. Someone else might have looked at the Kemmar and decided it wasn't worth it. The Reivers would have been sacrificed, but the Hermes would survive. Some might consider that action correct. But it was cowardly, and he was no coward. Not since his thirteenth year.

Yet he had sacrificed his crew. His friends. How long had he known Kevin? How many missions had they gone on together? He had killed him. Sure as if he shot him himself. Kevin and the rest of the Marines died because of his decision. They were warriors. They were all prepared to die. They knew the risks. But he was the one who sent them to their deaths.

I'm a killer, he thought. That's all I'll ever be.

It was easy to say the creature made him a killer, but he was one long before the Diakans put that thing inside him. He had been a killer since his thirteenth year when he had been baptized in blood.

Thankfully the creature had been quiet since Doctor Ellerbeck treated him. How long would that last? She said there was an adjustment period. The Diakans were supposed to give him the treatment, but they didn't. Instead, he had to battle the symbiont for control of his own body. The Doctor assured him that he wouldn't have a problem with the symbiont after the treatment period. It would remain quiet for a while and then they would work together. As one. That was how it was supposed to work. He hoped she was right.

He reached the galley entrance and silenced his thoughts. The past was no help to him now. It had to be buried. It was the only way to keep his sanity. He straightened his back, took a deep breath, and walked in.

The galley wasn't a large room like what they had on board the Hermes. It was rather small, which wasn't surprising considering the size of the freighter's crew. Like the rest of the ship the walls were a drab battleship gray with no adornments. A few tables and chairs were spread about haphazardly, and a disproportionately large food dispenser stood at the far end of the room.

The only person seated was Captain Seiben, who waved and gestured for Jon to join him at his table. Jon nodded, but first went to the food dispenser and selected a meal. The food wasn't as good as what they got on the Hermes, but it was light years better than the paste they had to eat on the lifeboat. He took a meat plate, not sure what type of meat it actually was, and afraid to ask. The plate had a side of greens, but those weren't familiar either. It didn't matter. He was hungry. He took his plate and walked to Captain Seiben's table.

"Please Jon, sit," said Seiben, waving his hand at the empty chair on the other side of the table from him.

Jon set his plate down, pulled out the chair and sat down.

"We will be arriving at the station in a couple of days," said Seiben.

"Then what?" said Jon, stabbing a piece of mystery meat with his fork, and shoveling it into his mouth. It looked like mystery meat, and it tasted like mystery meat.

"Then we talk to Mr. Jansen," said Seiben. He looked at Jon's shirt and said, "How do the clothes fit?"

"They're fine. Thanks."

"It's nothing. You must've been wearing that uniform for a long time."

"It's been a while," said Jon, after swallowing another forkful.

"That was a military uniform?"

Jon paused for a moment, studying Seiben, then speared another chunk of meat and nodded yes.

"Were you in some kind of battle?"

Jon took another bite and didn't answer the question.

"I mean, you were covered in blood, and in an escape pod…."

"Yes, we were in a battle," said Jon. Why lie? Everything indicated that they came out of a battle.

"I've done a fair bit of traveling in my time, and I've never seen those military symbols before. Where are you people from?"

"I can't answer that question. Sorry."

"I understand. Still, you are far from home. Very far. Maybe hundreds of light years away."

Jon continued to eat. If Seiben wanted to speculate, that was his business.

"The question is," said Seiben. "How did you get here?"

"Can't answer that either," said Jon, putting down his fork. "Now it's my turn."

Seiben nodded.

"I haven't heard you talk about any authorities. Don't you have to report the raider attack?"

"I've already told Mr. Jansen. That's all I need to do."

"I keep hearing that name," said Jon.

"That's because Mr. Jansen is the authorities."

"I thought you said he was your employer?"

"That's right. Mr. Jansen manages the station."

"Isn't there some form of government?"

"The station is owned by DLC. They govern everyone who lives on the station."

What's DLC?"

"You really aren't from around here. DLC is a corporation. All permanent residents on the station work for DLC."

"Is the corporation not bound by any regional power?"

Seiben shrugged. "No. DLC governs itself. Always has."

A corporation governing a million people living on a space station. It wasn't the oddest thing he'd ever heard, but it was different. "How do they defend themselves? Those raiders didn't look too friendly."

"The raiders? Those criminals wouldn't dare attack the station."

"Is the station armed?"

"Not only is the station armed, but it also has its own military."

This corporation sounded more and more like a government. "Sounds impressive. Mr. Jansen is in charge of all this?"

Seiben nodded. "He wants to meet you.

"Jansen?"

"Yeah. I told him about how you killed all the raiders. When we get to the station you'll be able to ask him your questions in person."

# Chapter 16

The DLC station hung in space like a gigantic spinning top. It was conical in shape and looked like it consisted of hundreds, if not thousands of rings stacked on top of each other. Each ring's diameter increased steadily all the way up to its widest point at the top. The station shimmered in the darkness, light from the nearby yellow star reflected off it in every direction as it turned.

Jon watched their approach from inside the lifeboat on the freighter's hangar bay. Breeah and Anki stood behind him.

"I can't believe how big that thing is," said Breeah.

"Seiben says that a million people live there," said Jon.

"That's a lot," said Anki.

Jon smiled. His affection for the little girl had continued to grow and he now regarded her with the same love he would show if she was his own daughter. Breeah and Anki had become his family. They were more than that. They were his redemption. For the first time since he lost his family he wanted to live.

"A million people living in a space structure. Incredible," said Breeah.

"It's also not orbiting a planet," said Jon. "Most stations I've seen orbit a planet, or at least a moon. This one doesn't. It's acting more like a planet itself, orbiting the star. I haven't seen anything like that before."

"It seems like it is too big, even for a million people," said Breeah.

"They need to feed all those people. I'm sure a lot of that extra space is for food. Agriculture. Livestock. Water. Then there's power generation. They need to keep the lights on somehow."

"Amazing. Maybe we can live here."

Jon turned and looked at Breeah. Her eyes sparkled back at him, a sly smile spreading across her beautiful lips. It made him feel good. Settling down somewhere with her and Anki seemed like a priceless treasure. Could he do it? Could he live a quiet life? Anki's eyes bounced excitedly between them.

"Are those ships? Those little specks out there," said Breeah, her eyes squinting at the screen.

"Yes."

"There's so many of them," said Anki.

"It's a busy place."

The hulking freighter crawled steadily closer to the station. On the screen the structure grew steadily larger as time passed. When they came within range a pair of smaller ships arrived to escort it to its designated dock. The station now filled the display, blocking everything else from view.

"Who built this?" said Anki.

"We're not sure," said Jon. "Probably the ancestors of the people living there today."

"They're good at building," said Anki.

Jon wondered about what they would encounter once they docked. "AI, can you transfer your core to my comm?"

"Yes, Captain," said the AI. "I am capable of even greater compression if needed."

"Transfer to my comm and make sure no data is left behind on the lifeboat's systems. If anybody comes snooping around I don't want them to find anything."

"Understood. Initiating transfer."

"You think these people are a threat?" said Breeah, her face now hard.

"I don't know, but I'm not going to take any chances. We don't need anybody telling the Kemmar where they can find us."

"Yes, that would be uncomfortable," teased Breeah.

Jon smiled.

"Transfer complete. All records of Space Force and the Hermes have been deleted from the lifeboat's systems."

"Good. Let's find Captain Seiben and see who is waiting for us on the station."

# Chapter 17

The hatch opened with a bang and a hiss. Captain Seiben and Milo stepped out onto the gangway, followed by Jon, Breeah and Anki. A tall thin man in a gray suit waited for them. Two armed men clad in black stood on either side of him. Jon took note. They carried energy weapons and had sidearms strapped to their thighs. Their posture wasn't threatening, and they didn't seem to be expecting any trouble. Bodyguards.

The tall man approached Jon and with a rehearsed smile stretched out his hand.

"My name is Mr. Kulberg," said the man, in the same language Seiben used. His speech was translated instantly.

Jon shook Kulberg's hand. It was like gripping a limp piece of lettuce. He immediately developed a dislike for Mr. Kulberg. "I'm Jon Pike," Jon replied. "This is Breeah and Anki."

Kulberg nodded at Breeah and Anki, still smiling, and said, "I am pleased to meet you." Kulberg paused, looking at the railguns Jon and Breeah were carrying. "I'm sorry Mr. Pike, but you can't bring the weapons with you."

Kulberg tried to keep his smile, but the demand obviously made him nervous. The bodyguards shifted their posture ever so slightly. Their hands rested on their weapons. It was all mildly amusing. If Jon had hostile intent none of them would have a chance. But he didn't have a reason to be hostile. Not yet anyway. He looked at Breeah, who stood relaxed yet ready, waiting to follow Jon's lead. She had noticed the guards' change in posture too and watched them warily. Jon nodded, telling her it was okay, and handed his weapon to Milo. Breeah did the same.

"Milo, please take those back to our vessel."

"Sure," said Milo

Kulberg looked relieved and the smile grew again. "Mr. Jansen is eager to speak with you. If you will all please accompany me."

Kulberg turned and walked down the gangway with his two guards. Jon, Seiben, Breeah and Anki followed. Milo watched for a moment and then went back into the ship.

At the end of a long corridor a craft waited, idling quietly off the ground. It was shaped like a passenger vehicle and used jets of forced air to make it float. The two guards sat in the front seats. Kulberg gestured with an "after you" wave of his hand for the group to enter the vehicle. In the back were two cushioned bench seats facing each other with ample room for all to sit comfortably. They entered and the doors slid closed. The vehicle set off, barely making a whisper as it went.

They glided through a maze of corridors until a door slid open and they were outside.

"If I did not know we were still in the station I would think we were outdoors," said Breeah.

Kulbeg gave her that same meaningless smile. "It is important for the wellbeing of all who live here that they experience the outdoors. A human being cannot stay indoors their whole life without suffering a myriad of psychological disorders. The station tricks the brain into believing it is in the open air. The blue skies. The daylight. All engineered to perfectly mimic the real thing."

The craft turned upwards and glided into the impossible azure sky. Jon, Breeah and Anki all looked out their windows at the scenery below.

"Look at all the trees," said Anki. "Is that a park?"

"Yes," said Kulberg. "The station has several parks and every street has vegetation of all sorts. Trees, shrubs, flowers, they all assist in putting our people at ease, completing the illusion of being outdoors. Our filtration system keeps the air fresh, but the trees and vegetation do their part as well."

Jon pointed to a skyline of buildings in the distance. "Is that a city?"

"Yes. That is where the bulk of our population lives. As you can imagine, the station doesn't have an infinite amount of space. Clustering the population has proven to be most efficient."

"Like an ant hill," said Jon.

Kulberg gave Jon a questioning look, like he didn't understand, but said nothing.

As the buildings drew nearer Jon realized that the structures were taller than he first thought. They all seemed to be roughly the same height, although the shapes varied to provide some semblance of diversity. The craft closed in on one of the buildings and circled it, waiting for its turn to land. A few moments later it had its opportunity. It positioned itself above the roof, its air jets maneuvering to allow a gentle drop onto the roof.

"You have a lot of air traffic," said Jon.

"It is more convenient to travel by air in the station. At a certain altitude the gravity drops off substantially, to almost zero g, requiring very little energy for propulsion. All our vehicles use air jets for lift and acceleration. We do not allow any other systems to be used on the station. As you can imagine, we take air pollution very seriously. "

The vehicle moved to its allotted parking space and came to a stop. Its doors slid open and Kulberg got out first. Jon followed, jumping out on the platform and quickly scanning the perimeter. No visible threats. The guards were already out of the vehicle, both watching Jon. Studying him. He had already assessed that they weren't anything to worry about, armed or not. He wondered if they felt the same about him.

The rooftop platform was quite large, littered with several other vehicles. They were surrounded by other buildings, with their own rooftop traffic. At the far corner of the platform was a glass structure enclosing what looked like a lift.

Kulberg walked toward it and the group followed. Reaching the structure they all entered the lift and immediately a female voice said, "Hello Mr. Kulberg."

"Mr. Jansen's office," said Kulberg.

The lift began dropping. It gave them a view of the surrounding structures. Several had giant displays providing a mixture of news reports and advertisements.

"How do you construct these buildings?" asked Breeah. "It must be difficult to build inside the station."

"Everything is made to be light and versatile," said Kulberg. "We use a lot of polymers in construction. Everything is modular, and prefabricated floor by floor. When demands for space increase, we build another module and stack it on top of the existing structure."

"Like my building toys," said Anki.

"Arriving at Mr. Jansen's office," said the lift's female voice.

The door slid open exposing a busy office surrounded by windows. Rows of desks spread out across the floor with men and women seated, busily working. A young woman approached with the same fake smile. She was blond, thin, almost as tall as Kulberg, and wore a gray suit similar to his. Jon wondered if the suits designated status.

Kulberg spoke first. "Mr. Jansen is waiting to see our guests."

"Of course," she said, still smiling. "Right this way." She moved effortlessly across the floor, her long legs covering the distance with ease and elegance. The guards had now fallen behind the group, keeping sight of all their guests. Jon could feel their eyes on him the whole time.

They approached a door, set in a wall of mirrored glass. No doubt Mr. Jansen was watching from the other side.

The door slid open and the woman entered. "Your guests have arrived Mr. Jansen."

At the far end of the room a middle aged man sat behind a large desk. He nodded at the woman as they approached. Unlike the woman and Kulberg, Mr. Jansen's suit was black. His white collarless shirt buttoned tightly up his neck. His perfectly coiffed dark hair accented by quick, piercing eyes.

The woman turned to the group and said, "Please come in." She walked up to Jansen's desk and motioned to a row of four chairs. When they were all seated she turned and left the room with the same long graceful strides.

Kulberg and the two guards remained, but stood back in front of the door. Jon glanced at them and acknowledged that they were doing their job. The guards stood a good distance apart from each other, with Kulberg in the middle. They could easily put the group in a crossfire if needed. Jon wondered if Kulberg was armed. He didn't carry himself like the guards, like a soldier, but that didn't mean he wasn't a threat.

"Welcome aboard DLC Station," said Jansen. There was no fake Kulberg smile. Jansen was obviously comfortable with his power and didn't need to put on an act. "I understand I am in your debt, Mr. Pike."

Jansen met Jon's gaze. He didn't flinch. He didn't seem intimidated by Jon like most people. Instead his eyes seemed to probe Jon's, trying to discover what hid beneath the surface. They were patient and deadly, like a cobra's. This man had killed. Of that Jon was certain.

"I merely reacted to the threat," said Jon. "I did what I had to do."

"Singlehandedly disposing of a raider boarding party is no small task, Mr. Pike. Even my best men couldn't do what you did."

"I don't know your men."

"Are you a soldier?"

"Yes."

"But you are far from home."

"Yes, we're new to this region of space."

"Where exactly is home, Mr. Pike?"

"If it's all the same to you, I'd rather not say."

"Yet you speak the old tongue."

"What do you mean?"

"I can tell, even with your translator, that you speak the old tongue. Very few know how to speak it anymore."

Jon stayed silent. He didn't like the direction the conversation was headed.

"I understand Captain Seiben picked you up in a life pod. Were you in a battle?"

"I'm sorry, I'm not at liberty to discuss that either." Jansen's questions were direct and unsettling. The comment about the 'old tongue' had unnerved him. He didn't know how much these people knew about Earth, but he couldn't risk revealing himself until he better understood what he was getting into.

Jansen sat back in his chair, lacing his fingers together in front of his chin. His eyes were still locked on Jon's, still probing for answers. "You are quite a mystery Mr. Pike."

"Is that a problem?"

"No. You saved me a great deal of money, wherever you're from," said Jansen. "Captain Seiben, you were quite fortunate to pick up this man when you did. There's no telling what the raiders would have done to you and your crew."

"Yes, we were very lucky," said Seiben, a hint of annoyance in his voice.

"What do you think of our station, Mr. Pike?"

"It's very impressive."

"Mr. Pike, I am a direct man. I don't like wasting time or playing games. I need someone like you. How would you like to stay here for a while?"

"You just met me. How would you know if you needed me for anything?"

"I did say I didn't like playing games, didn't I? Your abilities speak for themselves. No ordinary man could do what you did. You are obviously extremely well trained. So I'll repeat my question, would you like to stay here for a while?"

"That all depends on what your needs are."

"The raiders you encountered have been plaguing our shipping lanes for some time."

"I'm sure someone with your resources can deal with a few raiders," said Jon.

"There are more than a few of them, Mr. Pike. Killing a few raiders doesn't remove the scourge. What we really need to do is locate their base."

"I still don't understand why you need me."

"You said you were a soldier. What rank?"

"Captain."

Seiben turned and looked at Jon, surprised. Jansen simply nodded like he already knew the answer.

"But you're a special type of soldier, aren't you. The type that goes on difficult missions. No ordinary soldier could've done what you did on that freighter."

"Your point?" said Jon, increasingly irritated by the cat and mouse game they were playing.

"You could succeed where we have failed. You could find the enemy base for us. Then we could eliminate the raider scourge once and for all."

"That sounds like a suicide mission."

"I'm sure you can handle it, Captain Pike. You would be well rewarded for your efforts."

"You already said you were in my debt."

"I did. And I am." Jansen leaned forward. "But I can give you so much more. You can remain here and want for nothing. Or, if you wanted to leave I can provide you with a starship and anything else you needed. Just name your price."

The offer was tempting. It could allow him to start a new life. What was one more mission? Still, he needed time to think. "I'm tired. Do you mind if I think it over?"

"Of course. I've had some housing allocated for you. Mr. Kulberg will escort you to your apartment. We'll talk again, and in the meantime please make yourself at home on our station."

# Chapter 18

Kevin sat in his cell. Waiting. He wondered about Singh. What happened to him? How could he betray Earth like that? He didn't know Singh that well, but he never expected him to turn into a traitor. With jump system technology the Kemmar could launch a surprise attack against the Sol System itself. Singh had even promised to give them Earth's location. Earth wouldn't know what was happening until it was too late. They wouldn't have time to mount an effective defense. The Kemmar could take the Sol System with lightning speed.

The only hope for Sol would be a Diakan counterattack, but the damage would have been done. Even if the Diakans could push the Kemmar out of the system, Earth would be in ruins. After the Wars of Liberation and all the hard work to rebuild, this was the last thing Earth needed.

Singh had to be stopped.

Kevin had already decided to escape, but now he needed to capture Singh as well. They weren't leaving Kerces without him. He had to make a move, and he had to do it today. So he waited for the doctor's daily visit. He had only one chance and he couldn't make a mistake.

He didn't have to wait very long. When he heard the door to the cell block open, he readied himself. He lay down on the floor and closed his eyes, listening to the footsteps getting closer. As he expected, the doctor and the guard soon appeared in front of his cell.

"Get up," said the guard, clear menace in his voice.

Kevin didn't budge.

"Get up."

Kevin stayed on the floor. The guard growled.

The doctor said something to the guard, but Kevin couldn't make it out. He heard he guard respond, sounding angrier than normal. After the doctor finished speaking the guard touched his belt and the cell door slid open. Both Kemmar entered the cell and the door slid closed behind them.

The guard strode up to Kevin first and kicked him hard in the ribs. Pain surged through Kevin's side, but he didn't flinch. Another kick. Still nothing from Kevin. The guard kicked him two more times, the pain almost overwhelming, but Kevin didn't move. He hoped no ribs were broken. He couldn't afford anything slowing him down.

"I better examine him," said the doctor. "They still want him alive."

The guard grunted and the doctor bent forward to check Kevin's pulse.

The act was working. The guard didn't even put restraints on him. The doctor crouched down beside him, the putrid smell of rotting flesh on his breath. Kevin waited until he felt the hand touch his neck. Then he struck.

He shot out his right hand, fingers tight, and speared the doctor's throat. The force of the blow sent the doctor reeling backward, gagging, hands clasping his neck. He fell into the wall and dropped to the ground, still gripping his throat, struggling to breathe.

The guard moved fast, surging forward at Kevin. But Kevin moved faster. He kicked a leg out and caught the guard on the side of his knee, sweeping his legs out from under him.

The Kemmar guard hit the ground hard, smacking his head on the cold floor. Kevin was on him. The speed of his attack surprised the guard, his eye slits growing wider than he had ever seen them. Kevin dropped a bomb of a punch into the Kemmar's face. It felt good. He hit the guard two more times and the Kemmar responded with a weak swing of his baton. Kevin blocked the strike and stripped the baton from the guard's hand.

"Let's see how this thing works," said Kevin.

He smashed the guard in the face with the baton, sending a powerful electric current into the Kemmar's skull. The guard's body convulsed. Kevin thought of Private Denney. Thought of how these animals ripped the flesh off his bones while he screamed. He hit the guard again and his body seized. Then again. And again. The blood splattered and squirted with each blow. The skull opened up before him. Again. He bludgeoned the guard repeatedly until there was no movement, no doubt he was dead.

Kevin got up, and heard the doctor gagging behind him. He turned to see the doctor still holding his neck. Kevin had struck him with intent to kill, but he didn't want to take any chances. He stepped forward and the doctor raised a hand in a feeble attempt at defense. The first kick hit the doctor in the elbow. The satisfying sound of breaking bone filled the cell. The second kick finished the job. A powerful blow to the doctor's throat, crushing whatever was left of his windpipe. The doctor's head bounced off the wall behind him and then fell forward, blood gurgling from his mouth.

Kevin walked over to the guard, took off his belt, and strapped it around his own waist. He had watched the guard carefully, and memorized all the different ways he manipulated the belt. He touched the belt and smiled when the cell door slid open. Now he had to get his men.

Kevin walked out of his cell and looked at the row of cells. He touched the belt, half guessing this time, and all the other cell doors slid open.

The rest of the Marines walked out of their cells. They looked rough. Tired. Hungry. But not beaten. He knew that most had been tortured. He also knew they were tough. Well trained. The Fleet's best. They knew how to stay focused under extreme conditions. There wasn't a quitter among them. Each one of them would rather die than fail.

Kevin raised his hand, telling them not to make any noise. They had lost some good men, but there were still enough left to make this work. They needed weapons. Kevin had the guard's baton, but that wouldn't be much good against an energy weapon.

He crept up to the door at the end of the hallway, the Marines following close behind. Sergeant Henderson came up beside him. He looked just as tired as the rest, but his eyes were fierce. A tiger freed from his cage. Kevin whispered, "I saw two guards stationed on the other side of this door. They're armed with energy weapons. I can open the door with this belt. When I do we need to take them out fast."

"No problem, Chief," said Henderson. He turned and gave a couple of hand signs to the rest of the Marines, letting them know what was going to happen. He nodded. They were ready.

Kevin took a deep breath. There was a pain in his ribs where the guard kicked him. They were only bruised, not broken. It wouldn't slow him down. Already the adrenaline coursed through his veins, numbing the pain. Reviving him. He bent his knees. Prepared to pounce. He touched the belt and the door opened.

Henderson moved first. He had always been quicker. The Sergeant unleashed a flurry of strikes at the guard to the right of the door. The element of surprise worked perfectly, and Henderson obliterated his target, disarming him before he could fire a shot.

Kevin, a split second behind Henderson, struck the other guard in the arm with the baton, the electric shock forcing him to let go of his weapon. The guard seized up and Kevin's arm firing like a piston with another strike to the back of the head. The guard dropped to his knees. Three precise strikes followed with lightning speed, all to the back of the neck. The guard fell to the ground. Limp. The vertebrae in his neck broken beyond repair.

The rest of the Marines were flooding through the door. They quickly took positions to secure the room. The guards had carried two energy weapons each. Kevin and Henderson each took an energy weapon and gave the other two to Burke and Reynolds. The guards also had ion blades which were given to two more Marines. Kevin passed the bloody baton to a third.

Kevin checked his weapon and nodded to Henderson, who was doing the same.

"At least we have a fighting chance now," said Kevin.

"Yeah, and the element of surprise," said Henderson.

"They aren't wearing combat suits."

"They're comfortable."

"Uh-huh," said Kevin. "That gives us an advantage. We need to move fast before they figure out what's happened."

At the other end of the room were more doors. He remembered the route to and from the interrogation room. That was their first stop. He stepped up to the doors and the Marines took position along both sides. He leveled his weapon. Henderson, Burke and Reynolds did the same. He pushed a button on the belt and the door slid open. There were no guards on the other side. The Marines entered the room like a quiet brook filling a pond.

"Through the next set of doors it's gonna get busier," said Kevin. "There's a corridor that branches off. We stay to the right. That'll take us to the interrogation room."

The door opened without Kevin touching the belt. Four Kemmar appeared, two walking toward them and two walking away. The first two saw the Marines and raised their weapons, but the Marines fired first, hitting both Kemmar in the chest with multiple energy bolts. Hearing the discharges the other two Kemmar turned to face the Marines, but were hit before they could act.

The Marines raced down the corridor. The four fallen Kemmar were stripped of their weapons, and Kevin was starting to feel better about their chances now that they had some firepower. They reached the interrogation room without further incident and gathered outside the door.

"Chief Engineer Singh might be in there," said Kevin. "Make sure you don't kill him."

The Marines nodded and Kevin opened the door.

# Chapter 19

"I don't think this one can be trusted," said Lynda.

"Why?" said Singh.

"Who are you talking to," said the Kemmar interrogator.

"He plans to use you so he can improve his position," said Lynda. "He'll let you rot in here. Don't tell him anything."

Singh looked at the interrogator and said, "I need to speak to your top engineers."

"You can speak with me," said the interrogator.

"No. Only an engineer will understand. It would have to be someone very advanced."

"I think you are crazy. I do not think you have any knowledge to share."

"That is a mistake."

"So is not telling me everything you know. You obviously need motivation. Have you ever had needles inserted underneath your fingernails? I consider that mild persuasion."

"Your superiors wouldn't be happy with you if you harmed me."

"My superiors aren't here," said the interrogator, showing off his teeth. "It is just you and me."

"Don't be afraid," said Lynda.

But he was afraid. He was not a Marine. He hadn't been trained for this. He knew he couldn't withstand even the mildest torture tactics. He also knew the Kemmar saw right through him.

The interrogator looked at the two guards in the room and said, "Seize him."

They grabbed his arms, holding him like a vice. He frantically tried to move, futilely wasting energy.

"Don't panic," said Lynda, her cool blue eyes reaching out to him.

He tried to borrow her strength, but he didn't know how.

"Look at me," said Lynda. "Focus on me. On my voice."

"Hold his hands down on the table," said the interrogator.

Singh tried to resist. Tried to hold his arms back, but the Kemmar were too strong. His muscles strained as he tried to pull away. A cutting pain surged up his forearms, across his triceps, right up into his shoulders. The pain was so great he thought his ligaments would tear. Yet with all that effort he couldn't break his arms free. Each guard took a hand and steadily moved it forward, forcing it flat on the table.

Lynda stood close. So close he felt he could kiss her. How he longed to just kiss her. She said, "This is a test. That's all. You can do this." Her eyes were calm, soothing. He wanted to lose himself in them.

The interrogator approached with a handful of six inch long needles. He took one and held it close to Singh's face. Touched his cheek with the sharp point. Sliding it up the side of his face and then circling his eye.

"Do you like it?" said the interrogator. "As I said, this is one of our milder techniques. But that does not mean it is not fun." He bared his teeth again, snarling.

Dread climbed up his spine, its cold fingers filling him with terror.

"Don't listen to him," said Lynda. "Stay with me."

He tried, but the cold point of the needle pressed against his cheek kept his attention. His hands trembled, even with the guards holding them in place. He wanted to cry out. To scream. But he couldn't even draw in a breath.

The interrogator lay the rest of the needles down on the table, in between Singh's hands. He released the pressure against his cheek and showed him the needle again. "You are going to be very surprised to see how much of this I can get in under your fingernail. I can make it go right up your finger to the knuckle. It took some practice to perfect. At first the needle kept piercing through. Your species has very thin skin. But, fear not, I have perfected the procedure. The needle will remain inside your finger the whole time." He bared his teeth again at Singh and let out a chilling growl.

Singh couldn't look at the creature. He turned to Lynda, trying to avoid the interrogator's gaze.

A strong hand gripped his chin and pulled his face back so that he was looking at him again. "Are you not impressed?" said the interrogator.

Singh tried to look away, but the hand wouldn't let go.

"I understand. You believe in action, not words. An admirable quality. Very well. Action it is."

"You're going to get through this Raj," said Lynda. "Believe me."

"I believe you," said Raj.

The interrogator turned around. "Who are you talking to?"

Raj didn't answer.

"I admit, it will be interesting breaking an already broken man," said the interrogator, placing the tip of the needle under the nail of Singh's index finger.

Explosions could be heard in the distance and the building shook from the power of the blasts.

"What was that?" said the interrogator.

One of the guards accessed a computer link on the table. "We are under attack, Lord."

"Under attack?"

"Yes, Lord. There is a squadron of fighters firing on us."

"That makes no sense. Where did they come from?"

"There is a warship in low orbit, Lord. The fighters launched from the warship."

"How is that possible? The human ship was destroyed."

"This is a different ship, Lord."

"Our defenses?"

"Our fighters were destroyed in the battle with the human ship. As were our towers and batteries. Our forward units are responding with mobile ground to air weapons."

The interrogator turned his attention back to Singh. "It appears our conversation will have to be postponed." He snarled at Singh, showing off his teeth again.

An energy bolt hit the interrogator in the shoulder, spinning him around. A second bolt caught him in the back, in between the shoulders, sending him face first into the floor.

A barrage of energy bolts ripped through the two guards, dropping them before they had a chance to return fire. Marines surged into the room, several weapons now pointing at Singh.

"Don't move, traitor, or I'll burn a hole through your goddamn face," said one of the Marines.

Chief St. Clair marched passed him, heading for the interrogator who was still moving, trying to reach for his weapon. St. Clair took the weapon from him, rolled him over, and pointed the weapon at his muzzle.

The interrogator growled when he saw St. Clair.

"Still hungry?" said St. Clair.

"You won't-"

St. Clair fired the weapon, sending a crimson bolt tearing through the interrogator's face.

"See? You made it through," said Lynda, a bright smile on her face. "Didn't I tell you would get through this?"

"Yes, you were right. But it's not over yet," said Singh.

"Stop being so negative," said Lynda.

"Who the fuck are you talking to?" said the Marine pointing the weapon at him. "Chief, I think the traitor's lost it."

St. Clair turned, reached Singh in two steps and drove a heavy fist into Singh's solar plexus. Singh collapsed. On his knees, hands on the floor, gasping for air. He couldn't remember ever being hit that hard before. He desperately tried to suck in some air, but nothing came. He panicked, wondering if he would suffocate to death.

St. Clair pressed the muzzle of his weapon against the back of Singh's head. "Fucking traitor. I should just execute you now and get it over with."

Lynda knelt beside him, making eye contact. "Don't be afraid Raj. Remember what I said. We're going to get through this together."

He wanted to tell her he loved her, but he couldn't breathe, let alone speak. He believed her now.

Chief St. Clair pushed his head down with the weapon, almost to the floor, but Singh knew he wouldn't fire.

"Chief," said Henderson. "We've got to move."

"I should kill you," said St. Clair. "But I might need you."

The pressure on the back of Singh's head eased and left as St. Clair pulled his weapon away. He also felt his diaphragm filling, and relief washed over him as he was finally able to take a breath.

# Chapter 20

The building shuddered, and the sounds of battle thundered in the distance.

"Who do you think they're fighting?" said Henderson.

"I don't know, but I'll take what I can get," said Kevin, his ribs aching. "How many troopers are armed now?"

"We've got eighteen energy weapons, and nine ion blades."

"That's good. Enough to take out any resistance we come up on. We can arm the rest as we go."

"Chief? Have you got any idea how we're going to get off this ice cube of a planet?"

"We'll have to find a ship."

"There's the orbital defense grid too."

"Yeah, that's going to be a challenge. We'll figure it out."

"Yes, Sir."

Henderson was right. Getting off Kerces was going to be tough, but getting past the Kemmar would be tougher.

"I've got it, Chief," said Private Chen, looking up from the Kemmar computer link. "Building schematics. This is the route we take to get out of here."

Kevin and Henderson walked over to look at the display. There was a floorplan of the station with an escape route already highlighted by Chen.

"Good work, Private," said Kevin.

"Thanks, Chief."

The rest of the Marines scanned the display and each committed the map to memory.

"Ok, we know where we're going. Let's move out," said Kevin.

He strode to the door, weapon ready. The rest of the Marines followed. They formed two groups, flanking the door on both sides. They were going to make it. They had to make it. One way or another they were going to get off this rock. Kevin tried hard to believe it. *But the defense grid. How do we get past the defense grid?* The thought tormented him. He couldn't answer the question, but he had to stay positive. His men couldn't see any doubt.

Henderson touched a panel on the wall, opening the door. Burke and Daniels checked the corridor and sounded all clear. The rest of the Marines flowed out of the room. They moved steadily down the hallway in the direction of the exit. They held Singh in the middle of the group, ensuring he couldn't escape.

They didn't encounter much resistance. A lucky break. It was obvious that most were preoccupied with the larger battle taking place. They reached a junction where the corridor branched left and right. They needed to go left for the exit. The troopers lined up against the wall. Burke swept his weapon slowly around the corner, scanning for any opposition. He was answered with a salvo of red energy bursts, forcing him back behind the wall.

Leaning against the wall he said, "There's at least four Kemmar back there. They're wide open. No cover."

Burke stuck his weapon out and fired a couple of quick bursts.

"A grenade would be nice right now," said Burke.

Daniels crouched beside Burke and added fire. The shots coming from the Kemmar paused slightly each time Burke and Daniels fired. Patel and Johns took advantage of this and joined in. The fact that the Kemmar had no cover handicapped them. Their fire started to slow, as the Marines picked them off.

Soon there were larger gaps in the rate of return fire. With the four Marines laying down covering fire, Reynolds and Krukov ran into the corridor. Two Kemmar had already been killed and now the charging Marines took out the other two.

"All clear," said Reynolds. The rest of the Marines came around the corner and rushed down the long corridor. They stripped the Kemmar corpses of their weapons, adding more firepower to their team.

The larger battle raged, louder now as they got closer to the exit. The pain in Kevin's side got stronger and made him short of breath. He didn't know who the Kemmar were fighting, but for now he decided that the enemy of his enemy was his friend. He had expected more opposition to their escape. Whoever attacked the prison did them a great favor. Most of the Kemmar they would've faced were surely now engaged in the larger battle.

Not surprisingly, they didn't encounter anymore resistance to their escape. They had almost made it to the exit and Kevin knew the large atrium at the front of the building lay up ahead. The sound of battle was almost deafening. He ordered the Marines to stop their advance, unsure of what they were about to face.

He turned to his men. "Our first objective is escape. Remember that. Whatever we find out there, we take out the Kemmar first."

All the Marines nodded.

"Daniels, Burke, you're on recon."

"Yes, Sir."

The two Marines crept down the corridor while Kevin and the others waited.

Kevin looked over at Singh who was talking to himself again. What did it take for someone to snap like that? Would that be him one day? Would he see one thing too many? He'd already seen plenty, and he still held it together. Maybe that's what made him a Marine? He looked at the rest of his men. All were pretty beat up, but none of them looked like they were going to break. He felt privileged to be fighting alongside them.

The sound of boots caught Kevin's attention. Burke and Daniels were rushing back.

"Looks like at least a hundred Kemmar, half are wearing combat suits," said Daniels. "They're dug in behind some barricades. If we attacked we'd have their backs."

"Who are they fighting?"

"Couldn't see them, but whoever it is they're hitting the atrium hard. The Kemmar look like they're barely hanging on."

Kevin knew they wouldn't get a better opportunity. They were outnumbered, but they had the element of surprise.

"Okay, we're going in," said Kevin. "Fast and silent. We get behind them and put them in a crossfire."

"Oorah," said the Marines in unison.

"We don't know who they're fighting. With any luck they'll appreciate our help. But we need to keep our guard up in case they don't."

Kevin looked around, all the men nodded their agreement.

"Hold your fire until we all get in behind them. Move out."

They crept down the corridor and silently entered the atrium, spreading out behind the Kemmar line. The Kemmar were focused on the enemy in front of them and the roar of the firefight ensured they didn't hear the Marines. Kevin leveled his weapon and took aim at the back of an enemy skull, held up his hand, and gave the signal to open fire.

The Marines unleashed a storm of red lightning. Almost half the enemy line collapsed under the weight of the attack. The Marines continued to fire relentlessly, their rage insatiable. They first targeted the ones not wearing combat suits, which was easy enough. Now came the hard part. The rest wore armor and the energy fire didn't drop them as easily. They would have to weaken the suits first before their fire had any effect.

Many Kemmar turned to fire at the Marines now, and quickly picked off several troopers.

"Focus your fire on the ones facing us," ordered Kevin.

The tactic worked. Many of the Kemmar had to stay focused on the attackers in front of them and couldn't turn their attention to their rear. The Marines concentrated their fire on the direct threats, weakening their combat suits at an accelerated rate until finally destroying them.

Several of the Marines who didn't have energy weapons charged towards the fallen Kemmar, seizing their weapons and attacking from the Kemmar flanks.

Confusion swept through the enemy line allowing their attackers to also advance. Moving with speed and ferocity, armored soldiers leaped over the barricade, shredding the Kemmar combat suits with railgun fire. As the line fell apart, more attackers sailed over the barricade and closed with the enemy.

Between the armored attack from the front, and the Marine attack from the rear, the Kemmar didn't have a chance. The battle soon turned into a mop up, with the armored attackers finishing off what was left.

Kevin had been so focused on the Kemmar that he didn't pay attention to the attacking force. He was just grateful that they advanced when they did, or he might have lost more men. That gratitude disappeared now that he had a better look at the attackers. It was the insignia on their combat suits that filled his veins with ice. One he had encountered in battle before.

The mark of the Juttari.

# Chapter 21

Colonel Bast of the Chaanisar leaped over the barricade, into the carnage on the other side. Dead bodies lay all around and his men were adding more to the list, as they killed the last of the Kemmar defenders. Satisfied that the threat had been eliminated, he turned his attention to the Marines. They had surprised him when they entered the battle. He had expected them all to be imprisoned. That they escaped and helped defeat the Kemmar showed their value as warriors.

Scanning their line he identified their leader and stepped toward him. He halted his advance when the leader and the rest of his men pointed their weapons at him. Their hostile stance prompted a similar response from his own men.

"Hold your fire," said Bast over his suit's comm system. He wanted to take a less threatening posture and had his suit retract its helmet. He hoped that the Marines would relax when they saw that he was human as well.

He addressed their leader, who still pointed his weapon at him. "I am Colonel Bast of the Chaanisar. We mean you no harm."

"Bullshit!" said the leader. "You're the ones who attacked us when we began our mission. You attacked our Captain on Earth and on board our ship."

"I assure you those were different circumstances. Please, lower your weapons."

"I assure you that is not going to happen. Take one more step and I'll burn a hole through your face."

The reaction prompted a more aggressive posture from his men, and he repeated his order for them to hold their fire. He understood the Marines' mistrust. He couldn't blame them for it. But he needed them to listen, so he did something he would have never done before. He ordered his men to lower their weapons. His men obeyed, even though he knew it went against their every instinct.

"There, you see. We are not a threat to you. Now can we all just calm down before someone makes a tragic mistake?"

The Marine commander nodded in agreement, lowered his weapon, and ordered his men to do the same.

"Thank you. May I ask your name?"

"Chief St. Clair."

"Thank you Chief St. Clair. As I said before, we mean you no harm. In fact we came here to help you."

"Why would Juttari want to help us?"

"Because we are not Juttari. We are human. Like you."

"You're Chaanisar. You're nothing like us."

"We were born on Earth, just as you."

"Until the Juttari took you. Turned you against your own people. Your own families. You're an abomination."

"The Juttari did take us. They kidnapped us when we were children. Stole us from our families. Violated us with their technology. Enslaved us with their brain chips. Our every action since then has been forced on us by the Juttari."

"So? How is this any different?"

Bast smiled. "The Juttari no longer control us. We are finally free."

"I don't understand."

"We have mutinied. The warship that attacked you was under Juttari command. The Juttari on that ship are all dead. The ship is now under our command. Human command."

# Chapter 22

Kevin tried to process what he was hearing. "I find that hard to believe. No Chaanisar has ever mutinied."

"And yet here we are," said Bast.

"That means nothing. Do you think we went to the trouble of escaping to become Juttari prisoners instead?"

"While your escape today was impressive, how did you plan to leave this planet?"

"That's not your concern."

"Chief St. Clair, you cannot escape this planet. There are no ships for you to commandeer. Even if there were, you would never make it past their defense grid."

Kevin knew the Chaanisar was right, but he didn't want to admit it.

"You are trapped here until the next Kemmar ship arrives, at which point you will become Kemmar prisoners again. I imagine that hasn't been a pleasant experience."

"We'll take our chances."

"I offer you freedom. We have a jump system, just like your Hermes did."

"Technology you stole from us."

"Technology the Juttari stole from you. Technology we have now captured from the Juttari."

Part of Kevin wanted to believe Bast's story. But how could he trust someone who had been his enemy his whole life?

"Look Chief," said Bast. "You are outnumbered. Outgunned. We are all wearing combat suits. Even without the combat suits the Juttari have augmented us, giving us superior strength and speed. You know this. If we wanted to kill you, you would all be dead. If we wanted to capture you, you would already be our prisoners. The Chaanisar do not play games. We are telling you the truth."

While Kevin hated to admit it, Bast was right. They were facing overwhelming odds and they both knew it.

"Okay, we'll come with you on one condition."

"And that is?"

"We're not giving up our weapons."

"Agreed."

"Make one wrong move and you'll have a bloodbath on your hands. Outnumbered or not."

Bast smiled. "I like you, Chief St. Clair."

# Chapter 23

Kevin and his men boarded a Chaanisar shuttle as fighters streaked across the sky. The smell of fire, oil, and death surrounded them. Bast and a handful of his men boarded the shuttle as well. When all the Marines were on board the shuttle rocketed away toward the waiting Juttari warship.

Henderson sat next to Kevin and spoke in a quiet voice. "What do you think, Chief?"

"Honestly, I don't know what to think," whispered Kevin.

"How do you think they did it?"

"Did what?"

"Overcame the Juttari mind control?"

"I can answer that question, Sergeant," said Bast, seated a fair distance away from them.

"You've got good ears," said Henderson.

"Juttari augmentation," said Bast, pointing to his ears.

"So how did you do it?"

"One of the first things the Juttari did after they kidnapped us was to implant their chips into our brains. Those chips allowed them to control everything we did. They took away our free will."

"What changed?"

"After our battle we lost your ship. We jumped around for days searching for you. Finally we retraced our steps and jumped back into the binary system. It was there that we found you, only you were already engaged in battle with the Kemmar battleship. Fascinated, we hid and watched the events unfold. Watched your ship jump after being boarded. Watched the Kemmar take the colony your ship was obviously trying to defend. And watched the Kemmar activate a jump gate and leave. A jump gate we never knew existed.

"The Juttari Master ordered us to cross through the gate and follow the Kemmar battleship. We did, staying back a safe distance so as not to be detected. We followed the Kemmar to this planet. Watched them drop off their prisoners and waited. The Master was convinced that you would again try and rescue these colonists. And he was right. So we watched your tragic attack. And your eventual defeat."

"That's all very interesting, but you still haven't told us how you managed to overcome your Juttari masters," said Henderson.

"That, Sergeant, is the fascinating part. Every Juttari ship carries a system that emits a powerful broadcast intended specifically to exert control over our chips. These systems are in place throughout Juttari space. Without going into too much detail, suffice it to say that these systems go wherever we go. They are our shackles.

"On this particular mission, however, something went wrong. The system stopped broadcasting. The effect, as you can imagine, was quite a shock. After all those years our thoughts were once again our own. At first we expected the malfunction to be discovered. There was no way it would last. But it did. And something else happened. As we watched you battle the Kemmar against such overwhelming odds, we were inspired. We wanted to fight with you. To fight for humanity."

"Why didn't you?"

"We had to fight for ourselves first. We had all spent a lifetime under the control of the Juttari Empire. To rise against the Juttari seemed... insurmountable. After your defeat on Kerces, our Master gave the order to head back home, and that was when we knew we had to act. Regardless of the malfunction on our ship, we knew the moment we were back in Juttari space we would fall under Juttari control again. So we rose up and killed every Juttari master on board. Then we decided to rescue you."

"What if the system on your ship starts broadcasting again?"

"It won't. We destroyed it during our uprising. The only thing that will control us again is a return to Juttari space. Which is why we need your help."

"You said that before," said Kevin. "What is it you think we can do for you?"

"We want our chips removed."

Kevin laughed. "We're soldiers. How are we supposed to do that?"

"You can't, but your doctor can."

"Our doctor isn't with us."

"No, she isn't. But your people escaped from the Hermes before it was destroyed. We believe your doctor escaped too, and we're going to find her."

# Chapter 24

"Are you going to do it?" said Breeah.

"Jansen's mission?" said Jon.

"Yes."

"I haven't decided. We know nothing about what is going on here."

Breeah walked over to a window and looked out at the cluster of buildings surrounding them.

"It is very crowded here. They all live on top of each other."

"A big difference from the parks and trees we saw on the flight in," said Jon.

"If you go on this mission I am coming with you."

"What are you talking about? I can't bring you with me. What about Anki?"

"She will come along. We are Reivers. We do not sit at home while others fight."

"I won't put you in harm's way."

"It is not your choice to make."

Jon exhaled sharply. He had developed strong feelings for Breeah and Anki. They were the closest thing he had to a family since he lost his own. He wasn't prepared to take them on a dangerous mission.

"I'm not a Reiver. I can't bring a child into a hostile situation." Jon got up and walked over to Breeah. "I work alone, Breeah. I always have."

"Not anymore. We are your family now. We go wherever you go." Breeah's hand reached up to his face, her finger tracing its way down the long scar on his cheek.

Jon wrapped his hands around her waist and pulled her close. She felt good and he didn't ever want to let go. "I can't lose you," he whispered.

She looked up at him with those dark eyes, shattering his defenses. "Do I appear helpless to you, Jon Pike?"

"No, of course not."

"Perhaps you would prefer Kulberg and his guards by your side?"

"No. Don't be silly. I told you I work alone. If I fail I am the only one who suffers the consequences."

"And I told you that is in the past. Everything is in the past. Your old life, the Hermes, everything. There is only us now. And we stay together."

"But what if something happens to you and Anki. I couldn't bear it. Not again."

"You must forgive yourself. Do not focus on the past. Do not worry about the future. There is only now. Only us."

"I like the sound of that." He reached down and kissed her. Her body warm against his, her lips soft, his doubts and fears disappearing, the giggles like a song.

Giggles?

Jon released Breeah and turned to see Anki watching them, beaming, a huge grin on her face.

Breeah smiled. "So what do we do?"

Jon looked across the room to a computer link. "We get more information."

# Chapter 25

"AI, can you interface with the computer link in this room?" said Jon.

"Yes, it is a public terminal. There is open access to a specified level. Do you need me to access more secure information?"

"Not yet. Let's see what we can find out without raising any alarms."

"These systems are not sophisticated enough to detect my activity, Captain."

"I'm sure they're not, still, just stick to the public database for now." The AI was probably right and wouldn't get caught, but he didn't want to take any chances.

"Understood. Interface complete."

"Good. Do you have any information on the history of this station?"

A cross section of the station appeared on the display. "The station was constructed more than six centuries ago by the DLC Corporation. DLC acquired rights to this region of space from the Sol government at that time."

The answer confirmed Jon's suspicions, but was astounding nonetheless. "So they were one of the original colonies?"

"Yes, Captain. That is correct. Early colonization consisted of migrant workers. Resource mining provided ample employment and many came on contracts to work a number of years, after which they would return to the Sol System. Others took on permanent positions and settled on the station."

"Are there other stations like this?"

"Not this size. This region is resource rich, but there are no habitable planets." The display cycled through different regions of space, showing multiple star systems and planets. "Other corporations obtained rights to regions more hospitable to human life." The display zoomed in on one of the planets to show numerous cities. "Those corporations developed planetary settlements and had more permanent immigration. Over time, most of these worlds developed their own governments, which established laws and took control of the population away from the corporations."

"Are the other colonies as large as DLC?"

"They are larger. Population growth on the other colonies is not as constrained as it is on the DLC station. On the planets there is much more room to thrive and grow."

"So there are millions of people living in the other colonies?"

"Billions, Captain."

Jon blinked, trying to grasp what he just heard. Billions of people? If that was true, the number of people living in the colonies outnumbered the population of Sol itself. The Juttari invasion had wiped out much of Earth's population. The survivors lived in squalor for centuries. Not ideal conditions for population growth. Out here, however, they flourished. It made Jon wonder what would happen if Sol and the colonies were ever reunited. How would the colonies see Sol? Earth may have been the birthplace of humanity, but compared to the size of these worlds, Earth would be seen as a province at best. They were in for a major wakeup call back home.

"AI, what happened after the Juttari invasion?"

"The corporations shut down their jump gate and travel between Sol and the colonies ceased. Trade had already developed between the colonies and continued. The other colonies replaced Sol as the main customers for DLC exports."

"What about war? Five hundred years is a long time. Did the colonies fight against each other?"

137

"There have been many disputes as the colonies expanded their influence. These disputes have been mainly over territorial rights. In many cases full scale battles have been fought, but it was agreed early on that war would never be waged on the core worlds, including DLC station."

"So they don't always play nice with each other. War usually escalates, why didn't anyone break the treaty?"

"After the Juttari invasion there was no way of knowing what happened to life in the Sol System. Before closing their gate, the colonies received reports of Juttari ruthlessness. They knew of the orbital bombardment and didn't know if anyone had survived. There was a real possibility that the colonies were the last outposts of humanity. That was considered too precious to destroy through warfare."

"So they keep the fighting away from the civilian populations?"

"Yes, Captain." The display showed various warships and fleet formations. "If there is a dispute over a region of space between two parties, they may resolve the dispute through the use of force, but the conflict is restricted to unpopulated regions."

"Like a duel."

"Yes, Captain. Precisely, albeit on a much larger scale."

"Is that why I didn't see much military activity in this system when we arrived?"

"A couple of DLC warships are usually kept in the system to deal with the raider threat, but the main fleets patrol their valuable resource rich regions."

"Are these regions unpopulated?"

"No, there are mining communities, but their populations are so small that none of the parties consider fighting there a violation of the treaty."

"Is there any information on the raiders?"

"The raiders were originally a DLC mining community." The display showed a mining operation on a barren planet.

"A DLC mining community?"

"Yes, Captain. DLC miners worked in some very inhospitable places. Injuries and loss of life were common. Much of the hardship was blamed on long work hours and outdated equipment. There were several strikes, which were ended each time through the use of force."

"DLC sent in troops?"

"The company used armed security personnel to end the strikes."

Like those two prima donnas with Kulberg, thought Jon.

"Then there was an uprising. The miners killed their managers, seized any available vessels, and disappeared."

"Was there a specific incident that sparked the uprising?"

"The source says they suffered from Miner's Fever. A type of mass dementia."

"Sounds like bullshit to me."

"Would you like me to access the restricted sections to verify this information? It would be child's play."

"No."

"As you wish, Captain."

"When did this happen?"

"Almost one hundred years ago."

"A hundred years? And they still haven't found them?"

"That is correct, Captain."

"Sounds like more bullshit. What about aliens?"

"Interaction with alien populations is limited. After the Juttari invasion of the Sol System, the colonies adopted an isolationist policy."

"So there are no aliens on any of the colonies?"

"No, Captain. Citizenship is only granted to humans."

"What information do they have on the Kemmar?"

"They know of the Kemmar Empire, but there is no formal relations. The colonies share borders with an alien race known as the Otan. The Otan are Kemmar trading partners. As such, Otan space is a natural buffer between the colonies and the Kemmar Empire."

"What are relations like between the colonies and the Otan?"

"There are diplomatic relations between the colonies and the Otan. The Otan are not an agressive society. They do have a sizeable military, but this is maintained primarily for defense. This has kept the relationship peaceful."

"Thank you, AI."

"You are most welcome, Captain."

"What do you think?" said Breeah.

"I think we need a spaceship so we can travel to the other colonies."

"So we are going to accept Jansen's offer?"

"Yes, we are."

# Chapter 26

Anki walked with her head held back, trying to see the tops of the buildings, but she couldn't make them out. The buildings were so tall they looked like they joined the sky. She had never seen anything like it before. There wasn't anything close to it back home.

She imagined the buildings were sleeping giants, towering all around them. They had to be careful not to make too much noise or the giants would wake up and eat them. The giants took very long naps, and were very grumpy if they were woken up.

She decided it would be safer to walk on her tip toes. She slunk down the street with Jon and her mother, trying hard not to make a sound. The people walking by her weren't so careful and she wanted to warn them that the giants would wake up, but they didn't look at her. The giants must have hypnotized them. They couldn't be saved. Even worse, they might notice she wasn't hypnotized and capture her for the giants. It wasn't safe to look at the people anymore.

"Anki, this way," said her mother, pointing to a set of doors.

She stopped staring at the giants and ran to catch up with her mother and Jon. She followed them into a bright, noisy room with plenty of tables and chairs and people eating. Their meals smelled delicious, making her stomach growl. She stopped and stared at a table filled with heaping plates of food. Her mouth watered. The people sitting there didn't seem too eager to eat, though. The talked and laughed, but all that wonderful food just sat there. She wondered if they needed her to show them how to do it.

"Anki," said her mother. She walked back to her with one of those looks on her face. The ones that told her she wasn't happy with her. Anki tried to imagine what she had done. Nothing. She was just looking at the food. Her mother grabbed her hand and said, "I need eyes in the back of my head with you child. I know everything is interesting, but you need to stay with me." Breeah pulled her along by the hand and Anki followed. Up ahead she saw Captain Seiben sitting at a table, waving at them. They all went over and sat down. Sitting in front of her were two little girls, one about her age and the other looking at least a year or two older.

Captain Seiben rose from his seat and stepped behind the two girls. He reached down and seized them, wrapping his thick arms around them, and kissing both on the cheek.

"Daddy!" each girl complained. Anki didn't blame them. Captain Seiben's face was full of whiskers which would make it very scratchy. Captain Seiben kept kissing them, laughing loudly as they complained.

"Anki, these are my daughters," said Captain Seiben. "This is Alina," he said, pointing to the one who looked the same age as her. "And this is Otka."

"Hi," said Anki.

"Hi," said the girls.

Captain Seiben smiled at Anki and went back to his chair.

"My father says he found you in space," said Otka.

"Yes, he did."

"He said you were going to die if he didn't find you."

"It was boring and the food was bad," said Anki. "But we weren't going to die."

"Well that's what my father said, and he knows about things like that," said Otka.

"Do you have any dolls?" said Alina.

"No, do you?"

"Yes, I have lots of dolls."

"That's because you're still a baby," said Otka.

"No I'm not!"

"I don't think you're a baby," said Anki.

"Thanks," said Alina. "What type of games do you like to play?"

"Humans versus aliens."

"How do you play that?"

"You have to zap the attacking aliens."

"What kind of device do you need for that?"

"Just your imagination."

Both girls stared back at Anki with a confused look on their faces.

"That doesn't sound like it's any fun," said Otka.

"What games do you play?" said Anki.

"I play Rise to the Top," said Otka.

"How do you play that?"

"You start off as a worker on the first floor, and you have to do your job better than everyone else so you can level up and advance to the next floor. Then you get a new job and you have to be the best at that job so you can move up again. You get bonus points for reporting on bad people who don't do their job well."

"How do you win?"

"You have to get to the top floor. Then you become the CEO and win the game."

Anki nodded, trying to be nice, although the game didn't sound like it was much fun.

"My father said that your father killed a bunch of raiders on his ship."

"He isn't my father."

"He's not?"

"No, he's my friend."

"Did he kill the raiders?"

"Yes, he killed most of them, but my mother killed one too."

"Wow," said Alina.

"My father says you're soldiers," said Otka.

"Jon is. My mother isn't."

"But she killed a raider."

"Yes, she's good at that."

The two girls stared back at Anki with that same confused look, but said nothing. Anki was glad that Otka stopped asking questions. She didn't think she liked her very much. Then, before Otka could think of anything else to say, a man appeared with a tray full of food. He set a plate down in front of Anki and it smelled wonderful. Anki grabbed her fork and without another word began shoveling the hot food into her mouth.

"Slow down, child. Take a breath between your bites," said her mother.

"I'm hungry."

Her mother frowned at her. "Anki…"

"Okay," said Anki, and slowed down a bit till her mother went back to speaking with Captain Seiben, then she returned to shoveling the food back into her mouth.

"Will you go to school here?" said Alina.

"I don't know," said Anki. "I don't know how long we'll be staying."

"If you come I'll introduce you to all my friends," said Alina.

"Thanks," said Anki. She liked Alina much better. She hoped she would get a chance to play with her.

"Did you go to school where you came from?" said Otka.

"Yes."

"What was it like? What did they teach you there?"

"Normal things. Reading, writing, math, hand to hand combat."

The two girls looked back at Anki with their mouths open. It reminded her of her food and she went back to wolfing it down.

"They teach little girls how to fight where you're from?" said Otka.

"They teach everyone how to fight. Don't they teach you?"

The two girls looked at each other. "No," they said in unison.

"Oh, that's too bad. I hope your school improves."

# Chapter 27

"I'll find the base for you," said Jon, holding eye contact with Jansen. Kulberg had taken his position behind Jon, flanked by his two guards. Jon wanted to deal with Jansen alone and had left Breeah and Anki back at the apartment.

"Excellent," said Jansen. "I will arrange more permanent living arrangements on board the station for you."

"We won't be staying."

"Oh?"

Jon wondered if Jansen would go back on his word. "You said you would provide us with a spaceship if we chose not to stay."

"That's right, I did say that. You are planning on moving on then?"

"Yes. We want to explore the other worlds."

"Of course, Captain. That is understandable." Jansen went quiet for a moment and looked like he was silently debating something with himself. "Captain, I have another proposition for you."

Jon leaned forward and gave Jansen a cold look. "Are you trying to change the deal on me?"

"No, Captain, of course not. My offer stands. You find the raider base for us and I will give you a spaceship in return."

"Good," said Jon, relaxing his posture.

"What I am going to do is offer a performance bonus."

"What does that mean?"

Jansen accessed his console and a three dimensional holographic image of an older man appeared above his desk. "This is Durril Tai. He is the leader of the raiders, and not a very nice man. He deals in murder and extortion."

"He doesn't sound like a fun dinner guest."

Jansen ignored the comment. "If Durril Tai was eliminated the raiders would lose all cohesion and structure.

"Something you can accomplish once you know the location of their base."

"If we know their location we can certainly damage their operations," said Jansen. "Without Tai's removal, however, I fear they will establish a base elsewhere."

"How?"

Jansen sat back into his chair and looked at the holograph. "The raiders were fugitives at first. They were miners and went into hiding to avoid being captured after murdering their managers. They disappeared and weren't heard from for decades. Then they returned and began plaguing our shipping lanes. They even attacked some of our mining colonies. Their resurgence was the direct result of Durril Tai's leadership."

"So this Tai keeps outsmarting you?" said Jon.

"He is an elusive opponent."

"And you're afraid that he'll find a way to get out of any trap you set."

"The thought does trouble me."

"He doesn't sound like an easy man to find, let alone kill."

"You will be rewarded handsomely if you succeed, Captain. I will not only give you a spaceship for your travels, but will also give you one million credits as a bonus. This will be more than enough for you to live comfortably wherever you choose to go."

"You do realize you are asking me to commit murder."

"Come now, Captain. Let's not play games. I am a good judge of people and I can tell you have done this before. In any case, this would be a DLC sanctioned mission, so it is not murder."

"An assassination then."

"We can play with words all day, Captain. Durril Tai is the murderer. You would be merely carrying out his death sentence."

"What kind of spaceship?"

"I'm sorry?"

"What kind of spaceship do I get if I provide you with the base's coordinates?"

"A Journeyman Class passenger ship. It has an FTL system that is fully capable of travel between the worlds you want to visit and beyond."

"Armament?"

Jansen frowned. "Captain, this is a civilian vessel. It doesn't carry weapons."

An idea came to Jon and he knew what he needed. "Ok, here is what I want. If I manage to take out this Durril Tai, you give me the million credits and you upgrade the spaceship to one that can actually defend itself."

Jansen folded his arms over his chest and studied Jon for a few moments, then nodded like he had made up his mind. "I can provide you with an Interceptor Class spaceship." He manipulated his console and the holograph changed from the raider leader to an image of a sleek military vessel. "It has energy weapons and an armored hull. There is an FTL system, but it is also designed for speed and maneuverability allowing you to outrun an opponent you can't fight."

Jon smiled.

"Do we have a deal, Captain?"

"We have a deal."

"Excellent."

"I'm going to need full access to any intelligence you have on the raiders."

"Granted."

"I'm also going to need a freighter."

"A freighter?"

"Yes. Preferably one with a crew and some valuable freight."

"You are hoping the raiders will come to you."

"That's right. Then I'll convince them to take me with them."

"What if they don't comply?"

"I'll show them my persuasive side."

Jansen nodded. "I believe you've become familiar with Captain Seiben and his crew already. I will assign them as your freighter crew."

"I don't think that's such a good idea."

"Nonsense. He's already seen you handle yourself with the raiders. He's had time to get to know you, too. He's the perfect choice."

"I'm sure he'll be happy to hear that."

# Chapter 28

"I should have never picked up your goddamn lifeboat!" said Captain Seiben. "I should have let you rot in space." He glared at Jon, wanting to punch him in the face for getting him involved in this suicide mission. "You'd be dead if it wasn't for me."

"I understand you're upset. I asked for someone else, but Jansen insisted. I wanted to tell you myself."

Seiben had a bad feeling when Jon said he needed to speak to him, especially when he insisted it had to be in person. He glanced over at Breeah who hadn't taken her eyes off him, but her face didn't betray any emotion. Anki played with some toys and seemed uninterested in the adult discussion taking place.

"Are you comfortable with this?" Seiben asked Breeah. "You will be putting Anki and yourself in danger."

"Yes. Where Jon goes we go."

"You would willingly put your child in danger?"

"We do not shield our children, Captain Seiben. They learn through experience."

Seiben shook his head. Frustrated. What kind of people were these?

"You're all insane. All of you. And now you've pulled me into your crazy plan."

"I'm sorry," said Jon.

"I have kids too. I'd rather they grow up with a father."

"I won't let anything happen to you."

"Forgive me if your promise doesn't make me feel better."

Jon didn't say anything.

"What about Milo? He's barely a man. You're putting his life at risk too."

"I know."

"You know? You know?! Do you also know that his father, my brother, is going to kill me?"

"He can't know about the mission."

"Why?"

"The mission has to stay secret. The raiders may have spies on the station. In fact, we're counting on it.

"You're counting on raider spies?"

"That's right. The freighter will be loaded with very expensive cargo. We're hoping that word will get to the raiders about it and encourage them to act."

"Wonderful," said Seiben, the venom dripping off each syllable.

"Mr. Jansen has agreed to make it worth your while. You're all going to get hazard pay for this mission. Triple your normal salary."

"What the hell good is that if I'm not around to spend it?"

"Look, I know this is hard, but like I said, Jansen insisted. We have a few days until we depart. Try to relax and spend some time with your family. You'll be back with them in no time. You'll see."

Seiben still had the urge to punch Jon, but he knew it would accomplish nothing. He also knew Jon could likely knock him into a coma with one strike. He couldn't refuse Mr. Jansen either. If he disobeyed Mr. Jansen he would be out of a job and that would leave his family destitute. He had no choice.

# Chapter 29

His Eminence, Daag Tsogt, Grand Sovereign of the Kemmar Empire wanted to kill something. He looked from the battle on his display to his intelligence adviser, thinking the taste of his blood might be relaxing. It would certainly help calm the rage building up inside him. Unfortunately, he still needed the little man.

"Who are these creatures who dare attack a Kemmar planet?" said Tsogt.

"Based on information obtained from one of the captives, they are called humans," said the adviser.

"Humans. Where do these humans come from?"

"They come from a system known as Sol. We do not know its exact location, but it exists beyond the recently discovered gate."

"Yes, the gate. A remarkable piece of technology. A technology these humans appear to have mastered. Their ships use this knowledge to travel great distances in the blink of an eye. Why have our ships not been upgraded to do the same?"

"The gate technology is beyond our understanding, Eminence. We had captured a human engineer who was to reveal the technology, but lost him during the second attack on Kerces."

"Why was such a valuable asset left on Kerces?"

"The planetary commander overstepped his authority, Eminence."

"I want him executed."

"He was killed during the attack."

Tsogt grunted his approval. "What else do we know about these humans?"

"We know nothing more about their civilization beyond the gate."

"What are you holding back? Do not test my patience adviser."

"We have intelligence indicating that there is a species beyond Otan space that is identical to the humans, but we don't believe they are connected."

"Of course they are connected."

"With respect, Eminence, we feel that the distances between the two are too great."

"How do you imagine these humans ended up there?"

"We do not have sufficient intelligence to answer that question."

"That is because you simply do not have intelligence. There is another gate, you fool."

The adviser looked at his feet, but did not answer.

"If there is one gate, there must be more. That is the only explanation."

"Yes, Eminence."

"These gates are a great discovery, but they reveal a great threat at the same time," said Tsogt. "The humans have used this technology against us. They have taken position on opposite sides of the Empire. That gives them the ability to attack the Empire on two fronts. With the advanced technology of their gate ships it's a wonder they haven't attacked us already."

"They are wise to fear the might of the Kemmar Empire."

Tsogt growled, showing the adviser his teeth. "Idiot. The only answer is that the technology is experimental."

"Eminence?"

"It is obvious. Otherwise the humans would've sent a fleet to attack Kerces, not one solitary ship. And when they attacked a second time it was again with only one ship. After losing their first ship they would have to come back in force. That they risked coming back with a similar ship means they have no more."

"Perhaps their other ships were engaged elsewhere?"

"Do you think they would risk the Kemmar Empire gaining access to this technology? We had their engineer. They knew this. They knew we would soon have their secrets. They would have no choice but to attack with overwhelming force. They had no choice. That they didn't can only mean that there is only one gate ship."

"His Eminence is indeed wise."

"We need to capture that ship."

"All posts are on alert. The next time they appear we will be ready."

"We also need to prepare for war."

Tsogt looked back to his display and made a quick gesture with his right hand. The battle vanished from the display and a Kemmar face appeared in its place.

"How may I serve you, Eminence?"

"High Lord Toth, mobilize our forces along the Otan border."

"Yes, Eminence. May I ask our purpose?"

"Yes, High Lord. You are to annex Otan space."

# Chapter 30

Kevin felt strange standing on a Juttari bridge. After spending most of his military career fighting against the Juttari, he never thought he'd find himself here. He knew he took a chance trusting the Chaanisar, but what else could he do? Colonel Bast proved to be true to his word so far. The Chaanisar had in fact risen up against their Juttari masters and Bast had even showed Kevin their bodies to prove it. Now they were on an impossible quest to find Doctor Ellerbeck. The odds were against them. She could be anywhere. She might not have survived. But finding her was the only option for the Chaanisar. If they went back home, the Chaanisar would return to being Juttari slaves. Not a friendly thought.

What about Captain Pike? Did he survive? If so, where was he? If they searched for Ellerbeck they might find the Captain. Either way, he figured they owed it to Colonel Bast to help as much as they could. Without his help they may never have gotten off Kerces alive. The reality was Bast didn't need Kevin's help. Kevin had no idea where the doctor would be, so how could he help find her? The Chaanisar had also searched the prison and rescued what was left of the Reivers. Why?

It baffled him. These people had spent a lifetime fighting against their own kind, cruelly suppressing any human attempt at freedom. Could they really change just like that? Even if they were forced to commit all those atrocities, wouldn't the action itself change them? He didn't know the answer but he wanted to believe that they were in fact trying to make things right.

"Jump complete, Sir," said the Chaanisar at the helm.

The Chaanisar bridge was more of a pit, compared to the Hermes. There were multiple levels, with platforms that jutted out from the walls, but the center was open. Most of the action took place on the bottom level where an impressive array of technology and officers controlled the ship, but a considerable amount of activity took place on the upper level terraces. And then there were those symbols. Everywhere he looked the walls were covered in strange Juttari symbols. It was the same throughout the ship. Strange symbols covering every inch like wallpaper. It unnerved him. He didn't know if it was the fact that he didn't understand any of it, or just how weird it all looked, but it kept him from relaxing leaving him permanently on edge.

The viewscreen showed a massive debris field floating in space, seizing Kevin's attention.

"That is what's left of your ship, Chief St. Clair," said Colonel Bast, coming up beside him.

Kevin was speechless. His stomach hollowed out and a cold fist clenched around his heart. Bast had told him that the Hermes had been destroyed, but he didn't want to believe it. Now, seeing the debris in front of him, he knew in his heart it was true.

"Your escape pods dispersed from this location. We will search for your crew, and hopefully find your Doctor Ellerbeck. Of course any members of your crew we find will be welcome on board."

The escape pods. Bast had said the most of the crew escaped. They could still be alive. There was still hope. Still, the sight of the wreckage broke his heart. "I can't believe the Hermes is gone," said Kevin.

"She was a fine ship. With an even finer crew," said Bast.

"The best I've ever served with," said Kevin.

"Fear not, Chief. We will find them," said Bast.

"Sir, reading multiple Kemmar vessels on an intercept course," announced one of the Chaanisar officers.

"Initiate jump to search vector Alpha," said Bast.

"Initiating," said the helmsman.

"We have plotted the escape pod trajectories. We know which directions they took. We will have to search them one by one, however," said Bast.

"That won't be easy," said Kevin. With the amount of time that had passed, they could be anywhere. They had to try, though. They had to have hope.

"Unfortunately it will give the Kemmar time to do the same," said Bast. "The jump system gives us an advantage, but there are many escape pods. We'll need some luck too."

The Chaanisar ship landed near a yellow star system.

Bast turned to Kevin and said, "The escape pods engaged their FTL drives and would have traveled a significant distance before their FTL bubbles had to disengage. We have jumped ahead to where we believe that happened."

"You think they ended up in that star system?"

"It is possible."

The warship steadily advanced on the star system. Kevin had no idea where they were. They were way beyond unexplored space now. Were they still in Kemmar space? Were there other aliens to worry about? The Chaanisar probably didn't know either.

"Picking up Space Force beacon, Sir."

"Location?" said Bast.

"Far side of the third planet."

"Jump to third planet."

Kevin liked that. Bast didn't waste time. Why wait the countless hours it would take to reach the coordinates when you could just jump there? In an instant they were in orbit around the system's third planet.

"Are there any signs of civilization?"

"Negative."

"Prepare a rescue team," said Bast.

"I should go down too," said Kevin. "They may not trust your men, but they will recognize me."

"Agreed," said Bast.

# Chapter 31

"You can wear this one," said Lieutenant Jarvi, the Chaanisar soldier leading the rescue mission. He pointed to a Chaanisar combat suit. "I have disabled some of the suit's features to make it more compatible."

"What kind of features?" said Kevin.

"Our combat suits take advantage of the Juttari augmentation. I have modified yours to adapt to your reduced strength."

Kevin wondered if that was intended as an insult, or merely a statement of fact.

"Your suit will display your vital signs on your visor. For us the suits display vital signs and information on the health of our implants. Our brain chips allow us to further manipulate the suit's features through thought. I have modified your suit to function through verbal commands only."

"Those brain chips sound like they can be pretty handy."

"These brain chips have enslaved us, Chief," said Jarvi, the irritation clear in his voice.

"I apologize. I meant no offense."

"They do have numerous advantages," Jarvi said, his tone softening. "Although I would gladly give them up to prevent the Juttari from controlling me again."

"I can't imagine what that was like."

"Your imagination couldn't begin to comprehend the reality of our existence. Consider yourself lucky for that."

Kevin wanted to change the subject. "What else can this suit do?"

"Other than those features it is very similar to your own. It will protect you from most hostile environments, including space. You have access to an energy weapon, a rail gun, plasma grenades, and an ion blade. Do not access the weapons unless absolutely necessary. I do not want any of my men accidentally injured."

"Lieutenant Jarvi, I assure you I am more than capable of handling these weapons," said Kevin. It was his turn to be irritated now.

"These are Chaanisar weapons. They are not the same as your Space Force toys."

"Do we have a problem, Lieutenant?"

Jarvi ignored the challenge. "We can all communicate with each other over our own network. The network will provide you with information on the team's vital signs as well. Now if there are no more questions, we need to get started."

"Fine by me," said Kevin, still bristling from Jarvi's remarks.

The combat suit stood upright with its front section completely retracted. Kevin stepped into the boots and leaned back stretching out his arms. The suit powered on and encircled Kevin's frame with several whines, hisses and bangs as it locked into place. Finally the helmet closed in around his face and his visor came to life. He could see everything around him combined with an overlay of information. He saw his own vital signs and information on his suit's health. When he looked at the other Chaanisar the visor showed him their names as well as all their vital signs.

"Chief, can you hear me?" Lieutenant Jarvi's voice came through Kevin's helmet.

Kevin looked at the combat suit with Jarvi's name on it and said, "Loud and clear, Lieutenant."

"The rest of the team is ready. We will board the shuttle now."

"Understood."

Kevin followed Jarvi and the other Chaanisar out onto the adjoining hangar bay and the waiting shuttle. They entered the shuttle, five in total, and Jarvi pointed to a seat for Kevin to sit down. Loud bangs reverberated as his suit was locked into place. More bangs accompanied the other Chaanisar as they took their seats.

When all were seated the hatch closed and the shuttle's engines came on. The shuttle taxied across the hangar bay, bypassing other shuttles, fighters, and maintenance crews until it came to its launch point. Ahead of the shuttle was open space. The engines roared. The shuttle cleared the Chaanisar warship, and headed toward the planet below. It blazed through the atmosphere and descended toward their destination.

The planet looked like a massive rainforest. Trees reached several hundred feet into the sky. Their canopy seemed impenetrable. The shuttle used its thrusters to burn an opening through the leafy barrier, then continued its descent down into the jungle below.

When the shuttle landed, its locking system released the combat suits. Jarvi stood up and shouldered his energy weapon. The rest of the Chaanisar did the same and Kevin followed their lead, not caring how Jarvi felt about it. The Lieutenant exited the shuttle first, the other three Chaanisar followed with Kevin bringing up the rear.

Outside they entered one of the thickest jungles Kevin had ever seen. The shuttle's thrusters had burned a clearing for them, but beyond was dense foliage. It felt good to wear a combat suit again, even if it was a Juttari model. The powered armor made him feel almost invincible. He knew he could still get killed, but he always got the same feeling whenever he put one on. From his first days as a recruit donning a suit made him feel like he could take on any enemy. And why not? The suit gave him super human powers. He could move at incredible speeds, lift objects many times his own weight, and take an insane amount of punishment. He could also deploy a frightening amount of firepower. The increased strength of the suit allowed him to carry massive heavy weapons. How could you not feel invincible? The only problem was that the enemy often had combat suits too.

Jarvi's voice came over the suit, "Ion blades."

The Chaanisar kept their energy weapons in one hand and used their blades with the other. Kevin did the same, thinking they should call it an ion sword instead. They used the long powered blade to hack away the thick vegetation. It made for slow progress, as the jungle was deceptively resilient. All around him Kevin heard sounds of life. The forest itself seemed alive. Movement was everywhere. He couldn't shake the feeling that he was being watched. No, stalked, by some unseen enemy. Kevin looked around but didn't see anything. His visor picked up the heat signatures of local wildlife, but they weren't stalking them. The men in front of him started to look around more actively, showing that they felt the same thing.

When it happened, Kevin almost didn't register it. The speed and stealth of the attack surprised the entire team. A creature pounced from a nearby tree onto the second Chaanisar in the line, knocking the man face down to the ground. It was enormous and looked like some monstrous version of a tiger. Its body shimmered and it was covered in long nasty looking things that looked like knives.

The rest of the team immediately opened fire with their energy weapons and the creature roared in protest. The shimmer in its coat seemed to act like a reflector, making the energy bursts disperse on contact. It turned toward one Chaanisar, lowered its head and arched its back. The blades stood up and shot at the man like porcupine quills. A cluster of them hit, knocking the man backward, but his combat suit held. Still, Kevin noted the report on his visor showing that the quills had caused some damage to the suit's armor.

The animal circled, still holding the man underneath its front legs, firing daggers at the rest of the men. Several hit Kevin. The force of their impact stunned him, backing him up a few steps. One hit his helmet, jerking his head backward and narrowly missing his visor. With that kind of force it could easily penetrate the visor.

"Rail guns!" Jarvi ordered.

Kevin switched weapons, stepped forward and resumed firing at the beast. The others did the same.

The focused rail gun fire seemed to do the trick. The creature jumped away back up into the trees. It climbed up at incredible speed and was soon gone from view.

The fallen man got up, his helmet sporting several deep claw marks. Short of some damage to his suit's armor, he hadn't been hurt. It occurred to Kevin that the creature's heat signature had somehow not shown up on his visor. All around him he could see wildlife, even though many were hidden, because the visor picked them up. But that creature didn't even register. He assumed the strange shimmer

174

had something to do with it. Either way, it was one hell of a trick and some pretty effective camouflage.

The team continued on their path, with all men now looking up in addition to everywhere else. They steadily moved forward toward their target. Kevin wondered if there were more of those creatures. It looked like they were solitary hunters, but if they hunted in packs they could have their hands full quick. He didn't feel quite so invincible anymore. There was a rustling sound above him and he swung his weapon up, but didn't see anything. That damn thing could be hiding right over his head, waiting to strike. He kept walking, but he watched the trees, not the path before him.

They cut through some more undergrowth and saw the escape pod. It had created a small clearing where it landed. They cautiously approached the vessel turning as they stepped, making sure nothing crept up on them. The escape pod looked like it had been in a battle. Only when they got closer did Kevin realize that it was covered in claw marks. Those creatures were trying to get in, trying to break the craft open like a squirrel going after a nut.

"Okay Chief, get them to open the hatch. They'll probably recognize your voice," said Jarvi.

The Chaanisar fanned out around the escape pod, and watched the jungle warily. Kevin approached the hatch and knocked on it with a metal glove. He turned on his suit's speaker and said, "This is Security Chief Kevin St. Clair of the Hermes. We're here to rescue you. Please open your hatch."

The hatch unlocked and swung open in response. Kevin immediately recognized Ensign Petrovic and Ensign Yao. Unfortunately they didn't recognize him. All they saw was a Juttari combat suit. Petrovic moved first. He seized a rail gun and pointed it at Kevin.

"Don't shoot," said Kevin, putting his hands up in the air. "I'm telling you the truth."

"Retract your helmet," said Petrovic.

"Ok, just relax." Kevin retracted his helmet to show his face, shaking his feelings of vulnerability.

"Chief," said Petrovic, relaxing for a moment. Then he pointed the gun at Kevin's head. "Why are you wearing a Juttari combat suit? And who are the rest of these men?"

"I can explain. It's a long story, but you have to trust me."

Petrovic looked from Kevin to the other Chaanisar who were now looking back at him. Kevin hoped none of them would do anything rash.

Jarvi approached and Petrovic pointed the weapon at him. "I am Lieutenant Jarvi of the Chaanisar. If we wanted you dead, you wouldn't be breathing. Put down your weapon."

"The Chaanisar? Chief?"

"I'll explain everything. It's not what it looks like. But right now we need to get the hell out of here, before one of these animals kills us."

Kevin's comment registered and Petrovic dropped his weapon. Nodding he and Yao got up and walked out of the escape pod.

Yao grabbed a rail gun as she left. She looked up at Kevin and said, "Insurance."

Kevin smiled and said, "Let's go." He then retracted his helmet, feeling a little less exposed. He worried about Petrovic and Yao, though. If one of those things attacked them they'd be dead instantly without a combat suit.

Lieutenant Jarvi led the way back to the shuttle. Kevin walked behind Petrovic and Yao and two Chaanisar moved beside them to offer better protection. They all kept wary eyes on the trees.

"Those giant tiger things have been attacking us nonstop since we got here," said Petrovic. "Ensign McDougal was with us in the escape pod. He went out to look around when we got here and they got him. One second he was there and the next he was gone. The creature just grabbed him and raced up the tree. Then they came after us. We haven't opened the hatch since."

"Let's hurry up and get out of here before one of those things shows up again. You don't have combat suits to protect you."

They retraced their steps back to the shuttle, making faster progress with the path already cleared. When they reached the clearing and saw the Juttari shuttle Petrovic and Yao froze.

"Chief, what the fuck is going on?" said Yao.

"Madness," said Kevin. "Let's go, I'll fill you in on the ride up to the ship."

"That wouldn't be a Juttari ship up there, would it?" said Petrovic.

"It would," said Kevin.

Petrovic shook his head. "Okay, it's not like we've got anything to lose."

# Chapter 32

"So the Chaanisar are our allies now?" said Petrovic, his face twisted in disbelief.

"These Chaanisar," said Kevin.

The four Chaanisar on the shuttle had retracted their helmets and were looking at Petrovic and Yao, nodding in agreement.

"I can't believe it," said Yao.

"It is true," said Lieutenant Jarvi. "We are no longer Juttari slaves."

The other Chaanisar grunted their approval.

"One day the Juttari will pay for their crimes. Sadly, that day is not today," said Jarvi.

Petrovic and Yao looked at Jarvi with their mouths open. Kevin knew it was a tough idea to swallow. But they would have to accept it. Just as he and his Marines had.

"Tell me about the Hermes. What happened?" said Kevin.

"It was crazy, Chief," said Petrovic. "There was some kind of interference. I don't know if it was something the planet gave off, or if the Kemmar had some way of jamming our sensors, but we were blind up there."

"I remember the Hermes couldn't target the prison's defenses, or take over the prison's network," said Kevin.

"The interference created problems with several systems. The shuttles tried to compensate, but they were attacked by Kemmar fighters."

"Fighters?"

"They came out of nowhere, Chief. They started taking out our shuttles. They were too fast. The shuttles didn't stand a chance. So the Captain ordered the Hermes to enter the atmosphere."

"Sounds like something Captain Pike would do."

"It was a bold decision, and it should have worked."

"What went wrong?"

"One of the fighters got through our defenses and rammed us. That created an opening for the rest of the fighters, and they did the same."

"A suicide attack," said Jarvi. "These Kemmar do not fear death. That makes them formidable warriors."

"There was a massive hull breach and propulsion was knocked out. The Hermes went down," said Petrovic.

"Why didn't the Captain jump away?" said Kevin.

"It would've been a blind jump," said Yao. "There was no way of knowing where we would end up, and your team would've been stranded."

"That's Captain Pike for you," said Kevin. "No man left behind."

"Then Kemmar troops stormed the Hermes," said Petrovic. "Hundreds of them. There must've been an entire battalion down there."

"It appears the Kemmar had anticipated your rescue attempt," said Jarvi. "Your Captain should have planned better."

"The Captain did the best he could under the circumstances," said Kevin. "He had no way of knowing those troops were down there."

"Excuses are a sign of weakness," said Jarvi.

Kevin glared at Jarvi. The Lieutenant was treading dangerously close to his last nerve. He barely managed to keep his temper under control.

"With most of the Marines gone," said Petrovic, trying to diffuse the tension. "We didn't have a chance of defending the ship."

"And that was when the Captain ordered the jump," said Kevin.

"A blind jump," said Yao. "Unfortunately we ended up in a Kemmar system."

"We still had the Kemmar boarders to deal with," said Petrovic. "On top of that a Kemmar warship now raced to intercept us."

"So the Captain destroyed the Hermes," said Kevin.

"Yes, Sir."

"One big cluster fuck."

Petrovic and Yao nodded.

"What happened to your team, Chief?" said Petrovic.

"Some died in firefights. They had EMP weapons. Knocked out our combat suits and captured the rest of us."

A look of shock spread across Petrovic and Yao's faces. Kevin saw that they understood. For Kevin and his men being captured was a fate worse than death.

Kevin nodded and thought about Private Denney. "They're sick, ruthless bastards. We were able to escape. We fought our way out of our cells and then the Chaanisar showed up."

"Your Hermes had softened the Kemmar defenses," said Jarvi. "We battled the remaining Kemmar and Chief St. Clair's Marines successfully attacked them from the rear, ensuring their defeat."

Did Jarvi just give him credit for something? Kevin figured he should return the favor. "We're lucky the Chaanisar showed up when they did," said Kevin. "Or we would probably still be on that damn planet."

"What happens now?" said Yao.

"We find the rest of the crew," said Kevin.

# Chapter 33

Colonel Bast monitored the landing party's progress on his display. They had found two members of the Hermes crew, but neither of them were Doctor Ellerbeck. He couldn't help but feel some disappointment. He knew it would take time to find the Doctor, but he also hoped for some luck. Each additional second he had to live with the Juttari chip in his brain was a second he lived in fear.

What if the chip started working again? They had slain the Juttari officers and destroyed the broadcasting device, but what if they missed something? The thought haunted him. He and his men were free for the first time since childhood. Human once again.

185

But what did that mean? Could he ever be fully human again? He didn't know. That scared him almost as much as the thought of the Juttari controlling him. If they found the Doctor, and she was somehow able to remove the brain chips, then what? Return to Sol? To Earth?

Nobody would trust him there. He would still be Chaanisar. An abomination. They would blame him and his men for the atrocities committed while under Juttari control. Some would even suggest that they didn't do enough to resist. Of course they could not know the power of the Juttari brain chip, but would anyone care? Would they try to understand? Or would they be consumed with hate and a thirst for vengeance? They would be called war criminals. They might even be forced to stand trial for their crimes.

What about his family? Surely he had some relations left. Would they want to meet him? Would they consider him family? Or would they hide in horror, afraid of what he might do to them in a moment of relapse?

Deep down inside he knew there would be no place for him back on Earth. He had committed horrific crimes. Even if another controlled him, the blood still stained his own hands. He could not return to Earth. After a lifetime away he could not even consider it home anymore. He had no home.

A comm request brought him back to reality. It was his science officer, Lieutenant Schade. He had tasked Schade with investigating the ship's systems to determine if there was any hidden way to control the brain chips. Bast brought up Schade's face on his display.

"Yes, Lieutenant."

"Colonel, I have found something interesting."

Dread crept up the back of Bast's neck. "Do the Juttari have a fail-safe device?"

"No, Sir. I have not found evidence of any backup mechanism to re-initiate the broadcast."

Relief washed over Bast. "What did you find?"

"I believe I've found the source of the broadcast's malfunction," said Schade. "It appears that the broadcast failure was not an accident."

Bast leaned forward in his seat, closer to the display, as if Schade was about to whisper his next sentence.

"I almost missed it, Sir," said Schaude excitedly. "It was incredibly well hidden. A brilliant piece of work."

"Go on."

"It attacked in slow, quiet waves. A change here, a modification there, and nobody noticed a thing. Extremely sophisticated. The question is how they inserted it."

"How did who insert what?"

"Space Force, Sir. They managed to insert a virus into our systems. One that specifically attacked the Juttari broadcast device."

Bast leaned back into his chair, stunned. "How can that be possible? Space Force did not know about our mission."

"Someone did. The virus is clearly a Space Force design."

Bast knew the Juttari had spies in Space Force. There was no reason why Space Force, or the Diakans, did not have assets in place as well. But for someone to pull this off? They would have to be very high up to know about the mission and to even have access to the ship's systems. Unless Space Force knew there was a Juttari spy in place. The spy could have turned. Or, Space Force could have planted the virus in the Hermes systems. If they had uncovered the spy they would've known the Juttari ship would get infected. But why give up the jump system technology? No, they probably didn't know who the spy was, but had suspicions that there was a spy. The virus was a Space Force fail-safe in case the jump system was compromised.

"Could the virus have been inserted in the stolen Hermes technology?"

"Yes, that is possible. They could have inserted it into the jump system code. It could have been programmed to lay dormant in stealth mode. That way it wouldn't have been detected. Since the Juttari copied the Hermes jump system design, the virus was able to make it into our systems."

"But why didn't it affect the jump system?"

"That is the beauty of its design. It was programmed to be activated after a certain number of jumps. That would ensure the ship was far enough away from any backup Juttari broadcasts. Once activated, it traveled through our network, sought out and attacked the ship's broadcast system."

"Wouldn't it have done the same on the Hermes?"

"Yes, but it could easily have been programmed to not do any damage if there was no broadcast system."

"Fascinating. They assumed that the Chaanisar would mutiny once the Juttari lost control of their brain chips."

"Yes, Sir."

An ingenious tactic. Could Space Force have plans to liberate the rest of the Chaanisar? If the Juttari lost control, the Chaanisar would surely revolt. How many ships could be seized? It could potentially cripple the Empire.

If they had their brain chips removed, they could return with the virus and cripple the Empire themselves. Then Juttari blood would flow. Then the Juttari would know the meaning of Chaanisar justice.

"Do you possess the complete virus?"

"Yes, Sir."

"Safeguard it. It may still prove useful."

"Yes, Sir."

Bast switched back to view the landing team's progress. Their shuttle was almost aboard. He opened a comm with the bridge. "As soon as the landing team is on board, jump to the next search vector."

There would be no rest until the Doctor was found.

# Chapter 34

Singh stared at the Chaanisar guard watching him on the other side of the bars. There was cold malice in the guard's eyes. Why? He hadn't done anything to the Chaanisar. He shuddered. He wasn't built for this. He figured out puzzles, like starship reactors and jump systems. He was an engineer, not a soldier.

"Forget him," said Lynda. "He doesn't exist."

He looked away from the guard, and focused on Lynda. She was more beautiful than ever. Radiant. "Of course he exists. He's right there. Armed. Looking right at us.

She leaned closer and whispered in his ear, "There is only us. Only our love is real. Forget the guard. Forget this ship. Focus on me."

"The guard is real. So is this ship. Those are Chaanisar. They're going to kill us."

"No they will not."

"Why not?"

"They need you. They have a jump system don't they?"

"Yes."

"And your jump system expertise is second to none."

"Yes, that's true."

"So use it. Offer your services."

"They'll never trust me."

"Maybe not right away, but the time will come."

"How do you know?"

"They are in hostile space. Sooner or later they will find themselves in a battle. Jump systems often become damaged in warfare."

"Surely their own engineer can fix it."

"Do you think so? This is revolutionary technology. The Juttari wouldn't trust it to a Chaanisar."

"The Chaanisar killed all the Juttari. They have no engineer capable of repairing their jump system."

Lynda smiled, her blue eyes sparkling like precious gems. "Sooner or later, they will need you."

# Chapter 35

Jon thought about Jansen's mission. How was it that he was thousands of light years away from home and back to doing black ops? Only now he was taking Breeah and Anki along for the ride. He had really lost his mind. There was no other explanation. Not only would he be putting Breeah and Anki in danger, but they would also hamper his effectiveness.

His success at these missions was always directly related to his mindset. He truly believed he could succeed. He also resolutely accepted death. Even if he performed perfectly there was always the possibility of being killed. If he feared death he wouldn't function properly. Instead he embraced death. He laughed at the reaper. Defied him to come.

He looked over at Breeah and Anki. How could he be effective with the two of them coming along? He would constantly fear for their safety. That fear would make him second guess his actions. Make him hesitate. That could lead to mistakes. It was a bizarre irony that his fear for their safety could get them all killed in the end.

He couldn't allow that. He would have to leave them behind. Captain Seiben was a good man. He would leave them on the freighter with Seiben and he would complete his mission alone. Breeah would be angry with him, but she would understand.

A sound caught his attention. A feint sound that any other human wouldn't hear, but Jon's enhanced hearing picked it up. It was a common sound in the station. The faint whisper of forced air jets. What was out of place, however, was its location. The sound was directly outside their building. Above them now, but descending quickly. From what he had seen the station vehicles primarily used the rooftops, and didn't often descend down to the street.

His instincts warned him of the threat before his mind could register it. He knew from experience to obey his instincts. Breeah and Anki were getting their things ready and hadn't realized anything was wrong. The craft had almost reached their floor. Seconds away.

"Get down!" said Jon.

Breeah gave him a confused glance, but thankfully she trusted him enough to grab Anki and drop to the floor. Jon dropped as well, just as the vehicle came into view outside their window. It was similar to the craft that had brought them into the city, except for one difference. This one was armed.

Two Gatling guns jutted out from its sides. The craft stopped its descent in front of their apartment's windows and opened fire. Orange flashes spewed bullets at the windows. Anki screamed as the glass shattered and bullets ripped through the walls and furniture, shredding everything in their path. Breeah lay on top of Anki, using her body to protect her. The craft turned from left to right, flooding the room in a metal torrent. The pilot hadn't seen them on the floor and fired high, targeting someone who would be standing or sitting on a chair. Soon he would find their heat signatures and spray the floor.

Jon regretted leaving his railgun behind on the freighter. Now he was completely unarmed. They had to move.

"Breeah, I'm going to draw its fire. When I do you and Anki run in the opposite direction and get out of the apartment."

Breeah looked at him, concern on her face, and nodded.

Jon sprang to his feet and ran toward the bedroom, adrenaline coursing through his veins. Just as he anticipated, the guns followed. His speed gave him an edge and the guns missed him, but not by much. The guns changed direction as the pilot realized Breeah and Anki were escaping, and fired to block their escape. Breeah turned just in time and took Anki back to the floor, the little girl crying in fear.

Jon jumped up and ran straight toward the  attack craft, giving it something more threatening to worry about. That caught its attention and it shifted toward Jon again. Breeah seized the opportunity, jumped up and rushed Anki out the door.

Jon moved to evade the gunfire. He dove, the fire retargeted, he leaped, the craft moved with him, he rolled, bullets followed. Jon bounced around the room like a rubber ball, changing directions with inhuman speed. His assailants expected an easy kill, but his abilities caught them off guard. How long could he keep this up? He couldn't run for the door without getting hit. Sooner or later the gunfire would catch him. He needed to change tactics.

He spotted a round sculpture that had decorated the apartment. An odd looking thing. He had noticed it when they first arrived. More importantly, he knew it had some weight to it. He dove near it, evading another strafing attack, and snatched it as he rolled by.

Coming out of his roll he jumped up and threw the heavy object at the hovercraft. His strength and accuracy sent the orb smashing though the hovercraft's window and hammering the pilot in the chest. The craft's front end tilted up and its guns fired harmlessly away from the apartment. It lurched backward at the same time, moving further away.

Jon had hurt the pilot. If lucky he killed him. But there was a second passenger. He might be able to gain control of the craft and resume the attack. Confirmation came when he saw the pilot's body pushed out of the craft and fall to the ground below.

He had mere seconds now, and he had to reach Breeah and Anki. He bolted for the door and made it out just as a fresh salvo exploded behind him. The bullets ripped through the wall like it wasn't there, spraying debris in all directions.

Jon turned and ran down the hallway, but the bullets didn't follow. Maybe his attackers weren't willing to fire on other apartments. Or, the hovercraft was repositioning itself. Anticipating their next move.

Jon turned a corner and saw Breeah and Anki. Breeah had taken off her lariat belt and whipped it around at a black clad attacker. That was why the guns didn't follow him, they were afraid of hitting their men in the hallway. The man ducked and the weighted ball on the end of the rope belt just missed connecting with his head.

On the floor lay a second assailant, who had apparently underestimated Breeah's skill. The man standing held a long blade in his hand. A gun lay at his feet. Breeah had managed to dispose of one attacker and disarm the second. She always found ways to impress him.

He almost wanted to just hang back and watch, confident in her abilities. But they weren't safe yet. He ran toward her just as the attacker lunged, thrusting his blade at Breeah's chest. She deftly sidestepped the strike and at the same time swung her lariat around striking the man in the temple with the heavy ball. The blow dropped him instantly.

She turned, still swinging the lariat, as Jon approached, almost striking him as well, but changed the ball's direction once she recognized who it was.

"Easy. I'm one of the good guys," said Jon.

"Sorry," said Breeah, a wry smile forming on her lips, her eyes softening just slightly.

Jon reached down and grabbed the two energy weapons on the floor, tossing one to Breeah. She took the weapon and slung the lariat belt back around her waist. Even the simplest things could be deadly weapons in the right hands.

He looked back at the assailants. They were dressed in black military garb, but had no patches or insignias. Whoever was after them didn't want to be identified.

"Who are they?" said Breeah.

"I don't know," said Jon.

"Are they raiders?"

"They don't look like the raiders we encountered on the freighter. They could be mercenaries."

"You think this Durril Tai hired them?"

"Maybe. I don't think the Kemmar would use human mercenaries, but anything's possible. Still, how would the Kemmar know we were here?"

"You could ask the same thing of the raiders. How would Durril Tai know about us already?"

"Good question. Someone is talking. We'll have to worry about who that might be later. Right now, we have to get out of here."

He reached down and picked up Anki. She put her arms around his neck and gripped his torso with her legs.

200

"How are you doing, kid?"

She smiled. "I'm okay. Did you see my mom fight?"

"I did."

"Isn't she amazing?"

"She sure is," said Jon. "She's my hero."

"Mine too," said Anki.

Breeah rolled her eyes and gestured to Jon to hurry up.

"It's time to go now," Jon said to Anki. "I want you to hold on tight, okay? No matter what happens you hold on to me."

Anki's face went serious and she nodded. "I know how to hold on."

"Good." Jon looked at Breeah and said, "Ready?"

"Ready."

"Let's go."

They moved cautiously down the hallway.

"We can't take the elevators," said Jon. "That attack craft might still be out there, and those glass elevators are too exposed. We have to take the stairs."

They found the stairwell and headed down. The buildings on DLC station were extremely tall. The apartment was on the forty-fifth floor. A lot of stairs. Breeah was fit. In better shape than most people he knew. Hopefully she wouldn't be too winded by the time they got to the bottom.

Unfortunately they wouldn't find out right away. They descended several floors, heard a door swing open, and feet charging down the stairs from above. It sounded like five men altogether. They would have found the men Breeah disposed of. They would've seen that their weapons were missing and know that Jon and Breeah were armed. They would be more careful now.

Jon approached the door to the forty-second floor. He opened it and they ran into the hallway with Breeah close behind. He didn't want to fight in the stairway. He feared the possibility that more men would appear from the floor below. He didn't know how many there were, but knew that they were all on alert now. They had likely assumed that the attack craft would succeed in killing them. The rest of the men would have been intended to act as mop up, or back up. None of them would have dreamed that the attack craft would have failed. But now they knew different.

They rounded a corner just as the attackers entered the hallway. Jon swung his arm out from behind the wall and fired on the men, hitting one in the shoulder before they returned fire.

He had to get Breeah and Anki to safety. He could hold these men off while they escaped. "There should be another stairwell on the other side of the building," said Jon. "Take Anki and head that way. I'll catch up."

"No, we fight together," said Breeah, crouching down against the wall, swinging her weapon our and firing at their assailants.

"Can you not just listen to me for once?"

She pulled back behind the wall as a fresh round of energy bolts sailed by her. She looked up and fixed Jon with a threatening stare. "We fight together. We do not separate."

Jon cursed. He knew she was right, but again, he was worried that they would get hurt. Anki wisely stayed well back. Jon motioned with his hand for her to crouch down. She did. At least she listened. Breeah resumed firing and he swung his arm around to join her in the attack. The tactic took out another attacker, and seemed to take them by surprise.

Breeah shook her head. "They are used to attacking helpless victims, not people who can actually fight back," she said, disdain in her voice.

"Three left," said Jon. "Now it's more of a fair fight."

"It's still unfair," said Breeah, letting loose another volley. "For them."

Jon smiled and joined Breeah in firing back. He worried about her because he loved her, but he had to admit she was a hell of a fighter. He looked back to check on Anki. She was still crouched low and had a serious look on her face, but when she saw Jon looking at her she cocked her head and flashed him a smile. It was as if she was trying to reassure him. That kid was one tough cookie.

Their assailants had opened the door to the stairwell and were using it for cover. They fired haphazardly, with no real pattern. Jon and Breeah started taking turns, Jon firing, then Breeah. It was predictable. He knew the attackers would try to use it against them. Jon fired and made a mental note of an attacker's exposed leg. He put a hand on Breeah's shoulder telling her to wait.

Just as he expected, weapon fire came in low, anticipating that Breeah would jump out. Instead Jon fired again and picked off the exposed thigh. Ducking back behind the wall he heard the man screaming from the other end of the hallway, a fresh hole burned into his quads.

Jon yelled at the remaining men, "You hear that? Death is coming." A little psychological warfare never hurt. But he wasn't just playing head games. Death was coming for them. Right now.

He tapped Breeah again and she sprang out, firing on the last two. He surged forward and charged them. They had ducked behind the door to evade Breeah's shots, but when they realized what was happening one came out trying to fire on Jon. Jon was faster. He picked the man off before he could shoot. The door closed as the last attacker jumped back into the stairwell.

Breeah held her fire as Jon made it to the door. He stood back and opened it in case the man waited in ambush, but there were no shots. He entered and listened for footsteps. He heard them. The man ran down the stairs, trying to escape the reaper. It wasn't going to happen. Jon raced down the stairway, clearing five steps at a time, closing on his prey. As he gained ground on his quarry, he was greeted by panicked firing. He could still hear the man's footsteps and knew he was firing backwards blindly while running.

Jon looked over the railing and saw the man's hand gripping the railing below. He swung his weapon over the railing and locked onto the hand. He fired. The man screamed. He heard him tumble, obviously losing his footing. Jon rushed forward, moving in for the kill, and found the man's contorted body lying on a landing, already dead. The fall had broken his neck.

Above him he heard footsteps, and then Breeah's voice, "Jon?"

"Down here."

Breeah and Anki came down the stairs to Jon's location.

"Are you alright?" said Breeah.

"Yeah. You?"

"Fine."

He reached down and picked up Anki, who was looking at the dead man on the stairs.

"What happened to him?" said Anki.

"He tripped," said Jon.

Anki shook her head. "He should have held the railing."

# Chapter 36

Twenty more flights of stairs and Breeah still felt pretty good. Her legs didn't hurt. Her breathing wasn't strained. Thankfully her stamina had returned. After getting shot on the Hermes, she wondered if her fitness level would come back once she recovered. Jon had assured her it would, and he was right. She had made a full recovery, and none too soon.

She had needed her reflexes when the first two men came at her. A lifetime of training ensured that her body reacted with precision, and deadly force. Those fools saw a mother and daughter. Victims. She had always been taught never to underestimate an opponent.

Apparently those men never learned that lesson, and it cost them their lives. So many were like that. Never challenging themselves. Never pushing. Assuming their opponents would always be weaker. That wasn't how she was brought up. Her father always taught her to fight from a position of weakness. Always assume your enemy is stronger, he used to say. Always assume you are outnumbered. What will you do? How will you survive?

Ahead of her Jon came to a stop and raised his hand. Looking back at her he pointed to his ear and then pointed down the stairs. More attackers. Jon had told her about his special abilities, but it still amazed her. She heard nothing but knew not to question his senses. Then there were his physical abilities. Speed. Strength. Endurance. He still held Anki, down all those flights of stairs, and didn't have a bead of sweat to show for it.

Ahead of them was a door leading to the twenty-third floor. Jon pointed to it and they rushed through. They quietly moved down the hallway. She kept glancing back as they went, pointing her weapon behind her in fear that the enemy would come through the door and shoot them in the back. They rounded a corner. She pointed her weapon ahead. It was clear. They kept moving. She looked behind her. Still nobody. She was ready, but tense. Part of her wanted to be attacked. She wanted to face her enemy, not worry about phantoms and shadows.

Halfway through they came upon a walkway connecting their building to a neighboring one. An opportunity to escape? They hastened across the walkway. The glass surrounding them made her feel very exposed. They were suspended between two buildings, fully visible to anyone looking in their direction. She expected the attack craft to show up again and fire. She pointed her weapon up toward the sky. Swept it from side to side. She brought it down and panned left to right. Up and down. Nothing. She turned and aimed at her rear. Nobody came. She aimed up again, looking for the attack craft. It was nowhere to be found.

When she looked back to where their apartment was she saw several more wingless aircraft buzzing around it. Were they the authorities investigating the incident? Was that why the attacking craft left? Or were they the enemy too? Everything was unfamiliar. How could you tell friend from foe? The greatest enemy hides in the light of day, her father used to say. Did artificial daylight count?

They made it across the walkway without incident. Nobody followed. Jon slowed his pace a bit, turned back to her and said, "I think we can use the elevators now."

"I did not see anything when we crossed," said Breeah.

"Neither did I. Looks like the attack craft is gone."

"What about the men on foot?"

"They could be anywhere, but I'm guessing they're looking for us in that building."

"What do we do now?"

"We need to find Captain Seiben," said Jon. "If they know about us they probably know about his involvement in the mission."

"So you do think this is the work of the raiders?"

"We can't know for sure, but it's the most logical explanation."

"Well let's find Captain Seiben."

Captain Seiben was a nice man. A genuine man. You could count on him to be honest. She liked him and his family and hoped nothing happened to them.

They got onto the elevator and took it down. They both concealed the guns in their waistbands, under their shirts. The elevator stopped repeatedly, letting more people on with each stop. Before long the cabin was fairly crowded. She didn't mind mixing with the crowd. It would help them hide. She just hoped none of the other passengers were the enemy.

Their adversaries were a mystery. Who were they? Why had they come? They could only guess. She could be staring straight at one and not know until it was too late. She hoped Jon would know. She counted on it.

They made it to the ground level without incident and joined the throngs of people on the sidewalk. She tried to act normal, but could not help looking around constantly. She tried to stay calm, but her nerves were quickly becoming unraveled. Her suspicion of those around her bordered on paranoia. She couldn't help it. She did not want to be surprised.

But she was.

The crowd had pressed in around her making it difficult to keep a protective buffer between herself and others. A cold point pressed against her back. A knife.

Breeah didn't know if it would be pushed in and didn't want to find out. The second it touched her spine she spun. She timed it well. Even if the thrust came it would be partially deflected. It wouldn't be a killing strike. But the man behind her didn't thrust. He hesitated. Probably confident in taking her by surprise.

One of the first things she was taught growing up was to defang the snake. Your opponent has a weapon. Whether you have one or not you have to eliminate the threat. The snake's fangs. In this case the knife. She fluidly did this with three moves, taking no more than a second to execute.

Her arm came around first and hit the attacker's forearm, moving the knife away from her body. He still held the knife and would quickly come back at her with a slash, followed by a thrust. To avoid that her other hand followed and checked the man's elbow, taking away his attack. Control the elbow and you control the arm. The third thing she did as she came around was hammer her heel into the man's knee.

It takes just nine pounds of pressure to break a knee. The strike made the man buckle and instinctively reach for his leg. That split second loss of focus allowed her to strip the knife out of his hand. The man's eyes widened with shock as his own blade came back at him. She swung it across the side of his neck, slashing the artery, and then thrust it back like a piston, driving the point into his throat.

One of the other things she was taught early on: always aim for the soft targets.

But most importantly, know your target. Choose a target and go after it. Commit. A focused, decisive attack is more likely to succeed and will often overwhelm your opponent. Even a stronger opponent.

She quickly became aware of the crowd around her. People were now screaming in horror at the man falling to the ground, blood squirting in the air from the severed artery in his neck. And her standing there, still gripping the blood soaked blade.

Jon grabbed her by the arm and yanked her away. "We have to go. Now!" he said.

They ran down the street, the frightened crowd parting for them as they went. Breeah threw away the knife. She still had the gun, and she didn't think that carrying a bloody knife in her hand would help her cause.

# Chapter 37

"But you just got home," said Darla, Captain Seiben's wife. "You're not supposed to go out again for at least three weeks. It's in your contract."

"I know, but how can I refuse Mr. Jansen?" said Seiben. He understood her frustration, but he couldn't tell her the truth.

"It's not right. What about Alina and Otka? They've barely spent any time with you."

"I won't be gone as long this time."

"There are other freighter captains. Jansen should pick one of them."

"This freight is very valuable. That Mr. Jansen wants me to take this trip, rather than someone else, is a great honor. He is also paying me well for the trip. Three times my regular wages."

"We don't need the money. The girls need to see their father. I need to see my husband."

"It is only this once."

That set her off. "No it isn't," she snapped. She wagged a finger at him and said, "If you do it this time, Jansen will expect you to do it again."

"And what would you have me do? Say no? Lose my job? Where would that leave us?"

"We could leave the station," she said, her tone softening, pleading. "We could emigrate to one of the planets. The kids could feel what it's like to truly be outside. To breathe in fresh air."

"The air on the station is fresh," said Seiben, defensively. "It's constantly filtered. It's probably cleaner than any of the planets."

"You know what I mean," said Darla. "We could start a new life. This isn't the only place to live in the universe."

"And what would I do there? There isn't any demand for freighter captains on the planets."

"Do you have to haul freight?"

"Would you have me carry passengers then? Perhaps I should become a tour guide?"

"My point is there are opportunities there, so long as you are willing to look for them. We don't have to be trapped on this station."

"We aren't trapped. We have a good life here."

"Do we?"

"Yes, we do. All our needs are provided for. The children are getting a great education. I have a good position."

"A position that leaves no time for your family. And what about the last time? Those raiders could've killed you. You put yourself at risk every time you go out."

What would she do if she knew the risk he was taking with this mission? "Nothing would've happened. Even if Jon wasn't there Mr. Jansen would've paid the ransom and they would've let us go."

"And if he didn't pay? Then what."

"Don't be silly. The cargo and freighter are worth more than the ransom. Of course he would pay."

Darla stood there pouting. He knew he couldn't change her mind. She was a planet girl and always would be. She could never fully accept this life. He pulled her close and gave her a hug. She relaxed a little but he could tell she was still mad.

"Once I come back from this run I'll arrange for some extra time off. We'll take a vacation. Maybe we'll visit one of those planets you're so fond of. One with oceans and beaches."

"The girls would love that," she said, succumbing to the compromise.

The knock at the door interrupted them. Seiben threw his hands up. "Can we not find a moment of peace?"

He let go of Darla, walked to the door and opened it. Three men stood there, dressed in black. For a second he thought they were DLC security personnel, but didn't see the DLC insignia, or any other for that matter.

"Who the hell are you?" said Seiben.

One of the men pulled out an energy weapon, pointed it at Seiben's head and said, "May we come in?"

# Chapter 38

They reached Seiben's building without further incident. Were the attackers still in pursuit? Jon didn't know. Perhaps they didn't want to try anything else out in the open. He could only assume that they were waiting for a more discrete opportunity. Either way he had to warn Captain Seiben. They needed to leave their apartment and go somewhere safe, at least until they knew what was going on.

They got into the glass lift and took it up to Seiben's floor. Looking out of the elevator onto the city everything seemed normal. Yet every hovercraft floating above them could be a threat. Every person walking below an enemy. Every window in the buildings around them hiding a sniper.

He didn't know his enemy, and that left him feeling very vulnerable. Hell, he didn't know this city, this station, or this region of space.

They got out of the elevator and walked down the hall to Seiben's apartment. Before they reached his door Jon put Anki down and put a finger to his mouth, telling her not to make a sound. He gestured to Breeah to stay back with Anki. Breeah nodded and pulled out the gun from her waistband. Jon did the same and headed toward the door.

He stood beside the door and knocked on it. His fears were realized when weapon fire ripped through it. He backed up and waited. The door opened and a man stepped out, weapon drawn, his arm sweeping the hallway in a wide arc. Jon fired. The man dropped.

More gunfire burst through the open door. How many more men were inside the apartment? Had they killed Seiben? His family? There was no way of knowing without going in.

"Mr. Pike," said a voice from inside the apartment. "I have Captain Seiben. I have his wife. And I have his little girls. Cute kids. But not for long. Unless you come through that door."

Jon turned to Breeah. "I need your help," he whispered. "I'm going to go in and draw their fire. When they start firing at me I want you to take them out."

"What about Captain Seiben and his family?"

"Don't shoot them."

Breeah frowned, but nodded her agreement.

"I'm not a patient man Mr. Pike," said the man. "I am going to shoot one of these little girls now."

"Wait," said Jon. "I'm coming in."

Jon turned to the doorway, took a breath, and dove in. The men inside were waiting and fired immediately, barely missing him. He moved as quick as he could through the room. So long as the gunfire chased him it meant they were no longer facing the door.

Breeah appeared in the doorway and fired, hitting the first man in the head. She fired at the second, but he managed to duck. He jumped up, holding Alina in front of him, and pointed his gun at Breeah. She couldn't fire without hitting the little girl.

The man fired at Breeah and she jumped back behind the wall. The man pointed the gun at Darla and fired.

When Breeah had fired Jon had changed direction and headed for the gunmen. He didn't want to risk hitting the little girl so he didn't fire his weapon. He had to disarm him first. He lunged for the man's weapon as he aimed it at Darla. Then he heard the gun go off.

He had hit the man's arm and knocked it upwards, hoping the shot would miss. He hit it again, breaking it. The man dropped his gun to the floor, and dropped Alina, trying in vain to strike back. Jon easily blocked the strike, grabbed the arm, and broke it too. He was surprised when the man fell to the floor with Captain Seiben on top of him.

"You filthy scum," yelled Seiben. "I'll kill you." Seiben sat on top of the man clubbing him repeatedly with his heavy fists. After the second blow it was clear the man was unconscious, but Seiben kept hitting him.

Jon figured Seiben deserved some revenge so he let him get a few more punches in. He looked back and to his relief saw that Darla was still alive. The shot had missed her after all. Then he turned back to Seiben and said, "It might be better if you didn't kill him. We might find out who sent them."

Seiben stopped and looked up at Jon, a look of confusion on his face. He seemed to realize what Jon was saying and nodded in agreement. He looked down at the unconscious man and spit. Then he got up and went to his family. He took two steps toward them, turned and looked back at the man like he had an idea. He took a step back and unloaded a powerful kick to the man's groin. The force of the kick moved the man's body several feet.

Jon cringed. "Was that really necessary?"

"Something for him to remember me by," said Seiben.

# Chapter 39

"I don't understand how this could happen," said Jansen, his eyes intense.

Jon studied Jansen's face, but couldn't get a good read from the display. He didn't think Jansen was behind the attack. What motive could he have? There was no way it could be the Kemmar. That left Durril Tai.

"Well it happened," said Jon. "The raiders had to be behind this, which means you have a leak."

"Impossible. How could they have found out about the mission so fast? Or coordinate such a quick response?"

"I don't know, but it's the only explanation."

"Captain, surely a man with your particular talents has many enemies."

Jon didn't like Jansen's smug tone. "Even if that was the case, nobody knows I'm here."

"It is possible, though. Someone could have tracked you here."

Jon considered Jansen's words. Could it be the Kemmar? Would they hire human mercenaries? Considering the isolationism in the colonies, it would be easier to use humans than Kemmar. Did they somehow manage to track his escape pod? If so, why not just capture it in space?

"I don't think so," said Jon. "The only answer is the raiders. Otherwise why would they come after Captain Seiben?"

"What's he talking about?" said Darla, sitting behind Jon on the couch with her two daughters.

"Nothing dear," said Seiben, nervously.

"You're lying. What's going on? What's all this talk about raiders coming after you?"

There was a knock at the door and Seiben jumped up to answer it.

"Wait," said Jon. "I better check it out."

Seiben rolled his eyes. "Ok, go ahead," he said, and went back to his chair, smacking the armrest with his hand as he sat. He watched Jon approach the door, avoiding Darla's furious eyes.

Jon felt guilty about Captain Seiben. The mission was Jansen's idea, and Jansen was the one forcing Seiben's involvement, putting him in danger. Still, he felt responsible somehow.

Jon gripped the energy weapon in his right hand, pointed it at the door, and stood off to the side.

"Who is it?" said Jon.

"Kulberg. Mr. Jansen sent me."

Jon looked back at Jansen's face on the display. "Should we be expecting Kulberg?"

"Yes, he'll be arriving any minute," said Jansen.

Jon lowered his weapon and opened the door. Kulberg strode in with his two guards. Arrogance poured out of the man. From the fake smile on his face, to the way he carried himself, everything about him rubbed Jon the wrong way. But it wasn't just that he disliked him. Something about him instinctively set him off, warning him of some hidden danger.

"I've come to take your prisoner," said Kulberg, flashing Jon his PR smile.

"He's right over there," said Jon, pointing to the now conscious man propped up against the wall.

Kulberg looked at his guards and said, "Take him."

The two men walked up to the man and grabbed him by the arms. That woke him up and made him scream. The guards let go, a look of confusion on their faces.

"Sorry about that," said Jon. "I might have broken his arms."

The guards shrugged. They hooked their hands under his armpits and picked him up that way. The man groaned as they walked him forward, his head hung low, dragging his feet.

"Kulberg looked at Jon and smiled again. "Don't worry, Captain Pike, we'll find out what's going on."

"Good luck," said Jon.

Kulberg studied Jon for a moment, as if deciding how to respond, but said nothing. He simply turned and left, the guards following, dragging the prisoner with them.

# Chapter 40

The black vehicle lifted off the roof. Its jets swung around, propelling it forward. It sailed away from the crowded city, gliding quietly, a dark blemish in the cloudless blue sky. Beneath it the towering structures disappeared and were replaced by trees and green grass.

Inside the craft the four men were silent. The two guards were in the front, one piloting the vehicle. Kulberg sat in the back with the prisoner. He hadn't taken his eyes off him since they left. The man was a joke, thought Kulberg.

"Explain to me again how your team of so called soldiers, high priced soldiers I might add, managed to fail so spectacularly," said Kulberg.

"We-"

"One man," continued Kulberg. "One man, a woman and a child. How hard could that be for a team of skilled mercenaries?"

"That's no man I've ever seen," said the prisoner. "I've never seen any man move that fast. And the woman. She fights like a professional."

"What about the little girl?" mocked Kulberg. "How many of your men did she kill?"

"The girl didn't fight."

"Well aren't you lucky. Who knows what would've happened if they let the little girl loose on your men."

"Sir, I'm telling you the truth. These ain't no ordinary people."

"You know something? I'm tired of listening to your excuses."

"Next time we'll-"

"There is no next time. At least not for you."

Kulberg reached into his jacket and pulled out a small handgun. He pointed it at the man who looked back with terror. Kulberg waited while the man tried to move away, pushing with his legs until he fell off the seat onto the floor. There was nowhere for him to go.

"You want to get out?" said Kulberg. He pressed button beside him and the side door slid open. "Ok, out you go." Kulberg pushed the man with his foot. The man kicked back, trying to protect himself. Kulberg leaned in and fired the weapon point blank into the man's leg. Screams filled the cabin. Kulberg fired a second time, into the man's other leg.

"Broken arms and wounded legs," said Kulberg. "That makes you twice as useless." He returned the gun to his jacket, reached down and seized the man's ankles with his hands. He lifted till he had him upside down, then threw his legs out the door. The man tried to move his broken arms, but didn't have a chance, and his body followed his legs out of the vehicle.

Kulberg closed the door and accessed a panel. A display lit up in front of him and Durril Tai's face appeared.

"Is it done?" said Tai.

"We encountered some unforeseen resistance," said Kulberg. "This man is more formidable than we first assumed."

"I see," said Tai. He paused for a moment and then said, "No matter. Move forward with the poison pill."

"Understood. Leave it to me."

# Chapter 41

"Picking up Space Force beacon, Sir," said the Chaanisar officer.

"Have the Kemmar located the escape pod?" said Colonel Bast.

"Yes, Sir. Kemmar cruiser has dispatched retrieval craft. They have secured the escape pod and are returning to the cruiser.

Bast knew this would come sooner or later. "Sound battle alert."

A klaxon sounded throughout the ship alerting of the upcoming battle.

"Helmsman, initiate jump. Get us in between the Kemmar cruiser and the escape pod."

"Yes, Sir."

"Ready weapons. Fire on the retrieval craft the moment we land."

Chief St. Clair stood beside him, watching the viewscreen intently.

"We will prevail, Chief," said Bast, unwavering confidence in his voice.

"There's not a lot of space between that cruiser and the escape pod," said St. Clair.

"There is enough," said Bast.

"Initiate retrieval operations the moment we land." He looked over at Kevin and said, "We will block the Kemmar with our ship while we retrieve the escape pod."

"Ballsy move, Colonel."

"Ballsy?"

"Yeah, ballsy. It's a compliment."

Bast nodded. "Then we will endeavor to continue making ballsy moves, Chief."

St. Clair flashed a mischievous smirk.

Bast liked Chief St. Clair. The man was a warrior. As tough as any he had seen. But he was also a good natured person. He wondered what his childhood was like. Likely a happy time. He had tried repeatedly to remember something about his own childhood, but nothing came to him. There was only the Juttari. Only the Chaanisar.

They jumped and the Kemmar warship filled the viewscreen. The Chaanisar energy weapons fired and easily disposed of the Kemmar retrieval craft.

"Target the Kemmar cruiser. All weapons. Fire at will."

Energy weapons and missiles burst forth like merciless daggers, landing unopposed. The Kemmar warship had obviously been surprised by the attack. Explosions rocked the cruiser causing damage to its armor plating and some of its systems.

"Kemmar cruiser is returning fire."

"Keep firing," said Bast. "Launch countermeasures. Activate point defense system."

Missiles streaked towards the Chaanisar ship, glowing red like celestial demons. The Chaanisar ship spit out a cluster of drones, which scattered. They burned with disproportionate heat for their size, broadcasting the Chaanisar ship's signature. They fooled most of the missiles, making them chase the drones instead of the ship. The ones not pulled off course were destroyed by the point defense perimeter. A wall of exploding shells.

The two ships faced each other broadside, pounding one another like two ancient wooden ships of the line. Red and blue energy bursts lit up the void, pulverizing the hulls on both sides.

"Maintain position between them and the escape pod," said Bast. "What is the status of the retrieval operation?"

"Grappling drones are underway, Sir."

On the other side of the Chaanisar battle cruiser several drones raced toward the escape pod. Once within range they fired their grapplers, long arms with magnetic claws on the ends. The claws seized the escape pod, and the drones overpowered it, forcing it to follow them back to their ship.

"Kemmar cruiser is changing course," said the Helmsman. "They're turning toward us. They're trying to ram us, Sir."

"Ballsy move," said Bast.

"They're playing chicken," said Kevin.

"Chicken?"

"A game played on Earth. Whoever gets scared first loses."

The thought provoked Bast and a spark of defiance overtook him. "Let's play chicken then." He turned to the helmsman and said, "Hold position. Do not move until the escape pod is safely on board."

The Kemmar cruiser continued its slow turn towards the Chaanisar ship. Both vessels maintained constant fire on each other without pause.

"Reading hull breaches on Kemmar cruiser."

"Keep firing," said Bast.

"Colonel," said the Tactician. "The Kemmar vessel has passed the point where it can safely stop its turn. Collision is now imminent."

"Is the escape pod on board yet?"

"Negative, Sir."

"Time till impact?"

"Three minutes."

"Hold position."

Bast had developed some measure of respect for the Kemmar's willingness to sacrifice themselves in order to win a battle. They didn't fear death. That ship was going to ram them. Nonetheless, he would not run from them. They were not the superior warriors, and his crew would accept death just as readily as any Kemmar. If they wanted to test his will to win they would be sorely disappointed with the outcome.

As it turned the cruiser lost use of some of its batteries, reducing its rate of fire. The Chaanisar ship didn't budge. It stood toe to toe with the Kemmar ship and threw everything it had at it, like an exhausted heavyweight.

"Hull breach level three. Emergency field is in place."

The retrieval drones slowly approached the Chaanisar ship, hampered by the weight of the Space Force escape pod.

"Two minutes until impact."

"They're calling your bluff, Colonel."

"I am learning a lot today. What is a bluff?"

"A bluff is when you're pretending to do something you don't really intend to do."

"I see. You don't think I intend to let them ram my ship?" Bast locked eyes with the Chief, letting him see the resolve in his eyes.

The Chief seemed to turn cautious. "It doesn't seem like a desirable outcome."

Bast smiled. "Perhaps not. We can jump away to safety, but what if the Doctor is on board that escape pod? We would lose her to the Kemmar."

Kevin nodded. Understanding in his eyes.

"One minute till impact."

"The difference between success and failure often comes down to commitment. The Kemmar have shown they are worthy opponents, committed to victory. Are we less than the Kemmar?"

The question triggered a defiant posture from the Chief. He squared his shoulders and said "Hell no."

"Hell no," said Bast. "We will prevail, Chief."

"Thirty seconds till impact."

On the viewscreen the Kemmar ship seemed to already be on top of them. Energy bursts continued to criss cross the sky, ravaging the hulls of both vessels. They had each suffered heavy damage. Bast wasn't sure either ship would survive the coming collision. He had to admire the Kemmar resolve. They were a worthy foe.

"Ten seconds till impact."

"Escape pod is on board, Sir."

"Initiate jump," said Bast, calmly.

The Chaanisar ship jumped away, narrowly denying the Kemmar its suicide mission. The Chaanisar battle cruiser landed in a quiet region of space.

"Report," said Bast.

"Reading no threats present, Sir, Kemmar or otherwise."

"Undertake repairs immediately."

"Yes, Sir."

"Shall we go and greet our guests, Chief?" said Bast.

Chief St. Clair exhaled sharply, clearly relieved. "Let's go," he said.

# Chapter 42

The escape pod sat secured on the Chaanisar flight deck. Its hatch hadn't opened and there was no way of knowing who was inside. A couple of Chaanisar soldiers stood guard in front of the pod, and the rest of the flight deck personnel continued their usual activities.

Kevin wondered who was inside the pod, excitement surging through him. It might be the Doctor, or it might be the Captain. Whoever it was, he was happy to be retrieving the crew. The more they rescued the better. He felt like he needed to catch his breath after the battle with the Kemmar. Colonel Bast, however, seemed unshakable. Did anything get to this guy? No wonder the Chaanisar were so effective during the wars.

As they approached the pod Colonel Bast motioned to the soldiers to stand aside. They moved out of the way and Kevin stepped up to the vessel.

"This is Security Chief Kevin St. Clair of the Hermes. You are safe now. Please open your hatch."

Nothing happened. Kevin rapped his knuckles against the hatch. "I repeat, this is Security Chief Kevin St. Clair of the Hermes. Please open your hatch.

Nothing.

"Perhaps they are ill," said Bast. "Or they could have perished."

"Or they don't believe me," said Kevin.

"That is a possibility. Nonetheless, we must open that hatch to know for sure."

Bast summoned a salvage drone. It was normally used to dismantle damaged vessels and had powerful cutting tools, allowing it to open the escape pod like a tin can. It went to work on the hatch, shearing away the heavy metal, and soon had completely severed it from the craft, leaving a jagged opening behind.

Kevin took a step toward the hatch and was greeted with energy weapon fire. The bolt barely missed his head. He ducked and dove away out of the line of fire.

Getting up he shouted at the escape pod. "Hold your fire! This is Security Chief Kevin St. Clair of the Hermes."

No response.

The two guards were now flanking the craft, weapons drawn, ready to fire.

"This is Security Chief Kevin St. Clair, please acknowledge that you understand."

Silence.

Kevin looked at Bast and said, "They must be disoriented. Maybe they're delusional."

Bast stared at the pod. He then accessed his communicator. "I need a paralytic agent on the flight deck."

"Paralytic agent?" said Kevin, worried that Bast might be overreacting. "That could cause permanent damage."

Bast was expressionless. He scrutinized Kevin for a moment and said, "I assure you, Chief, the effects are only temporary. We can administer the counter agent as soon as they have been disarmed."

"I don't know how I feel about this, Colonel." Kevin heard the worry in his voice and stiffened. He still had trust issues. He wondered if he'd ever fully trust the Chaanisar.

"Don't worry, Chief. Your people will not be harmed."

Kevin grudgingly agreed.

A man soon appeared wearing an oxygen mask and a menacing short barreled rifle. Kevin's hands balled into tight fists, and the muscles in his back flexed. He felt his knees bend slightly and suppressed the impulse to tackle the man before he could shoot, but it wasn't easy. His job was to protect his crew, not leave them to the Chaanisar's tender mercies. He had no way of knowing what their gas would do to his men. How could he let Bast lull him into compliance?

He felt Bast's eyes on him. Scrutinizing him. Were his feelings showing through? Did it even matter what his feelings were?

"Proceed," said Bast, still focused on Kevin.

The man approached the pod from the side and fired repeatedly inside. Within seconds the interior of the pod filled with a deep blue smoke. It brought back memories of past battles. Ruthless battles where no quarter was given or received. Kevin resisted the urge to run into the pod and drag the people out of there. He tried to convince himself that they would be okay. That they wouldn't suffer any permanent damage. But the thought chewed at his mind, like some cruel ravenous beast.

The man looked at Bast and nodded. Bast sent in the two guards, who also wore masks now. Seconds passed, but they felt like hours. He would be one of the first things his people saw when they were brought out. They would be paralyzed, but their eyes would point at him. You. Traitor. Collaborator. How could you do this to us?

The guards soon emerged, dragging out the first body. He tried to make out who it was, but the smoke obstructed his vision. The

240

smoke cleared as they pulled the body out further, and he got a good look. Only there was something wrong. It wasn't a human. It was a Diakan.

It was Tallos.

"Motherfucker," said Kevin. All the pressure building up inside him spewed out like a geyser. He drew his sidearm and lunged forward with murderous rage, pointing the gun at the Diakan's head.

Tallos was immobile, but conscious, and he looked up at Kevin with those large, unblinking eyes.

"Chief!" said Bast. "Don't shoot."

After everything that happened, Tallos was still alive. Kevin couldn't believe it. And he was in one of the Hermes escape pods. He wondered which humans didn't get off the Hermes as a result of Tallos taking an escape pod. His finger tightened on the trigger. Soon Tallos would be no more.

"Hold your fire, Chief," said Bast, uncharacteristic alarm in his voice.

The words reached Kevin, piercing through the anger that enveloped him. "You don't understand, Colonel," said Kevin. "This piece of shit tried to take over the Hermes. Tried to kill a mother and her child. He doesn't deserve to live."

"I understand how you feel, Chief. But we need to keep him alive. We need to find out what he knows."

"He knows nothing."

"Let's be sure first."

Bast was right. He had to control his emotions. The guards had brought out two more Diakans. All three were paralyzed. They couldn't do much harm in this state.

Kevin holstered his weapon. "Ok, Colonel. It's your ship."

"Thank you, Chief," said Bast. Turning to the guards he said, "Take them into custody."

# Chapter 43

Tallos sat in the middle of a small gray room. An empty chair stood in front of him. He was no longer paralyzed, but had energy restraints on his wrists and ankles. Several cameras and scanners were trained on him from the walls. Colonel Bast studied him on a display from an adjoining room. This was a surprise he hadn't expected. A high ranking Diakan in his custody. Under the Juttari it would mean an instant promotion. Only in that case he would hand Tallos over to Juttari Intelligence. Things were different now, and they would stay different. What would he do with this treasure?

Bast walked out and entered the interrogation room that held the Diakan. He sat in the empty chair, and didn't speak. He merely stared, analyzing Tallos like a scientist studying a newly discovered species.

"You know, I've never seen a Diakan up close," said Bast, leaning in as if to get a better look. "After all the battles, you would think it would have happened. But no. This is the first time I've been face to face with one."

"Who are you?" said Tallos.

Bast's right hand shot out with unforgiving speed. His fist connected hard with Tallos's face, knocking him and his chair backwards onto the floor. He was surprised at how satisfying the blow felt. He had been trained to hate the Diakans. They were the sworn enemy of the Juttari Empire. Even with his new found freedom and his personal hatred for the Juttari, the conditioning stayed with him.

Tallos lay on his back, stunned by the ferocious blow.

"My name is Colonel Bast."

Tallos didn't respond.

"Release restraints," said Bast, and the energy bands around Tallos's wrists and ankles opened. "You will pick up your chair, place it back in its original position and sit in it."

Tallos slowly rolled off his back and got onto his feet. He lifted his chair, put it back on its legs and sat down, facing Bast. "You are Chaanisar," said Tallos.

244

Bast nodded. "And you are General Tallos."

"You know my rank? How do you possess this knowledge?"

Bast struck him again, sending Tallos back down on his back. The second strike confirmed his earlier observation. The Diakan's head was different. Softer. More flexible. His fist seemed to sink into the Diakan skull, before the tissue bounced back, like a rubber band. He wondered how much his blow actually hurt him.

Tallos got up without being asked and sat back into his chair.

"We have a database of all high ranking Diakans," said Bast. "It was easy enough to learn your identity. You have quite an impressive military record, General."

"All in the past," said Tallos, no noticeable change in his voice. If he was afraid, he did a good job hiding it.

"Yes, things have taken an unpleasant turn for you, General."

"Where are the Juttari, Colonel? Why is Chief St. Clair with you? Why am I here?"

The question surprised Bast. Tallos willingly risked taking another punch. It impressed him. "So many questions, General. This all must be very confusing for you. Why don't I ask the questions for a while and then I might decide to answer some of yours."

Tallos stayed silent.

"Or, if you don't want to speak with me, we can continue playing games. I assure you I have an unbelievable amount of stamina. I wonder if you can match it?"

"Ask your questions."

"What was your mission on the Hermes?"

"I was sent as an adviser, to assist the Captain."

"Come now, General. We both know that wasn't why you were there."

"The Captain needed guidance. He had no experience with starship command."

Bast unleashed another savage blow sending Tallos to the floor yet again.

"Don't you think you are a little overqualified for that role, General?"

Tallos picked up his chair, sat down and said, "I do not question my orders."

"Would you rather we do this the hard way, General?"

"I will answer your question if you tell me why you are working with the humans."

"Very well. Proceed."

"Diakus sent us to ensure the humans accomplish their mission. We oversaw their mission so that no harm came to the Hermes, or its jump system. If required, I was authorized to take command of the Hermes to keep it from harm."

"You failed in your mission."

"Captain Pike is a stubborn man."

"Why were you so interested in their mission?"

"Two reasons. The obvious being the jump system. Diakus considers the technology to be vital to the Galactic Accord. The second was the colonies. When the Hermes found the colonies, I was to act as an ambassador for Diakus and negotiate their entry into the Galactic Accord."

"Yes, the colonies. I wonder if they really exist."

"I answered your question. Now tell me what has happened here."

"Ah yes, there have been some changes on board. The Juttari no longer command this vessel."

"You mutinied?"

"Oh yes. We certainly did."

"But how? Your brain chips. How did you resist?"

Bast wondered if the virus had been part of Tallos's mission. "Don't you know?"

"Know what?" said Tallos.

"Juttari control of our brain chips failed."

"How did that happen?"

Bast stifled the urge to hit Tallos again. Wouldn't he know about the virus? Was it possible that Space Force kept the knowledge from the Diakans? Highly unlikely. Tallos knew something. Bast decided not to show his cards yet. If Tallos knew about the virus then he would surely be wondering how much Bast knew. Better to keep

Tallos wondering. "I'm afraid that information is classified," Bast said.

"I understand."

Tallos accepted that too easily. He does know something.

"How did Chief St. Clair end up on board?" said Tallos.

"We rescued him and his men from Kerces."

"What did you say?"

"Did the paralytic agent affect your hearing, General?"

"You attacked the Kemmar planet?"

"Yes."

"After the Hermes was destroyed trying to do the same?"

"Correct."

"To rescue Chief St. Clair and his men?"

"That sounds right."

Tallos leaned back in his chair. Bast knew he was trying to comprehend what he was hearing. Chaanisar mutinying against their Juttari masters, and then risking their lives to rescue Space Force soldiers. People they fought countless bitter battles against. How could any of that make sense to a Diakan? And what of the implications? Did this present a threat to Diakus? He could see the wheels turning in that odd looking head.

Tallos pondered silently, then said, "Why?"

"Unfortunately, General, we do not have enough time for me to answer that question. Now it's my turn. When you fled the Hermes and commandeered your escape pod, did you see Doctor Ellerbeck?"

"Yes."

"Was she on an escape pod?"

"Yes, she was."

"So she escaped the Hermes."

"I believe she did." Tallos went quiet again, and then said, "You want the Doctor to remove your brain chips. I understand now."

Tallos was living up to his reputation.

"Tell me Colonel," said Tallos. "What do you plan to do once your brain chips have been removed?"

Tallos wasn't stupid. There was no point lying about why they wanted the Doctor. "We will reassess our situation."

"What if you do not find the Doctor?"

"We will find her."

"You do realize that you and your crew would be an invaluable resource to Diakus and Space Force, don't you?" said Tallos. "I could ensure that you were repatriated. You could go home. You would be seen as heroes. The Chaanisar who rebelled against their Juttari masters. It would be a glorious homecoming for you and your crew."

Tallos hit a nerve. To return to Earth, to return 'home' seemed only a dream. Could Tallos do what he said? Could they come home as heroes, not monsters? He was a General after all. And Earth was beholden to the Diakans. Surely he could make things happen. As appealing as the offer was, however, he knew Tallos was trying to manipulate him.

Colonel Bast stood up and said, "Thank you, General. That is all for now. I will probably have some more questions for you later." With that he opened the door and two Chaanisar soldiers entered. Bast turned to them and said, "Take the Diakan to his cell."

# Chapter 44

"Fucking Tallos," said Henderson. He took a bite of some type of freeze dried meat and said, "Of all the people to rescue, we get the damn Diakans."

"I should've pulled the trigger," said Kevin. He hadn't touched his food the whole time they'd been seated.

"Bast was right. He could be a source of intelligence," said Henderson.

"I know he's right, but still."

"Are you going to eat your food? It tastes like crap, but you should keep your strength up. Who knows what's going to happen next."

"Yeah," said Kevin with a frown. He stabbed a chunk of mystery meat with his fork and wolfed it down.

"May I join you?" said Lieutenant Jarvi.

The request surprised Kevin. So far Jarvi hadn't been very friendly and he couldn't say that he liked him much. Maybe he should give him another chance. "Sure. Pull up a chair," said Kevin.

Jarvi set his tray down and sat with the two Marines. "You are discussing the Diakans?" said Jarvi.

"We are," said Kevin.

"An interesting development," said Jarvi. "Here we are, former enemies, now allies, and we pick up Diakans who were your former allies, yet are now your enemies."

"It's ironic," said Henderson.

"That's one way of looking at it," said Kevin.

Jarvi seemed to be enjoying his mystery meat.

"You like that stuff?" said Kevin.

"The food? Yes, this is one of my favorites."

"Do you remember anything about the food on Earth?"

Jarvi stopped eating.

"Sorry. I don't mean to pry."

"No Chief. You are not prying. I am trying to remember, but I can't recall anything about food. Although it doesn't concern me. I am a better soldier without these attachments."

Kevin figured this was as good as it got for him. It wasn't surprising that he couldn't remember a home cooked meal. The Juttari wouldn't have any reason to cater to Chaanisar taste buds.

"You've always eaten food like this?" said Kevin.

"Yes. It is all I know. If you gave me one of your meals I would probably find it disgusting."

"I know what you mean," said Kevin. "That's how I feel about this stuff. It tastes like cardboard."

"It is packed with nutrients," said Jarvi. "Everything the human body needs to function optimally is included. Your desire for flavor is a weakness you must overcome."

*There he goes again*, thought Kevin, *acting all superior.*

"Yeah, I don't see that happening anytime soon," said Kevin, rolling his eyes. "You know, now that you're free of the Juttari, you need to learn how to be a little more human, and a little less Chaanisar."

"There is no shame in being Chaanisar. Our human form has been optimized. So long as we are not controlled by others, we represent an evolved human form."

*As evolved as a robot,* thought Kevin. "I prefer flesh and blood to nuts and bolts, but that's just me," said Kevin.

"A Chaanisar is superior in every physical way, Chief," said Jarvi.

"Really? Do you have a girlfriend?" said Kevin.

Jarvi looked confused.

"Exactly," said Kevin.

"Do you remember any of your childhood?" said Henderson.

"Some. I remember my parents. My siblings. But I see them as pictures. I often see myself in the pictures. As if I am looking at someone else. But I don't remember my interactions with them."

Kevin thought back to his own childhood, the happiest time in his life. "It must be painful," he said. "Sorry for bringing the whole thing up."

"You have not caused me pain, if that is your concern. I want to know what my life was like before the Juttari."

"How about sports?" said Henderson. "Do you remember playing any games? Do you remember kicking a ball around? Or throwing a baseball?"

Jarvi's eyes turned up and to the right as he tried to access his memories. "No, Sergeant. I don't remember playing any games."

"They say smells are one of the longest lasting memories," said Kevin. "Do you remember what anything smelled like?"

"No."

"See that's another thing that might be a trigger," said Henderson. "If we had access to any odors from Earth, that could work."

"Perhaps," said Jarvi. "But I doubt we will find any familiar smells out here."

"Yeah, we'll have to get you back to Earth," said Kevin. "Or find the Doctor."

"You think your Doctor can help me remember?"

"If anybody knows how to do it, it'll probably be her," said Kevin.

"You think highly of your Doctor Ellerbeck."

"I do."

"All the more reason why we cannot rest until we find her," said Jarvi.

Kevin nodded, and forced another forkful of mystery meat into his mouth, wondering if he would taste Earth food again.

# Chapter 45

"I don't understand," said Jansen, his eyes barely hiding their rage. "How could the prisoner be dead?"

"He had an accident," said Kulberg, staying calm in the face of Jansen's impending anger.

"What type of accident?" said Jansen.

"He fell out of the vehicle."

Jansen's eyes went wide with disbelief. "How is that possible?"

"The door was open."

"Why would the door be opened?"

"Good question," said Kulberg. "I guess I opened it."

"You threw the prisoner out of your craft?" said Jansen, rising from his chair.

"I wouldn't say I threw him out. Nudged maybe." Kulberg tried hard, but couldn't resist smiling. A rare, real smile this time, not the practiced one he usually showed the world.

Jansen exploded. "You've gone too far this time. Guards. Take Mr. Kulberg into custody."

The guards didn't move.

Jansen stood, pointing at the guards. "Did you hear me? Take Mr. Kulberg into custody this instant, or I'll have you both arrested as well."

The guards stood their ground.

"Those are my guards, Jansen. Not yours. And you know what else? I've grown rather attached to this station. I think it belongs to me now."

"You're crazy, Kulberg," said Jansen, reaching for the communication link on his console.

Kulberg pulled out his energy weapon and shot Kulberg in the arm. The blast spun Jansen around, turning him a full three hundred and sixty degrees, and knocked him back into his chair. Jansen gripped his bicep, where a fresh hole smoldered, glowing orange like a tiny partial solar eclipse. "You shot me. Now you're done for. You just turned yourself into a fugitive."

"Why don't you let me worry about all of that."

Jansen groaned in pain, fear now filling his eyes.

"You know, all these years I've put up with your ego. The brilliant, all powerful Mr. Jansen." Kulberg laughed. "You think you're so bloody smart. Why do you think you've never found the raider base? Because I didn't let you find it. That's why."

"You're a traitor," said Jansen, his voice higher pitched than normal.

"Name calling. The last refuge of the defeated," said Kulberg. "Only you were defeated long ago. You just didn't know it. How do you think the raiders found all those freighters? If you had any intelligence you would question those around you. But your ego is too big for that. How could one of your assistants outsmart you, the great Mr. Jansen? Impossible. Do you have any idea how much money I have made over the years?"

Jansen stayed quiet.

"Of course you wouldn't. All this time you thought I was this little man who was happy with the meager salary you granted me. Well let me tell you, all those ransoms add up pretty quickly." Kulberg laughed again. "I've got more money than I know what to do with. So do my men. See, unlike you, I know how to reward those who are loyal to me."

"You're a foolish little man," said Jansen. "Money doesn't change any of that."

Kulberg fired his weapon again. This time it burned a hole through Jansen's forehead. Jansen's head snapped back from the blast, hit the chair and fell forward, his shoulders following until his head smacked against the desk. Kulberg stepped behind the large desk and pushed Jansen's body off his chair onto the floor. He sat down in the chair and swiveled around to face Jansen's body. "Remember what I said about name calling?" He then turned and faced the two guards who hadn't moved from where they stood. "Guards, Mr. Jansen has been murdered. Effective immediately I am taking control of DLC station. I am also issuing a warrant for the murderer, Captain Pike, and his accomplices."

# Chapter 46

"You're a liar," said Darla, pacing across the bedroom floor.

Seiben sat on the edge of the bed, watching her warily. He needed to choose his words carefully. Saying the wrong thing now would be like the opening shot of an all-out war.

"All you do is lie to me. I just can't trust you," said Darla.

"I didn't want to worry you," Seiben replied, trying desperately to save himself from Darla's wrath.

Darla stopped pacing and turned to confront him. "Worry me? You didn't want to worry me? What about turning me into a widow? Didn't that bother you?"

"I wasn't going to turn you into a widow."

"No, you weren't. Instead you just about got us all killed."

"How was I supposed to know any of that would happen?"

"Exactly my point."

Now he was confused. "What do you mean?"

"Do you think sporting the title of Captain makes you a soldier?"

"No, of course not."

"That's because you're not a soldier. You never were. Yet here you are accepting what amounts to a military mission, with no concept of what the repercussions could be."

"Are you saying if I had military training I could anticipate what happened?"

"No. I'm saying you should have turned down Mr. Jansen because you don't have that kind of training. Because you couldn't anticipate any of the possible outcomes, or prepare for them. Maybe Jon didn't anticipate being attacked, but at least he knew what to do when it happened. We just sat here praying we wouldn't be killed."

"If I turned down Mr. Jansen I would be out of a job."

"Do you love your job more than your family?"

"No. Of course not."

"Then?"

He didn't know how to respond, so he said nothing. Darla looked like she was about to unleash another verbal onslaught when an explosion interrupted him. The sound of gunfire followed in the adjoining room.

"The girls," yelled Darla, running for the door.

"Wait!" said Seiben, grabbing Darla. "I'll go."

Darla slapped his hand away, panic filling her eyes, and said, "We both go!"

The couple ran to the door and looked out into the living room where Jon and Breeah crouched behind toppled furniture and traded fire with a DLC security team.

Darla looked back at him and said, "What is going on now?"

"I don't know," he said.

Up ahead the door to the girls' room opened and Anki peered out of it. She was spending the night with Otka and Alina, while Jon and Breeah slept in the living room.

"Get back inside," said Seiben, motioning with his hands for her to go in and stay low.

Darla jumped out and ran into the room, taking Anki in with her.

Seiben looked back into the living room where the firefight continued and wondered how he could help. Darla could stay with the girls, but if Jon and Breeah couldn't hold off the security team they would all be done for. He went back into his bedroom and opened a drawer beside his bed. Inside it was an energy weapon Jon had taken from the men who had attacked earlier. He had given it to Seiben so he could protect himself if need be. Did he know more men would come? Was that what Darla was talking about?

He seized the weapon and headed back out. He may not be a soldier, but he did know how to fire a weapon. If you hauled freight you needed to know how to protect yourself. The raiders weren't the only dangers out there.

His mouth was dry with fear, and his heart banged against his ribs like a war drum. He dropped to the ground and crawled out of his bedroom, trying not to call attention to himself. He didn't want to fire from his doorway as he was afraid of drawing fire towards the girls' bedroom. Instead he crawled out along the floor until he made it to the kitchen, and took cover behind the kitchen counter.

He looked over at Jon who had spotted him and was motioning for him to stay down. Seiben shook his head no, and signaled that he was going to fire and that Jon should take advantage of the distraction. Jon frowned, clearly worried that Seiben would get himself killed. Seiben wondered if Jon wasn't right. He had to help. The security team didn't know he was there. He would catch them off guard, if only for a moment.

Seiben turned to face the counter. He tried to steady his hand and control his breathing. He readied his weapon, gripping it with both hands, just like he had been taught in the self-defense class he had taken. How long ago was that? Ten years maybe? Fifteen? Maybe more? He was a younger man then. Would he be quick enough now? Or would he get himself killed? Maybe Darla was right? What business did he have playing soldier?

*Your mind is playing tricks on you*, he thought. *Don't think. Just act.*

He sprang up from behind the counter and fired repeatedly at the security team. He hit one of the men, dropping him. He then ducked back behind the counter just as a barrage of energy bursts flew over his head. *I got one!* Adrenalin surged through him, overcoming the fear he felt a moment ago.

Seizing the opportunity, Jon and Breeah both jumped up and fired. Seiben couldn't tell if they hit anyone, but the weapon fire above him ceased. Should he risk another shot? They knew he was there now, and the odd energy burst flew by overhead. If he jumped up at the wrong time he'd be dead. He watched Jon and thought he could try the same tactic he used. The next time Jon fired, he would fire a second later. They would be focused on Jon and not targeting him. The best way to learn something is to emulate an expert, after all.

He watched Jon and waited. Jon fired back at the enemy, and a second later Seiben jumped up to fire too. When he did he saw the barrel of a gun pointed straight at him.

# Chapter 47

Anki watched Otka and Alina tremble with fear. She felt sorry for the two girls. They had never been in battle before and nobody had told them how scary it would be. But then they weren't Reivers.

At least their mother was here to comfort them. She hugged them close, which always helped. But she screamed and cried just as much as her girls did. She knew her own mother wouldn't do that. She would hold her close, but she would stay strong. That helped the most. She always felt safe with her mother. She couldn't imagine anybody beating her.

She wished her mother was here now, but she knew she was out there fighting the bad men. It was up to her to stay strong for Darla, Otka and Alina. Maybe if they saw her being calm they wouldn't be so frightened.

But Anki was scared. The sounds coming from the other room were close and terrifying. She had heard sounds like that before, and it did help, but she still wanted to run away from them and hide.

She decided that the sounds were nothing more than fireworks. Spectacular fireworks, like nothing anyone had ever seen before. These fireworks were so powerful that an entire planet could see them. They would shoot up so high that they were almost in orbit before going off. When they did, they would fire out in all angles, lighting up the night sky for as far as the eye could see.

Fireworks Day was the most important holiday of the year. All the schools and stores were closed and everyone celebrated all day long, feasting on the tastiest food and playing the best games. Then when darkness hit the sky would fill with brilliant colors and thundering explosions.

The sounds would be so loud that the smaller children would cry with fear while their parents told them to look at the beautiful lights. But the older children knew that while the sounds were loud, they weren't anything to be afraid of. That without the explosions, there wouldn't be any pretty lights.

Darla's voice pulled Anki out of her imagination. "Anki. Anki. Come here." She waved with her hand for her to come to them.

Anki thought she should go. It would be what her mother would do. They were all scared and needed somebody strong to make them feel better. So she got up and went over to Darla who reached out with a trembling hand and pulled her in to huddle with her and her girls.

"You poor thing," said Darla. "This must be terrifying for you."

Anki looked up at Darla and said, "Don't worry. The show will be over soon."

# Chapter 48

Jon had a feeling that whoever had orchestrated the previous attack wasn't finished. That feeling might have saved their lives. He and Breeah had prepared for the possibility of a second attack as best they could. They were armed and kept their weapons ready. They had positioned the furniture to give them a defensible position. Also, one of them stayed awake, while the other slept.

Jon had the first shift, and had heard the enemy approach the door. He woke Breeah and they both waited for the inevitable assault. The security force thought they were staging a surprise attack. Imagine their horror when they blew the door and charged into an ambush.

The first soldiers ran in blindly, trying to use speed to their advantage. Jon had let them get a few feet into the room before dropping them. Even with the door blown, the entrance created a natural bottleneck and kill zone. Jon and Breeah had positioned themselves to take full advantage of that. Letting the first men get a few feet into the room, before opening fire, ensured they would trap as many as possible in the kill zone before they could respond.

Unlike the previous encounter, there were many more men this time, and even after killing as many as they did, they were still outnumbered. If they didn't manage to break out soon, reinforcements would arrive. The craft that shot up his apartment might even show up again.

Seiben's actions were foolish. What was he thinking? But they did give them the break they needed. Seiben had gotten off a lucky shot and killed one of the enemy, but more importantly he confused them. Jon and Breeah took full advantage of the opportunity and shot several more. The odds were evening up.

He still wasn't sure who they were fighting, but whoever it was, they were openly using DLC security forces now. Could it be Jansen after all?

They had to get through this to find out. He continued firing on the enemy, looking to create an opportunity. That opportunity came when Seiben tried again to get himself killed. Jon gave him credit for bravery, but his lack of experience made him expose too much of himself.

Jon saw the man put Seiben in his crosshairs and knew it was now or never, so he charged. The man didn't get off a shot as Jon picked him off first. At the same time Breeah unleashed a torrent of covering fire. Surprisingly Seiben recovered quickly when he realized he wasn't dead and opened fire.

The attackers had suddenly turned into defenders, some taking cover, while others retreated. Jon crashed into their positions like a bull after a running matador. His speed and accuracy made short work of the disoriented security forces, and within seconds the siege was over.

Seiben came out from behind the counter and said, "What the hell is going on? Why are DLC security forces coming after us now?"

"That's what I'm going to find out," said Jon. "AI, can you access DLC security systems?"

"Those systems are restricted, Captain."

"I don't care anymore. Bypass security systems, but don't trigger any alarms. I don't want to tip anyone off to your presence."

"These systems are not sophisticated enough to see me, Captain."

"Of course, AI. I should know better," said Jon, shaking his head at the size of the AI's artificial ego.

"Who is this AI you're speaking to?" said Seiben.

"My ship's artificial intelligence."

"You mean a computer?"

"I am not a computer," said AI. "I am as self-aware as you are. Perhaps more so."

"Careful," said Jon. "You don't want to offend her."

"Uh, I'm sorry," said Seiben.

"Apology accepted," said the AI. "I have gained access to the DLC security systems, Captain. There is a warrant out for your arrest."

"My arrest? For what?"

"The murder of Mr. Jansen."

Jon was stunned. Of all things he hadn't expected this.

"But we spoke to Mr. Jansen today," said Seiben. "Jon's been here the whole time."

"I am merely relaying the information I have found. Protesting the Captain's innocence to me is pointless."

"AI, do you have access to DLC security deployments?" said Jon.

"Yes, Captain. I am monitoring their movements and communications."

"How long do we have until more show up?"

"There is a team approaching the building from the ground. I advise the roof as an optimal escape route. Several vessels are located there that can be commandeered."

"Get Darla and the girls. We have to leave now," said Jon.

"But if they're just after you then we can probably stay here," said Seiben.

"There is a warrant out for your arrest as well," said AI.

"Me? For what?"

"You and your wife are considered accomplices to the murder. As is Breeah."

"Wonderful," said Seiben.

"AI, who is in charge of the station now that Jansen's dead?" said Jon.

"Mr. Kulberg has taken Jansen's position."

"That slimy son of a bitch," said Seiben. "I should've known he was behind all of this."

"All the more reason why you or your family can't stay here," said Jon. "We have to go. Now."

"You don't have to tell me twice," said Seiben. He turned and headed to the bedroom to retrieve Darla and the girls.

"AI, track our progress and continue to feed me updates on DLC security movements."

"Understood."

Seiben emerged from the bedroom with Darla, who gripped her girls to her side. The two girls both cried inconsolably.

Anki came out as well and ran to her mother. Breeah took her into her arms and picked her up, giving her a big hug. She then looked at Anki and said, "This has been a scary day for you, little one. Are you alright?"

Anki tried to put on a brave face, and nodded. She then buried her face in her mother's neck.

Jon looked at them all. "Ready?"

They nodded. He turned and headed out of the apartment with the group following closely behind.

# Chapter 49

There were several vehicles on the roof, but the ones that caught Jon's attention were the DLC security craft. The team that attacked the apartment likely arrived in these vehicles. Jon led the group toward one of them, keeping a wary eye out for any hidden threats.

He was pleased to see that the vehicle was armed with two Gatling guns, similar to the one that shot up their apartment earlier. It also looked like it might have some armor plating on its body. He tried to open the doors but they were locked. Jon took off his comm and placed it on the vehicle.

"AI, can you access this vehicle's computer systems."

"Yes, Captain," said AI.

"Unlock and turn power on. Give me clearance to operate all its systems."

"Clearance granted. You may enter the vehicle."

Jon reclaimed his comm and ushered everyone into the vehicle.

"Captain, I am reading several security personnel approaching the building's roof."

The last of the group got in and Jon jumped into the driver's seat. He took hold of the security craft's controls and powered up its forced air jets. The vehicle lifted off just as the first of DLC security made it onto the roof. He immediately started taking fire, so he turned the craft around, pointing the nose at the attackers and accessed the Gatling guns mounted on either side.

He opened fire. The bullets ripped through the men foolish enough not to take cover and the glass structure housing the lift. He turned the craft to face the other security vehicles and fired, perforating them in mere seconds. Satisfied that he had caused sufficient damage, he turned the vessel and flew away from the city.

Breeah climbed into the passenger seat and looked over at him. "What do we do now?"

"We take everyone someplace safe, and plan our next steps."

"Captain, an attack drone has been launched and is closing in on your position," said AI.

"Are we being tracked?"

"I've disabled the hovercraft's tracking beacon, but DLC security can still track your vehicle without the beacon."

"Can you disable their ability to track us?"

"I can, but doing so will alert them to my presence."

"Will that be a problem?"

"Of course not, Captain," said AI. "They will try to remove me, but they will fail."

"I think it's time for you to come out of the shadows, AI. Take whatever steps necessary to destroy their ability to track us."

"With pleasure, Captain."

"Oh, and can you do something about that drone?"

"Unfortunately the drone has its own independent tracking system. I do not have access to its systems."

"Wonderful," said Jon. "Everybody brace yourselves, we're going to have a bit of a bumpy ride."

The drone approached at blistering speeds. Jon watched its progress on his dashboard display and waited. He hoped he was right about the craft having armor. His question was answered when the drone overtook them, strafing the side of the vehicle with gunfire. The vehicle's integrity withstood the attack. There was armor.

The drone sped off in front and then turned to face them. Hovering in front of them it fired its guns again. Sparks flew as bullets hit the armor plating. Jon knew that, armored or not, the vehicle couldn't withstand much more pounding. He fired his Gatling guns in return, scoring direct hits on the floating killing machine. That made it move to get out of the way, all the time still firing on their vehicle.

It circled the security craft, firing from all angles. Inside the sound of screaming from the back seat was deafening. Jon spun the craft the opposite way so he could have another shot at the drone. When it came into view he fired again. The drone took more damage, but didn't stop its advance. Alarms rang out from Jon's dashboard telling him that the drone had ruptured a critical system.

The security craft started losing altitude and the drone followed, still spraying it with gunfire. Jon banked the craft and got the drone in his sights. He fired and his twin guns finally did some significant damage. The drone started spinning out of control, still firing its guns, but now the bullets flew out in all directions. Jon fired again, killing the machine. He watched as it fell from the sky.

If he felt any satisfaction it was extremely short lived as the alarms told him they weren't out of danger yet. Their craft still lost altitude and he couldn't stop its descent. They were going down.

# Chapter 50

"Ship's sensors are not picking up any Space Force beacons, Sir," said the Chaanisar helmsman.

The Chaanisar Heavy Cruiser had jumped into an empty region of space following a pre-plotted escape pod trajectory.

"Is there anything on long range scans?" said Bast, hiding his frustration. The last few searches had found nothing. No beacons. No escape pods. He knew that finding all the pods was a long shot, but each one they didn't recover might be one that contained the Doctor.

"Picking up two contacts on long range scans, Sir."

"Could be a clue," said Chief St. Clair, with a hopeful expression.

"Agreed," said Bast. "Helm, jump us to the location of the two vessels."

"Yes, Sir. Initiating jump."

Bast knew that a warship appearing out of nowhere would be a surprise, but he didn't want to waste time playing games.

They appeared just in front of the two vessels. They faced each other, floating in space, not heading anywhere. One dwarfed the other in size. It was a gigantic commercial freighter that looked to have taken heavy damage. The other was smaller, but an obvious warship, and likely responsible for the scars on the freighter.

"Looks like we interrupted the party," said the Chief.

Bast nodded in agreement. "Hail both vessels," he ordered.

A human man's face appeared on Bast's console display. He glared at Bast, visibly angry. "What's wrong? One ship's not enough? You need two? I don't care if you bring a hundred, you're not getting my cargo!"

Bast hesitated, still stunned by the fact that he was looking at another human. "Slow down. We mean you no harm."

"Don't toy with me you raider scum."

"Am I correct in assuming that you command the freighter?"

"Very funny. Of course I command the freighter."

"What's your name, Sir?"

Bast's politeness seemed to surprise the man. His eyes seemed to reassess Bast, and some of the hostility dissipated. "I am Captain Santos. Is that some kind of military uniform you're wearing?"

"A pleasure to meet you, Captain Santos. I am Colonel Bast, and yes, this is a military uniform."

"So you're not raiders?"

"No, what are-"

"Sir, the warship is moving toward us," said the tactician. "They're firing weapons."

Bast switched to his tactical display. The warship fired energy weapons at the Chaanisar cruiser. Red energy bolts connected causing the floor to jolt under Bast's feet. His tactical display lit up as several missiles streaked toward them.

"Launch countermeasures and return fire," said Bast, calmly.

The missiles were not sophisticated enough to beat the Chaanisar drones and each one followed the decoys, exploding harmlessly in open space. The warship continued to strafe them with its energy weapons, but did not have enough piercing power to burn through the heavy armor quickly.

The Chaanisar returned fire, hitting the enemy ship with its own powerful energy weapons. At this close range the blue beam was at one hundred percent charge. The enemy's armor didn't prove to be much of a match and quickly melted under the intense heat. Cobalt colored lightning carved a long, broad gash across the ship's hull. Equipment and personnel were sucked out of the breach into the frigid void.

"Hold your fire," said Bast. He tried again to communicate with the warship. "Unidentified vessel, call off your attack or you will be destroyed."

No response. The warship came around for another pass and spit out a second round of missiles and energy weapon fire. The missiles were again tricked by the drones, and the bridge shook with the impact of the energy weapons, as they slowly degraded the armor's integrity.

Bast sighed. While the warship was weaker, it could damage his ship. That damage would eventually cost Chaanisar lives. He couldn't allow that. He had warned them of the repercussions. Now he had to make good on his promise.

"Return fire," he said, dejected by the unnecessary loss of life.

The Chaanisar Heavy Cruiser unleashed another powerful energy burst, slicing through an adjacent section of the enemy warship. This time the weapon caused multiple explosions on board the vessel. The warship broke off its assault, but the concussions continued to rock it, tearing open massive sections of its hull. The ship continued to lose integrity as its sections began to break apart. Where there was once one ship there was now only large chunks of debris, making any hope of survival for the crew impossible.

Bast looked over at Kevin who had an awed look on his face. "What do you think?"

"They're human," said Chief St. Clair. "You know what this means don't you?"

"Yes, we've found the lost colonies."

Kevin nodded his face looking like he had seen a miracle.

Bast switched back to Captain Santos, who's previously hostile countenance had changed to one of astonishment.

"You destroyed them," said Santos, his voice filled with wonder.

"It was an unfortunate outcome. We had no quarrel with these people," said Bast.

"No quarrel? But they were raiders?"

"What exactly are raiders, Captain?"

Santos eyed him skeptically. "You're not from around here, are you?"

"No, we most certainly are not."

Santos nodded, but he didn't seem to believe him. "Raiders are pirates. They prey on freighters in these shipping lanes heading for the station."

"The station?"

Santos raised an eyebrow. "DLC Station. It's the main commercial center in this region. It's where we were heading when the raiders attacked us and disabled our engines. Say, you wouldn't be able to help us with repairs, would you?"

"I'm afraid we are on a time sensitive mission. But we might be able to help you in another way. Let me look into it and I will get back to you."

Santos frowned, ending the transmission.

Bast turned to Kevin. "When you battled the Kemmar battleship and it split up into smaller ships, the Hermes jumped away while it was being boarded and took the Kemmar vessel with it."

Chief St. Clair nodded. Yes, that's true. You're not thinking of trying that with this freighter, are you?"

"Why not?"

"It's enormous. That thing's got to be three times our size."

"You don't think it can work?"

"I don't know, but I do know someone who might."

# Chapter 51

Former Hermes Chief Engineer Rajneesh Singh examined the room in which he found himself. He spotted some of the hidden cameras in the walls, and realized he had been taken to an interrogation room.

"They're going to torture me," he said.

"Stay calm, Raj," said Lynda. "Let's see what they want before we jump to any conclusions. Remember, they need you."

Singh tried to stay calm, but his anxiety levels were too high to get under control. The memories of the Kemmar interrogator and his needles were still fresh in his mind. He was lucky to have escaped that experience, but here things would be different. If they chose to torture him here there would be no last minute rescue.

"They won't torture you," said Lynda, as if reading his thoughts.

"I wish I could believe that," said Singh.

A door opened and a Chaanisar officer walked in. A colonel. Singh remembered him from the planet. He was the Chaanisar leader. The Colonel sat in the chair directly opposite Singh. There was no table between them, just the two of them facing each other.

"I am Colonel Bast, commander of this vessel."

"See, he is being polite," said Lynda.

"Hello," said Singh, clasping his hands together to keep them from trembling.

"I'm sure you are wondering why you were brought here. I wanted to talk to you and thought this would be more comfortable than your cell."

Singh stayed silent, waiting for the inevitable question, threat, punishment progression.

"I understand you are a jump system expert."

"Yes, that is correct."

Lynda bent over and whispered into his ear, "He needs you."

Singh turned to her and said, "You already told me that."

Bast had a puzzled look on his face. "Who is it you are talking to?"

"Commander Lynda Wolfe."

Bast looked in Lynda's direction and said, "I see." He turned back to Singh. "I need to ask you a couple of questions about the jump system, Mr. Singh."

"This is how you prove your worth to him," said Lynda.

"When the Hermes fought the Kemmar the Hermes had jumped away taking one of the Kemmar ships with it. Do you remember?"

"Yes, of course."

"How was that accomplished?"

Singh took a breath and relaxed. Perhaps Lynda was right. They weren't going to torture him. "The jump system creates a field around the ship. This is similar to an FTL bubble in theory. The difference being that the jump system is in effect folding space, and anything within its field travels with the ship to the other side of the folded space. The Kemmar ship had attached itself to the Hermes. As far as the jump system was concerned the two ships were one. It enveloped both ships with the field, transporting them to the other end of folded space."

"Do the two ships have to be connected for this to take place?"

"No, not necessarily. The field actually radiates out from the ship's hull, so anything within its radius would be affected."

"Are there limits to how much larger the other ship can be?"

"Yes, of course. The jump system emitters do not have limitless capabilities. I would say the other ship couldn't be much larger than jump ship."

"What would happen if the ship was too large?"

"Hmmm, that would be an ugly scenario. The field would expand to its limit. Anything larger than that would not make the jump. So in the case of a larger ship, part of it would travel across folded space, and the rest would remain."

"It would be destroyed."

"Yes, without a doubt."

"Well done," said Lynda. "Look at him. You have given him the answers he seeks. You've proven your value to him."

"Thank you for your time, Mr. Singh. I'll have someone take you back to your cell."

Colonel Bast rose from his chair and walked out the door.

Singh sat back into his chair and relaxed. Lynda was right. They did need him after all."

\*\*\*

Bast walked out of the interrogation room. Up ahead a door opened and Chief St. Clair emerged. Bast approached him and said, "What do you think, Chief?"

"I think Singh's crazier than I thought."

"Who is this Lynda Wolfe he sees?"

"She was the XO on the Hermes. The two of them were in a relationship, but from what Petrovic and Yao tell me, she died on the bridge."

"Interesting. Mr. Singh cannot accept her death."

"I think there's more to it than that. I think he blames Space Force for her death. That would explain him turning into a traitor."

A message came in over Bast's communicator. "Colonel, the Captain of the freighter is requesting to speak to you. He says it is urgent."

"Patch him through."

"Colonel?" said Captain Santos.

"Yes, Captain. I was just going to contact you."

"Colonel, we have a serious problem. Our reactor is overheating. We cannot get it under control."

"Understood. What can we do to help?"

"I'm afraid we'll need to abandon ship. Can you ferry us to-"

The ship suddenly shuddered as if it was hit by weapon fire.

"Captain? Captain?" Bast tapped his communicator trying to get Santos back without any luck. He contacted the bridge instead. "What just happened?"

"It was the freighter, Sir. She exploded. It looks like it was caused by a reactor breach," said the tactician.

"Were there any survivors?"

"No, Sir."

"Understood."

Chief St. Clair had a solemn look on his face. "That's terrible."

"Horrible," Bast agreed. He wished he had done more to help the freighter, but if he had sent some of his technicians to the freighter they would likely be dead now along with the freighter crew. The raiders had caused the destruction of the freighter, not him.

"What do we do now?" said Kevin.

"We go to the station," said Bast.

# Chapter 52

"Picking up Space Force beacon, Sir. It's coming from the station."

"Are there any Kemmar ship signatures?" said Bast.

"No, Sir. There are no signs of the Kemmar in this system."

"Very well. Approach the station. Steady as she goes. We do not want to appear aggressive."

Bast studied the station on the viewscreen. From this distance it looked like a child's toy, but he could tell that it was a massive structure. He wondered what surprises awaited them here.

Chief St. Clair appeared on the bridge, stepped up beside him and said, "You've found another beacon?"

Yes, Chief. It looks like the escape pod we're looking for made it to the station somehow," said Bast.

"That's a big station."

"My thoughts as well, Chief. Captain Santos was right. It is a busy place."

"Looks like it does a lot of business."

"Yes," said Bast. "Perhaps we can pick up some supplies."

"If we're lucky they might have some good food."

"Is the food on board not to your tastes, Chief?"

"It's okay. Let's just say I like a touch of spice with my food."

"I see. Then we shall try and obtain some spice for you, Chief."

The Chief smiled like he had made a joke. Bast couldn't help thinking that he missed many nuances when he spoke with Chief St. Clair. He tried to pick up as much as he could, but still felt inadequate when it came to the non-verbal cues. If he ever returned to Earth he didn't want to come across as alien.

"Colonel, can I ask you something?" said Kevin.

"Is it about the Diakan?"

"Yeah."

"Of course. What would you like to know?"

"What's he told you?"

"Not as much as he knows," said Bast. He turned and studied the Chief. "Tell me, Chief. How much do you know about this Diakan?"

"He came on board the Hermes with a team of Diakans. They were to act as advisers."

"Do you not think it odd for a Diakan General to be assigned as an adviser to a human Captain?"

The Chief looked confused. "Who, Tallos? He's a General?"

"You didn't know?"

"It's the first I've heard of it."

"He says his purpose was to negotiate with the colonies on behalf of Diakus, to add them to the Galactic Accord."

"You don't believe him?"

"I believe that was his assignment. I'm just not sure that was his only assignment."

The Chief's brow furrowed as he pondered the implications. "Any idea what that other assignment is?"

Bast wondered again whether Tallos had anything to do with the virus. "Unfortunately I don't."

The Chief pressed for more information. "Did he say anything else?"

"He offered to repatriate my men if we returned to Sol. To make us heroes."

St. Clair's eyes widened. "You do realize that if you return to Sol Tallos will have us executed."

Bast knew the Chief was in a precarious position. They had made Tallos their enemy. If the Chaanisar were to ally with Tallos then all hope for them would be lost. Tallos did make a desirable offer. In many ways the best option would be to take it. His crew were an invaluable intelligence source for the Diakans. But Bast had no desire to trade one alien master for another.

"Fear not, Chief," said Bast. "I will not do that to you and your crew."

The Chief appeared to relax, although Bast was sure he still had some doubts. Doubts about Tallos and doubts about the Chaanisar. He couldn't blame him for it. So long as Tallos was on board the Chief would feel threatened. For the Chief, the optimal solution to the problem would be to execute the Diakan. Bast was not going to allow that to happen. Tallos might still be of some use. Either way, neither of them could return home. At least for the time being.

Bast wondered how much the Chaanisar still threatened the Chief. He had rescued the Chief and his Marines. They were rescuing the escape pods. He had shown him nothing but good will. While the Chief did seem grateful, Bast knew there must still be some part of him that didn't trust the Chaanisar. It would be a challenging relationship, but Bast hoped he would win over the Chief and his crew in the end.

"We are being hailed, Sir."

"Acknowledge the hail."

To Bast's surprise, a human male appeared on his display. There could be no doubt that they had found the lost colonies now. "Identify yourself and state the nature of your business," said the man.

"I am Colonel Bast, of the Chaanisar ship 7249. We are responding to a signal from our escape pod on board your station. We are here to retrieve it and our personnel."

The man studied Bast for a moment, and then said, "Stand by." The screen then went blank.

"I guess we did find the colonies," said Chief St. Clair. Wonder in his voice.

"We found something," said Bast. "And so did one of your pods."

Bast's display flickered on again and a different man appeared. This one was dressed in a black suit and had dark, calculating eyes.

"My name is Mr. Kulberg. I am the manager of DLC station. What is your business here?"

Bast was sure the man had been briefed already, but he played along nonetheless. "I am Colonel Bast, of the Chaanisar ship 7249. Our escape pod and personnel are on board your station. We are here to retrieve them."

"I see," said Kulberg. "That will not be possible. Cease your approach immediately. You will not be granted access to the station."

Kulberg's words surprised Bast. He managed to retain his composure, however, and said, "I don't understand. We mean you no harm. Why do you deny us access to our people?"

"Because your Captain Pike is a fugitive. I will not allow you to come on board and facilitate his escape."

Chief St. Clair jumped at the display. "What have you done with Captain Pike?" he said.

Kulberg looked annoyed. "Who am I speaking to here?" he said.

Bast waved a hand at St. Clair, telling him to stand down. "You are speaking to me," said Bast. "May I ask what Captain Pike is charged with?"

Kulberg's eyes narrowed. "He is charged with murder, and he will answer for his crime. You are hereby ordered to leave this system. If you continue to approach, your actions will be considered hostile and you will be fired upon. I assure you this station has more than enough firepower to destroy your vessel. This is your only warning."

With that the screen went blank.

"Tactician, analyze the station's armaments."

"The station is heavily armed, Sir. We cannot hope to succeed in battle against it."

"Understood. Helmsman, turn us around. Set a course to leave this system."

The Chief looked like he was going to explode. "We're leaving?" he said, several veins bulging from his temple. "Didn't you hear? Captain Pike is on board. We can't abandon him."

"We are not abandoning your Captain, Chief," said Bast. "But we will need a different approach."

# Chapter 53

The Chaanisar ship steadily continued to leave the system. Kevin sat in Colonel Bast's office with Lieutenant Jarvi seated in the chair beside him. Kevin couldn't believe they found Captain Pike. On a human station no less. He wondered if he should be surprised that the Captain had gotten himself into trouble there. He knew the Captain wasn't a murderer. If he did kill someone, he had to have been defending himself somehow. If the Captain was on the station, who else was with him? Did he have Breeah and Anki with him? The Doctor? He couldn't be by himself.

He didn't like Mr. Kulberg, either. That man was a weasel, if he ever saw one. It was clear that things weren't right on that station. They had to do something.

Kevin and Jarvi sat quietly, waiting for Colonel Bast to finish what he was doing. He had said he had an idea, but needed to verify some of the details first. Obviously they were going to do something, or Lieutenant Jarvi wouldn't be here. Kevin's right leg vibrated, his heel tapping the floor in rapid beats. He was finding it hard to sit still. He wanted to take action now.

Colonel Bast looked up from his console at Kevin and Jarvi. "I think we have an opportunity to save your Captain, Chief," he said.

"You've found a weakness?" said Kevin.

"I've found an opportunity for a covert insertion."

Kevin liked what he was hearing.

"We cannot defeat the station in battle. It has too much firepower. But, as you pointed out on the bridge, it does seem to be a trading center. As we left the station I monitored the traffic coming and going and have identified clearly defined space lanes for commercial traffic. We will travel beyond the range of the station's sensors and intercept one of the commercial vessels. You and Lieutenant Jarvi will then take two teams and board. Once you have commandeered the vessel, you will use it to insert your teams onto the station."

Kevin smiled. "I like it," he said.

"With all due respect, Colonel, the Chief's Marines would hamper the success of the mission," said Jarvi.

Kevin was quickly getting tired of Jarvi's opinions. "Maybe you should sit things out this time, Lieutenant. My Marines can show you how it's done."

"Don't be foolish, Chief. There is nothing you can teach my men," said Jarvi.

"That's enough," said Bast. "Do you feel your Marines are ready for deployment, Chief?"

"Hell Yes. Especially if they know they are going to rescue the Captain."

"Good. I believe it is time we all work together, don't you Lieutenant?"

"Yes, Sir," said Jarvi, holding Bast's gaze.

Bast kept his eyes locked on Jarvi, like he was giving him an unspoken warning.

"Chief, you will lead a team of your Marines, and Lieutenant Jarvi will lead a team of Chaanisar. Once inside the station you will have two objectives. Chief, your team will be tasked with rescuing the Captain, and whoever is with him. Lieutenant, your job will be to disable the station's defensive systems. That will allow us to retrieve you."

"Understood, Sir," said Jarvi. "I will assemble my team immediately."

"I'll let my men know as well. We'll be ready."

Bast nodded. "Dismissed."

# Chapter 54

"We found the Captain?" said Sergeant Henderson. "That's great."

Excited chatter broke out among the crowd of Marines surrounding Kevin. They all looked good. Ready for battle. The time on board the Chaanisar ship allowed them to get their strength back. They had plenty of food, and while it didn't taste great, it was laden with all the nutrients they needed. Enough to help the Marines get back to peak health, especially after what they had gone through on the prison planet. They all took advantage of the Chaanisar training facilities too, exercising daily, getting themselves ready for the next battle.

"That's right, and he's in trouble," said Kevin.

Anger flowed through the crowd of Marines. A threat against the Captain was a threat against each and every one of them. There were many who wanted to know why they were still standing there. Kevin almost felt sorry for whoever was responsible. They had no idea what was coming for them.

"Listen up," said Kevin. "We're going to get the Captain. Here's our plan."

The Marines quieted down while Kevin explained the details of the operation. They were all seasoned veterans, fully capable of completing this mission.

"So we don't know exactly where the Captain is on the station?" said Henderson.

"No, that's the hard part," said Kevin. "This Kulberg said the Captain was a fugitive, which means they don't know where he is either. It doesn't surprise me. The Captain isn't going to make it easy for them. But really, it would be easier if they had him in custody. Then we'd just have to break him out."

"And we're dealing with humans?" said Henderson.

"Yeah. It looks like we might have found one of the lost colonies. It should make it easier for us to blend in though," said Kevin. "We play this by the numbers. We move quickly and quietly. Acquire information. And get to the Captain before the bad guys. Simple as that."

"Oorah!" said the Marines in unison.

# Chapter 55

The Chaanisar battle cruiser hid behind one of the planets in the station's system. The planet, a large gas giant, provided ample cover from the station's sensors. There they waited for their opportunity to strike. They had identified a commercial vessel leaving the system heading in the opposite direction. They monitored its speed and trajectory, identifying a potential intercept point. It would soon be on the far side of the system's star, which would blind the station's sensors to its fate. The Chaanisar would jump to the freighter's location, jam its communications, and board it. Once the vessel was under their control, they would return it to the station, complaining of a malfunction.

Kevin and Lieutenant Jarvi waited on the flight deck, already wearing combat suits. They each had a small group of men assembled. These teams would board and take control of the commercial ship. Once under their control, more men would travel across to the freighter. When the insertion teams were at full force they would turn the freighter around and head back to the station.

"When we board we need to move fast," said Jarvi. "My team will take over the bridge while your team takes Engineering. We can then mop up and find any remaining crew members hiding on board."

Jarvi thought he was in command, telling Kevin how things were going to happen. Kevin didn't like it much, but he had to remember he was on a Chaanisar ship and he needed their help. Better to play ball than get into a pissing match.

"No problem," said Kevin, wondering how things looked to his Marines. He knew they would only take orders from him. If Jarvi tried to tell them what to do it would not go over well. He needed to make sure they understood that the first priority was the retrieval of the Captain, not Marine/Chaanisar politics.

Colonel Bast's voice came over their comms. "We have jumped and intercepted the freighter. Begin boarding operations."

The Chaanisar and Marines stepped into the waiting shuttle and locked their combat suits into place. The vessel's engines came to life. With a roar, it exited the Chaanisar flight deck and thrust itself forward toward the helpless freighter. A display on board the shuttle gave the men a view of their target. It was a behemoth of a ship with no noticeable armaments. Even if it did have weapons they would be insane to engage the Chaanisar Heavy Cruiser blocking their path.

As the shuttle closed the distance the freighter's hangar bay came into view. It was open and waiting. Bast had likely told them under no uncertain terms to allow the shuttle access to their hangar bay or be fired upon. They would have to be complete idiots not to comply.

As the ship approached the hangar bay, Kevin looked over the men. Including himself there were eight Marines, and eight Chaanisar, all wearing combat suits. That should be more than enough to subdue the crew of the freighter. He didn't anticipate any resistance from a merchant crew, but you could never be sure.

His men were quiet. This was their first mission since Kerces. They seemed positive enough, but he wondered how they really felt about working together with the Chaanisar. They probably didn't fully trust their new allies. Kevin didn't expect them to. Hell, he didn't trust them completely himself. In a way he felt guilty about it. He knew he should be thankful for their help, but it was difficult to overcome years of conditioning. He wondered if he could ever trust them? And if not, what hope did the Chaanisar have of ever returning to Earth? If he couldn't let go of the past, after all they had done for him, why would anyone on Earth? The Chaanisar were trying to reclaim their humanity. But what if humanity rejected them? What would the Chaanisar do?

The shuttle entered the hangar bay and touched down with a thud. Its engines powered down, the combat suits were released from the locking system, and the hatch opened. The Chaanisar moved first, jumping out of the shuttle and establishing a security perimeter. Kevin and his Marines followed. The hangar bay was deserted. The crew was probably hiding. He didn't blame them. All they knew was that some hostile force was boarding their ship. They didn't know if they would be slaughtered, or just robbed.

One of the Chaanisar accessed the ship's computer systems and soon the ship's schematics appeared on everyone's visors.

Jarvi's voice came in loud and commanding over the comm, "Everyone move out. Go, go, go."

Kevin opened a comm with his team. "I've highlighted the direction we need to take to get to Engineering. It should be on your visors now. Let's move fast and wrap this up quick."

"Oorah," came the replies over his comm.

The Chaanisar had already left the hangar bay. The Marines raced out seconds later. They covered the distance to Engineering with extraordinary speed. Their combat suits allowed them to cover several meters with each stride. They must have sounded like a herd of bionic buffaloes to the freighter crew. The metallic pounding would certainly add to the intimidation. Kevin didn't want to hurt any of the crew. They were human after all and were simply in the wrong place at the wrong time. Hopefully there wouldn't be any heroics. They freighter crew should be intimidated enough not get any brave ideas.

Arriving at Engineering they found one man waiting. When he saw the Marines burst in his face blanched and he quickly raised his hands in the air. Private Chen reached him first, grabbed his arms and secured them behind the man's back. He grabbed him by the elbow and walked him over to Kevin.

"What's your name?" said Kevin.

"Marcus," said the man.

"Are you the Engineer, Marcus?"

"I am."

"Where is the rest of the Engineering team?"

"There's just me," said Marcus.

"Just you for this whole ship? That's a little hard to believe, Marcus."

"The rest of the crew knows how to complete repairs. We all pitch in where needed."

The Marines searched every corner of Engineering but found no one else.

Kevin opened a comm with Jarvi and said, "Engineering secured."

"Well done, Chief. We've successfully secured the bridge. I have signaled for the rest of the teams to come over. In the meantime we need to send out a team to search the rest of the ship and pull everyone out of hiding."

"Understood. I'll assign a few of my men."

Kevin closed the comm with Jarvi and spoke to his men. "Burke, Johns, Daniels, you've got search duty. Coordinate with the Chaanisar and make sure there are no hidden surprises on board."

"Yes, Sir," said the Marines, and left Engineering.

"The rest of you stay here until further notice. I'll be on the bridge."

The Marines established a perimeter around Engineering so that nobody could come or go without their knowing, and Kevin headed for the bridge.

When he arrived at the bridge he was surprised to see a number of injuries. One man lay on the ground unconscious with a bloody nose and mouth, and another had what looked like a broken arm. Jarvi spoke to another man who was obviously terrified and looked like he had tasted a metal glove too.

"What's going on here?" said Kevin, as he stepped up to Jarvi.

Jarvi looked at Kevin. "They tried to resist. That one there even fired an energy weapon at my men." Jarvi pointed to the unconscious man lying prone on the floor. "He should be thankful we showed restraint and didn't kill him."

"We thought you were raiders," said the man.

"We keep hearing about these raiders," said Kevin.

The man cocked his head at Kevin, the fear now mixing with surprise. "You don't know what raiders are?"

"We've had an encounter with them, but we're not from around here," said Kevin.

The man looked like he didn't believe Kevin, but played along anyway. "Raiders are outlaws. They prey on commercial vessels and do not hesitate to kill. We thought you were going to slaughter us."

"We still might," said Jarvi, eliciting another horrified look from the man. "We have deduced that this is the Captain of this vessel."

"What's your name?" said Kevin.

"Captain Neeman."

Kevin retracted his helmet in an effort to show Neeman that he was sincere. "We are not raiders, Captain. But we do need the use of your ship."

"What for?"

"We need access to that space station."

"Why don't you just go there? It's a busy place. Ships come and go all the time."

"We've been denied access."

"Why?"

"That is none of your concern," Jarvi barked, making the man jump.

Kevin raised his hand trying to signal to Jarvi to let him handle this.

"Unfortunately, Captain, our mission is secret. But I can assure you that neither you nor your crew will be harmed."

"And if we don't cooperate?"

Kevin frowned. "Let's not discuss such things. You seem like a reasonable man, Captain. We will gain access to the station. The only thing you should be concerned about is how much we have to persuade you to help us."

Neeman looked over at Jarvi again who looked ready to take another swing at Neeman if he said the wrong thing. Turning back to Kevin he said, "I will help you."

"Good man," said Kevin. He patted him on the shoulder with a heavy metal hand, making Neeman flinch. Kevin knew it must be terrifying for the man, to be surrounded by these metal Goliaths. He actually held up remarkably well, all things considered.

# Chapter 56

The station became larger on the viewscreen as the freighter drew closer. They had turned the hulking vessel around after the rest of the men had boarded. They came around from behind the star and were back in the system.

During the trip Kevin and Jarvi debriefed Neeman and accessed the ship's computer. They gathered as much intelligence as they could on the station, including maps and schematics. The station's main city was the logical place to look for the Captain. Unfortunately it wouldn't be easy. The Captain could be anywhere, and he didn't want to be found. There was likely a manhunt for him. They had to somehow gain access to that search and find the Captain first.

His team had taken off the combat suits and had donned clothing acquired from the freighter's crew, consisting of jumpsuits and coveralls. With the amount of commercial traffic on the station, freighter personnel should fit right in. The clothing was made with carrying tools in mind, making it ideal for hiding their weapons. Nobody would think twice about a group of big, muscular men in work clothes.

The additional men who boarded the freighter would be left behind with the combat suits, to guard the freighter and make sure the crew didn't tip anybody off. They would also serve as backup in case they ran into any real trouble and needed help. This was a covert mission, but if they ended up needing to fight their way out, the armored soldiers on the freighter could tip the scales in their favor. Kevin hoped it wouldn't come to that. This was not how he expected to see the lost colonies for the first time.

"We are being hailed, Sir," said the helmsman.

Neeman looked at Kevin who said, "Remember what we talked about. Audio only." He hoped Neeman wouldn't try anything stupid. Jarvi was scowling at him, reminding him of the very real danger present in the room with him.

Neeman nodded his head in quick movements. "Acknowledge the hail," he said to the helmsman. "Audio only."

"Captain Neeman," said the voice coming over the audio. "Why have you returned to DLC station? And why are you restricting communications to audio?"

"We've been plagued with system malfunctions since we left. It's affected everything from our viewscreen to our core. We need to perform a full diagnostic and have the ship serviced."

"Why wouldn't you just run your diagnostics at your destination? Why come back here?"

"DLC station was closer," said Neeman. "I was afraid if things got worse we might end up stranded in between systems. Vulnerable to any raider crew that might appear."

"This isn't like you, Neeman. You're not the type to panic about things like this. Is everything alright over there?"

Neeman gave Kevin a worried look. "Everything is fine. I'm just getting paranoid in my old age. This ship is not a young girl anymore either."

The voice laughed. "It sounds like you need a full diagnostic yourself, old man. Kill your engines and I'll have you towed in."

"Thanks a lot. Neeman out."

Neeman killed the connection and looked over at Kevin.

"That didn't sound too bad," Kevin said. "You did good."

"There will be an inspection," said Neeman. "It's standard procedure."

"How many inspectors?" said Jarvi.

317

"Usually two."

"Their inspection is going to be delayed a bit."

"How long does one of these inspections last?" said Kevin.

"Usually several hours. Sometimes longer. They go through the cargo to make sure we're not smuggling anything."

"Good. They shouldn't be missed for at least that long. That'll give us a good head start," said Kevin.

"They will be missed eventually," said Jarvi. "More will come to investigate. If we have not found your Captain by then things will become… complicated."

# Chapter 57

Kevin waited with his men and the Chaanisar as the freighter docked. The two teams were dressed like freighter crewmen. The rest of the Chaanisar and Marines who were to stay behind wore full combat suits. Two of those armored men stood by the hatch, flanking it on each side. The floor vibrated as the massive vessel slowly positioned itself. The clanging sound of connecting metal followed while the ship fastened itself to the station. Above the hatch a light had been flashing red. Now that they had successfully docked the light switched to a solid green, indicating that it was safe to open the hatch. With a bang and a hiss the hatch was unlocked.

It slid open with a moan and revealed two waiting inspectors. They had the same annoyed, self-important look on their faces that most bureaucrats have. The look said, I have power over you, so you better suck up to me if you know what's good for you. There was something corrupt about them. They were equipped with hand held devices used no doubt for checking the cargo. Kevin wondered how much it cost for these men to ignore certain things. Some things don't change, even a thousand light years from home, thought Kevin.

The two men stepped through and boarded the freighter. As they passed through the entrance a metal glove seized each man by the elbow. At first they acted outraged and threatened retribution. That act must have been a reflex because their protests quickly stifled when they had a real good look at the armored soldiers taking them into custody. Not only did they tower over the men, but the barrels of their oversized weapons were very persuasive. Their attitude changed so quickly from outrage to panic that Kevin was surprised neither of them pissed themselves. The armored soldiers took the inspectors away and the two teams prepared to board the station.

One of the Chaanisar walked out first, clearing the corridor. His weapons were concealed in his freighter work clothes and acted natural, like he belonged. Inside the freighter the rest of the men had their weapons drawn and ready, just in case. The Chaanisar scout whistled, signaling that the gangway was clear. The rest of the men put their weapons away, hiding them in the tool pockets of their work clothes, and stepped through the hatch out onto the gangway. Ahead was a long corridor which the two teams followed until they were outside. Or, more accurately, in a part of the station made to mimic the outdoors. Directly ahead was a parked vehicle, likely used by the inspectors.

"Chief, you take the vehicle and travel to the city," said Jarvi.

"What about you?"

"Our augmented speed will enable my team to reach our target quickly. The vehicle may draw attention to our approach. A craft like that heading into the city will not be suspicious."

"Understood. Good luck, Lieutenant."

Jarvi looked confused. Apparently the Chaanisar did not know what luck was. Probably for the best. Jarvi chose not to respond. He merely turned to his men and ordered them to move out.

"Chen," said Kevin.

"Yes, Sir."

"Figure out how that damn thing works."

Private Chen stepped up to the craft and produced a handheld scanner. He checked out the vehicle, walking around it and manipulating the display.

"Got it, Chief," he said, and opened a small panel on the craft's driver side. Behind the panel was a service display, providing access to the craft's systems. Chen used the scanner to bypass the system's security protocols, and within seconds the vehicle lit up and came online with a faint hum.

The Marines, eight in all, jumped on board. Chen sat in the driver's seat and Kevin set his large frame beside him. Sergeant Henderson and the rest of the Marines filled the back. Forced air jets powered on and lifted the team of Marines off the ground. A display came up on the dashboard indicating how many meters were remaining until they reached optimal altitude. It counted down as the vessel climbed until the display signaled success. Chen touched the controls and the vehicle turned and sailed away toward the city.

Everyone looked out the windows with wonder at the lush vegetation. The trees, grass and flowers were just like those on Earth. Even though Kevin knew they were not really outside, the effect of the landscape still touched a nerve. It reminded him of his island home, the tropical plants, the blue skies, the ocean. He hadn't realized how much he missed Mother Earth. He was sure the rest of the Marines felt the same. He also knew the question wasn't when they would be back, but if they would ever be back. He thought he had accepted that fact, but now he wondered if he ever could.

The people who lived here had probably forgotten Earth. It was probably something they were taught about in school. A subject that bored children, during which they daydreamed about what games they would play when the school day was done. They might retain some knowledge of Earth, something telling them that their ancestors came from Earth centuries ago. Beyond that it would likely be a subject for historians, irrelevant to the struggles and conquests of daily life. Yet when Kevin looked out the window he saw vegetation that had obviously been imported at some point from Earth. Sure, most of it was likely cloned, but where else would maple trees and oaks come from? Where did they find the rose bushes? The junipers? Or the cedars? Even out here, over a thousand light years from Earth, people still clung to home without even knowing. Whenever humans settled in alien environments they always tried to bring something of Earth with them. Kevin saw it on other planets, on space stations, and on starships. It was like people needed an anchor preventing them from drifting too far into the unknown.

He knew he needed it, and he suspected his men did too. But what about the Chaanisar? Where was their anchor? Certainly the Juttari didn't provide any. When it came to the Chaanisar, the Juttari's main goal was to extinguish any and all attachments to their humanity. The brain chips would have suppressed any negative reactions, like homesickness. But what would happen if the chips were removed? Kevin suspected that the chips regulated the Chaanisar's physiology, even without Juttari control. Every one of them seemed too composed. Too in control. It wasn't normal. But if the chips were removed? Then what? Would the weight of their experiences come crashing down on top of them, driving them insane? The Juttari had made them commit atrocities against their own kind. What would that knowledge do to them without the chips? And what of their childhood traumas? Would all those suppressed emotions, hiding deep in the dusty corners of their minds, come back like vengeful beasts to tear apart any hopes of normality? What do you do with an insane Chaanisar super soldier?

Leaving the chips in wasn't a better solution either. That brain chip was every Chaanisar's Achilles heel. If they went anywhere near a

Juttari ship again, that would be the end of their freedom. The Chaanisar would be turned back into ruthless slave warriors. The Juttari possessed the jump system technology now. How long would it take them to retrofit the rest of their fleet with the systems? How long until Juttari warships started showing up out here? That would mean imprisonment or worse for his Marines. An unacceptable risk. They had to remove those chips before that happened.

Up ahead he began to see the city's skyline. It was an incredible contrast to the landscape they had encountered so far. The city seemed as overcrowded and depressing as any back on Earth. Even here humans lived on top of each other. From a mere glimpse he saw that they clung to more of Earth than just its plant life. People were the same everywhere. Group large numbers together and they scurried around, thinking they were making progress, but really just finding different ways of securing their next meal. They compete with fervor in the contest of life, vying for rank and status, clamoring for a few golden hairs of Fleece. They believe themselves free and ambitious, but are blind to the true nature of their bondage.

As they entered the city's skies the air traffic became thicker. They flew around for a bit, looking out at the metropolis, trying to decide where to start their search. Then something caught Kevin's eye. There was a buzz of activity dead ahead. They approached cautiously, keeping a safe distance so as not to call attention to themselves, but getting close enough to survey the situation. What looked like official vehicles circled above more commotion below. On the ground lay a smoking craft with a crowd around it. The scene looked very out of place. Of course it could simply be mechanical failure, but something about it smelled of the Captain. They had no other leads so that made it as good a place to start as any.

Kevin had Chen land their vehicle on a nearby rooftop. They all exited and headed for the lift. The burly men crowded into the glass cabin and headed down to the ground level. Looking out at the forest of tall buildings, Kevin knew that the Captain could be anywhere, and they didn't have much time until they were found out.

"Chief, look," said Henderson, pointing to one of the buildings. The side of the building was illuminated with an advertisement. Only it wasn't a product being sold. On the side of the building was the Captain's face. A wanted sign. The image then transitioned to show Breeah's face. At least they now knew the Captain and Breeah were together.

"We don't have a lot of time," said Kevin.

"No, Sir," agreed Henderson.

When they reached the ground level they headed in the direction of the downed hovercraft. Soon they came upon the gathering crowd. Station security had cordoned off a perimeter and weren't letting anyone get close to the vehicle. Once Kevin got a good look at it he was convinced it had something to do with the Captain. The downed craft wasn't an ordinary civilian model. This one had guns attached and showed signs of recent combat. It was too much of a coincidence. The Captain either shot it down, or was shot down himself. Kevin looked around at the crowd and saw an older, talkative man. He seemed to know what was going on and looked too eager to share his knowledge with those around him. Kevin approached the man.

"What happened here?" said Kevin.

The man turned to Kevin and smiled, eager to tell the exciting story. "It was the fugitive. The one that killed Mr. Jansen. He was in the security vehicle. Making a run for it. But the drone got him. I saw the whole thing. They shot each other down."

"Where's the fugitive now? Did they catch him?" said Kevin.

"No. They didn't catch any of them."

"Them?"

"Yeah, the accomplices. They were altogether. The other man and the women."

"You saw them?"

"I sure did. A scary experience, let me tell you. He looked right at me. I've never seen eyes like that on a man before. Deadly eyes. I thought he was going to shoot me, but they just ran off."

"Which way did they go?"

"Just down that way and around the corner," said the man, pointing with his finger.

"Thanks for the info."

"It sure is something. But nothing like my run in with the raiders. Now that was a scary situation. I was hauling some freight and-"

"Sorry, but I've got to go."

"Suit yourself," said the man. He then turned to the man standing on the other side of him and said, "Those raiders are some dangerous people, I can tell you that much."

Kevin turned to Henderson and said, "Looks like the Captain was here. The question is where is he now?"

"They probably know," said Henderson, nodding his head in the direction of a couple of security personnel walking away from the crowd. "They'll have the most up to date information."

"Agreed," said Kevin, and they set off after the men.

Kevin and Henderson took the lead, and the rest of the Marines fell in behind. Kevin wondered if these guys were still on duty. They certainly didn't seem to be in a hurry to get anywhere and they acted too casual, like they were just out for a walk, rather than working. He decided they were just unprofessional. Men like that would never make it in his unit.

The men turned a corner and entered a building. Kevin signaled to the rest of the Marines to stay outside while he and Henderson broke into a quick jog and entered the building behind the men. Inside was a quiet open area. The two men stood just inside talking together. They both turned and looked at Kevin and Henderson, apparently not expecting to be interrupted.

"Excuse me," said Kevin. "We need some help."

The one man rolled his eyes and sighed, not hiding his annoyance with the request. "We're off duty," he said. "You'll have to find someone else to help you."

Kevin and Henderson quickly closed the gap between them and the two men. "It'll only take a moment of your time, Sir," Kevin said.

"Do you have a problem with your ears?" said the second man. "He said we're off duty. Now get the hell out of here before we find a reason to arrest you."

"I'm sorry for bothering you, but it's just a quick question" said Kevin, just steps away from the man now. He wasn't sure what it was that triggered the response. Maybe the fact that two very large men were still coming at them after being ordered to leave. Whatever it was, the first man got nervous and reached for his weapon.

Henderson was closer and reacted instantly, surging forward and landing the heel of his boot on the offending arm, connecting hard with the elbow, probably breaking the joint. Before the man could cry out in pain the Sergeant was on him, landing two heavy punches perfectly on the man's chin. The blows turned the lights out for the man and he fell backwards like a falling tree.

The second man tried for his own weapon, but Kevin had gotten too close. With a powerful low kick Kevin swept the man's legs out from under him and the man hit the ground awkwardly, not getting his hands up to protect his face. There was the ugly sound of skull crashing against unforgiving floor and a pool of blood quickly started to build around the man's head. Not taking any chances, Kevin seized the man's arm and held him in place with a knee to the small of his back.

They disarmed the men, stripped them of their clothing and identification, and found a storage room to hide them. They got as much information as they could from the men, including the Captain's last known whereabouts, and left them there. Most importantly they took their communicators. They now had access to the security broadcasts and updates.

Outside, they regrouped with the rest of the Marines and headed off towards the Captain's last location. They were closer now, but finding the Captain in time was still a long shot.

# Chapter 58

"AI," said Jon, accessing his comm.

"Yes, Captain."

"Can you take down those pictures of us they're showing on the buildings all over the city? They're really not helping."

"I believe so, Captain. Give me a few minutes."

Jon stood in a lift staring out the window at his face on the side of the building in front of him. Getting out of the city was going to be a lot harder now that everybody knew his face. They had run away from the crash and ducked into a building to stay out of sight. They needed another vehicle, otherwise getting out would be impossible.

The lift stopped and the doors opened. A small, gray haired woman shuffled inside. She looked at Darla and said, "Hello."

Darla forced a smile and returned the greeting. The woman scanned the group appraisingly. She stopped at the girls and said, "Hello children. Are you having fun today?"

The girls just looked back with blank faces and didn't respond. The woman chuckled and said to Darla, "They're shy huh? My grandchildren are the same way. I keep telling them not to be afraid of people, but they're young. They'll learn soon enough."

Darla smiled at the old woman again, but didn't say anything. The woman's eyes then rested on Jon. She had clever eyes betraying a quick mind. Jon wondered how many people she fooled with the grandma game she played. She also hid her thoughts well, and Jon couldn't gauge what her opinion of him was. She turned away from Jon and looked out the window. There, right in front of her was a giant picture of him, with a caption saying he was wanted for the murder of Mr. Jansen. The woman stood motionless staring at the picture. For all her slyness, Jon knew she was trying to come to terms with the information she had been given. She was trapped in this small lift with a murderer.

What would she do? Jon wondered. Would she try and play it cool? Pretend like she didn't see anything? It would be a little ridiculous considering the ten story tall picture of him. He was overcome with a cruel curiosity. How would this sly gray fox try to get out of the dangerous situation she found herself in? He had to admit he didn't expect her decision.

Without warning the woman screamed as loud as she could. She had to have strong lungs to belt it out like that. Jon put a hand on her shoulder to try and calm her, but she kept screaming. She turned around and started punching Jon as hard as she could. While she did have unexpected strength for someone her age, the blows didn't hurt too much. He let her bang away at his chest in hopes that she would soon run out of steam.

"Let me out! Let me out!" she wailed.

"Calm down," said Jon, in an even tone. "I'm not going to hurt you."

"Murderer! Help! Help!"

She swung at him like a windmill as she tried to reach the door. Jon stood in front of her, blocking her path.

"Look, just relax. Nothing's going to happen to you. We just need to get to the roof and then we'll let you go."

"What are you doing with these people?" she said. "Has he hurt you," she said, looking at the children.

"No," said Anki, shaking her head.

"You poor thing," said the woman. "Animal! You let these people go!"

Jon endured another round of windmill strikes. He looked at Breeah who had a mischievous grin on her face. "Really?" he said. "Are you enjoying this?"

"Surprisingly I am," said Breeah, giggling. Her mirth must have been contagious because Anki looked up at her mother and began giggling as well. Soon Alina and Otka joined in followed by Seiben and Darla.

The laughter shocked the old woman, and she stopped hitting Jon. She looked around at the smiling faces surrounding her. Wagging a finger at them she said, "You're all crazy. Every one of you."

"Just take it easy grandma," said Seiben. "You're not in any danger."

The lift reached the rooftop and the doors opened. They all walked out and left the old woman behind.

"See," said Seiben, turning back to speak to her. "I told you." He turned away and rejoined the group.

They headed to an array of parked vehicles up ahead. Jon hoped he would find another security vehicle, but there was nothing with any firepower. He settled on the first craft he saw and had the AI unlock the vessel to give him access. The rest of the group climbed in. Jon powered up the vessel. It hummed quietly, ready to take off. He eased the craft up off the landing pad and turned around so they could fly it out of the city.

As he did he heard screams again. He turned and saw the old lady standing near the edge of the roof waving her arms and screaming, "Help! Help!"

He looked off in the direction she was looking and saw a security craft floating above a nearby building. He cursed. His only option was to run and take advantage of whatever head start he had. The craft surged forward and he accelerated as much as it would let him. His vehicle had no guns and no armor. His only hope was that the security craft wouldn't notice the old lady until he got away.

"Captain," said the AI over his comm. "A security team has identified you and is in pursuit."

"Great," said Jon.

"And Captain."

"Yes, AI?"

"I've removed your pictures from all displays, including the ones on the buildings."

"Thank you, AI."

"You're most welcome, Captain."

# Chapter 59

"Fugitive has been spotted in hovercraft. Security team is in pursuit," said the voice over the security communicator.

"That's him," said Kevin. "They're on him. We need to get to one of those ships fast."

"In here," said Henderson.

The team ducked into a building and ran for the lift. The lift took them up to the roof where they could find a vehicle. The Captain and his pursuers had a head start but the security reports should point them in the right direction. He only hoped the Captain could elude capture long enough for them to catch up.

They reached the roof without incident and ran toward the parked vehicles. One happened to be landing as they approached. It was still powered on and the passengers had just disembarked. It looked as though the driver was about to take off. He waved goodbye to his passengers when he noticed Kevin's team running up. With curiosity, he watched and waited to see what the urgency was all about. When Sergeant Henderson came up to his door and opened it, that curiosity quickly turned to fear. Henderson reached in and grabbed the man by the hair. He pulled the wide eyed civilian out of the vehicle, throwing him to the ground. His passengers looked on in shock as the Marines climbed into the humming craft.

Henderson again let Chen into the driver's seat. Kevin sat in the passenger seat, the Sergeant and the rest of the men climbed into the back. Chen lifted the vehicle off the landing pad and headed in the direction of the chase. Inside, the Marines readied themselves for combat. The time for disguises was quickly coming to an end. They pulled their weapons out from their coveralls, and checked to make sure everything was in working order. They had outfitted themselves with Chaanisar rail guns, preferring to have the punch and armor piercing capabilities the energy weapons sometimes lacked. They wore armor underneath their coveralls for protection. Unlike a combat suit, the armor was lighter and not powered, and didn't offer the same amount of protection. It did shield them, however, and would allow them to take a few hits before it started to fail. It protected their torsos, arms and legs, but not their heads. Unfortunately it was the only option that allowed them to stay covert.

As they headed for the outskirts of the city a report came in over the security frequency. "Fugitive vehicle has been fired upon and hit. Craft is losing altitude."

"Damn it!" said Kevin. "Can't this thing go any faster?"

"Sorry Chief, it's maxed out," said Chen.

Kevin punched the dashboard. They were too far away. The security forces would get to the Captain first.

"Lieutenant Jarvi to Chief St. Clair," said a voice over Kevin's comm.

"St. Clair here."

"We have successfully disabled the station's weapons, Chief. What's your status?"

"We're in the air. We've located the Captain, but we're too far and station security forces are already on top of them."

"Understood. Send me the Captain's location, Chief. We'll try and reach them from the ground. Maybe our teams can flank the security force."

Kevin sent Jarvi the coordinates. The Chaanisar were fast, but were they fast enough?

Over the security frequency came another update. "Fugitive hovercraft has been grounded. Fugitives now on foot. We are giving pursuit."

Kevin ground his teeth and hit the dash again. "Come on! Let's go!" he said in frustration.

The voice came over the security frequency again, this time sounding panicked. "We are taking fire… Requesting assistance…" The Marines were all quiet, waiting for the next update. "We've been hit. Repeat, we've been hit. We are going down. Request immediate assistance."

Cheers broke out in the hovercraft.

"You're gonna need more than one of these damn flying toys to take out the Captain," yelled Kevin, releasing some of the tension that had built up inside him.

Another voice came over the security frequency. "Hold position, assistance is on the way."

The cheers quieted down at the sound, replaced by a grim determination. The Captain had bought them some time, but the battle wasn't over yet. Kevin knew it likely hadn't even begun.

# Chapter 60

Jon ran, but not at full speed. Not even at half speed. He was
slowed by the group, and the group was slowed by the children.
When it was just Anki he could carry her to pick up the pace, but he
couldn't carry all three, so they had to move slower than necessary.
Seiben and Darla carried their two girls which was taking its toll on
their mobility. At that speed it was a certainty that the security forces
would overtake them. He had shot down the last team that chased
them. He had been lucky. They weren't cautious when they
approached, thinking they had Jon at their mercy. Perhaps they
didn't think he was armed? Either way they were foolish and gave

him an opportunity to fire. The next round wouldn't be as easy. They had managed to leave the city and were now running through the acres of parkland that surrounded it. The landscape was serene and pleasant, woefully unsuited to their desperate circumstances.

He turned and looked at the sky behind him. He spotted more security forces in the sky heading towards them. They were mere dots in the distant sky, but that would change quickly. They were too exposed out here, and they had no hope of outrunning their pursuers. They needed to find another option fast. Up ahead he saw something that might work. A structure, standing behind a group of evergreens. It wasn't a house. Rather it looked to be used for maintenance supplies. It looked solidly built. It would have to do.

Jon waved the group over to the small building. It had a couple of small windows and a door. He tried the door, but it was locked. Jon pointed the energy weapon at the door and fired, burning a hole through the lock. The door swung open and he ushered the group inside. He shut the door behind him. Now they would sit and wait. The building smelled of soil and fertilizer. All around them were gardening supplies. There were bags of soil stacked up high in the corner. The building itself had thick walls and looked like it could resist the weaponry he'd seen the security forces use. If they used heavier weapons, however, the game would be up. They would need to get out of there before that happened, which would be hard to do with only one way in and out.

"What do we do now?" said Seiben, trying to catch his breath.

"We wait," said Jon. "With any luck they won't find us here."

"What are the chances of that?"

Jon sighed, "Not good, but we'll find out soon enough."

He looked out the window and saw three vehicles floating around the crash site. They began to land and DLC security forces emerged. They all looked like Kulberg's guards, dressed in black from head to toe, and carrying energy weapons. Jon counted twenty five men in all. They spread out into a long, wide line, intended to cover as much area as possible and started to move forward, weapons ready and pointed dead ahead. They would be on top of them in five minutes at most. Jon figured the chances of them not checking the building were about zero, so he got ready.

He had put Darla and the girls behind a pile of bags filled with soil, and told them not to move. He positioned Seiben in the rear to protect Darla and the children if anybody managed to break into the building. He had Breeah stand at one of the windows while he took the other. They were on opposite ends of the door, giving them the ability to put anyone coming through in a crossfire, while also allowing them to fire through the windows.

They waited a few minutes until the security forces closed on the building. He peeked out the window and cringed. The security craft were back in the air and floating just above the DLC soldiers. They were going to provide air support to the ground troops with those Gatling guns. How the hell was he supposed to get out of this one?

Any hopes that they might miss the building faded when a soldier approached the door and saw the hole burned through it. "In here," he yelled, and pulled the door open. Jon and Breeah fired in unison.

The soldier didn't have a chance. He fell to the ground with a thud directly in front of the door.

Jon heard soldiers running toward the building and turned to his window. He broke the glass with the stock of his weapon and opened fire. Breeah did the same. The soldiers outside scrambled for cover in response. From the window Jon caught a glimpse of an attack craft's nose pointing at him. He got out of the way just as its Gatling guns opened fire, sending a barrage of bullets through the window.

A second attack craft moved in and fired on Breeah's location, forcing her to take cover. They were pinned down. Trapped. The DLC soldiers would soon use the supporting fire from the hovercraft to break through. Jon pointed his weapon at the door, waiting for the inevitable onslaught.

More gunfire erupted from the other side of the building. Had they surrounded them already? Maybe he didn't give them enough credit? The attack craft stopped firing at his window and he carefully peeked out. There was still shooting, but it wasn't aimed at the building. They were fighting someone else. But who? He tried to get a better look at what was happening but didn't have a decent vantage point. He did spot another vehicle approaching. As it neared he realized that it wasn't armed. It was a civilian craft. Some thrill seeker wanting a better look at the action? He watched it set down. Saw the doors slide open, and gasped. Coming out of the vehicle, wearing coveralls and now engaging the DLC soldiers from behind was Kevin and a team of Marines.

He stood stunned, not believing his eyes. *How could any of this be possible?* he thought. *How did they get off Kerces? How did they find the station? It's impossible.* He looked out the window again. They were still there.

"Breeah," Jon yelled. "Do you see Chief St. Clair out there?"

Breeah looked out her window and scanned the landscape. She froze. A few moments later she pulled away from the window and looked at Jon with the same surprised look he imagined was on his face. "Yes, Jon. I see him. How-?"

"I don't know. But I think we should probably give them a hand, don't you?"

"I do," she said, still clearly confused, but adapting to the bizarre situation.

The two returned to their windows and joined in the fight. The security team ahead of them had forgotten the building and had turned to engage the force on their rear. That made them easy targets for Jon and Breeah, who had no qualms about shooting them in the back. They fell quickly and the Marines advanced.

"Captain? Are you in there?" came Kevin's voice, as they approached the building.

"Yeah, we're in here," said Jon. "Where the hell did you come from?"

"Hang on a minute, Sir. I'm just in the middle of something here."

Jon broke out into laughter. He laughed for joy. Not just at the joke, not just at the fact that they were saved, but at the fact that his best friend was still alive.

Outside the firing slowed, becoming more sporadic, until it finally stopped.

"You can come out now, Captain," said Kevin.

Jon walked out of the building with Breeah, Seiben, Darla and the children in tow.

Kevin walked up to him and saluted. "Chief St. Clair reporting for duty, Sir."

Jon returned the salute and laughed. He thrust out his hand and Kevin shook it.

"Chief, I've never been so happy to see anybody in my life," said Jon. He looked at the rest of the Marines who also sported wide grins and said, "That goes for all of you."

Jon became aware of more men approaching from behind and turned to see another armed group dressed like Kevin and his men, only he didn't recognize any of them.

One of them stepped up and said, "Captain Pike, I'm Lieutenant Jarvi. I know you have a lot of questions, but we have to go. Quickly."

"Lieutenant Jarvi? There was no Lieutenant Jarvi on the Hermes," said Jon.

"That's because we're not from the Hermes," said Jarvi. "We're Chaanisar."

# Chapter 61

They moved faster now. Jon carried Anki, Seiben carried Alina, and Private Daniels carried Otka. Even though the Chaanisar were capable of greater speed, they matched the speed of the group so as to better defend against any further attacks. Two Chaanisar raced ahead to scout for any waiting surprises.

*Chaanisar*, thought Jon. *What the hell are the Chaanisar doing here? And why is Kevin with them?*

Kevin ran beside Jon, and as if hearing his thoughts he said, "They rescued us from that planet, you know."

"Why would the Juttari do that?" said Jon.

"They're not Juttari anymore. They mutinied and killed all the Juttari on board."

"How? The Chaanisar have never mutinied before."

"Their brain chips malfunctioned. Actually they still work, but what stopped working was the Juttari's control over the brain chips."

"You believe that?" said Jon, the cynicism punching through with each syllable.

"I know. I found it difficult to swallow at first, too," said Kevin, in between breaths. "I still have my doubts. But they've come through. We've been chasing down the escape pods and picking up the crew. We've even fought the Kemmar over an escape pod. They've risked their lives for us a few times now. That goes a long way in my books."

"I don't know. The last time I ran into Chaanisar they were using me for target practice. Forgive me if I don't suddenly hold hands and sing songs with them."

"You are right to be suspicious, Captain," said Lieutenant Jarvi, from up ahead. He turned his head and looked back at Jon, not breaking stride. "I would not expect any less from you."

"You don't know me, Lieutenant, "said Jon. *Who was talking to you anyway? he* thought.

"Of course I do, Captain. We all know you. Our original mission was to destroy the Hermes. We have all been briefed on your career.

Your victories. Your assassinations. Your record is quite impressive."

"All in the past." *A murderer would be impressed by killing,* he thought. He felt ancient furies waking inside him and the past rushed at him in a torrent of deep seated hatred. He saw his wife, and his children, and how they died at the hands of Chaanisar like this Lieutenant Jarvi.

"Ah, the past," mused Jarvi. "The past is slavery. It is unchangeable. There is only the future, Captain." Jarvi slowed his pace so that Jon and Kevin could catch up to him. "Forget what you know of the Chaanisar, Captain. We are no longer puppets. We are reborn. We are human. You are witnessing the dawn of a new age."

"I'm witnessing something. I just haven't decided what it is yet." *Be happy I haven't decided to gut you.* His thoughts caught him off guard. He had decided to forget the past. To start anew with Breeah and Anki. But here was the past showing him that its icy hands still gripped him as tightly as ever. Would he ever be free?

"Of course, Captain. As I said, I wouldn't expect any less from you," said Jarvi.

"So you're from the Juttari ship we fought against at the beginning of our mission?"

"Correct."

"Do you still have the jump system? The one you stole from us?"

"Yes, Captain. We still have the jump system the Juttari stole. Not us."

"What's the difference?"

"As the Chief said, the Juttari do not rule us anymore."

"Yeah? Who does?"

"We rule ourselves."

*We'll see about that*, thought Jon. "Where's the ship now?"

"A safe distance away. The station's leader denied us access to its system. They did not want us to help you escape judgment."

"Escape judgment," Jon spit. "I didn't kill Jansen," he said, the anger dripping off each word.

"Whether you did or didn't is irrelevant. All that matters now is escape."

"Wait. How did you get on board if they denied you access to the system?"

"We commandeered a freighter," said Kevin, smiling.

"You did what?" said Seiben, who ran just behind Jon and listened to the entire conversation.

"This is Captain Seiben," said Jon. "He's a freighter Captain."

"Which did you capture?" said Seiben. "Who was the Captain?"

"Captain Neeman," said Kevin.

Seiben let loose a loud belly laugh. "Serves him right. I hate that guy. Did he shit his pants?"

"Daddy!" said Alina, a frown of disapproval across her face.

"Sorry, I didn't mean to swear," said Seiben, looking apologetically at his daughter. He turned back to Kevin and grinned, saying, "Well, did he?"

"There were a few moments I thought he might," said Kevin, returning the grin.

Seiben laughed hysterically. Jon looked back at him and smiled, happy that he was letting off some steam. He had never wanted to involve Seiben and his family in any of this. He knew it wasn't his fault, but he still felt guilty.

"The good Captain saved our lives when he picked up our escape pod," said Jon.

"Don't remind me," said Seiben. "I should've never let my nephew talk me into it."

"Nonetheless, you have my gratitude," said Jon.

"And look where that got me. You can keep your damn gratitude."

Darla punched Seiben in the arm. Alina copied her mother and punched her father in the chest.

"Why is everybody hitting me?" protested Seiben.

"Don't be so rude," said Darla.

"You're right," said Seiben. He turned to Jon and said, "Thank you for all the exercise you are giving me today. I was worried about how fat I was getting."

Darla and Alina both punched Seiben again, making Jon and Kevin laugh.

"Thank you for saving our Captain," said Kevin, still chuckling.

Seiben grunted.

Jon turned back to Kevin. "So who else have you rescued?"

"We got a lot of the Marines off Kerces. The ones who were still alive," said Kevin, his eyes turning grim. He looked at Breeah and said, "We got some of the Reivers out, too."

Breeah cocked her head at Kevin, but didn't say anything. Jon wondered why she was so detached when it came to her people. She never showed any emotion when the subject came up. She was generally stoic in nature, but you would think that she would be happy that some of her own were rescued. But there was no curiosity to know who had been saved. If they got off the station in one piece he'd try and find out why.

"We got Singh too," said Kevin, his voice full of venom.

"What's wrong with that?" said Jon, confused by Kevin's tone.

"He's a traitor, Sir."

Jon couldn't believe it. Chief Engineer Singh loved the Hermes. He hadn't known anyone more committed to their jobs than Singh. "That's got to be a mistake. How could Singh be a traitor?"

"He's lost it, Sir. I don't know what happened, but he showed up on Kerces and was telling the Kemmar everything about the Hermes and Earth. He was even going to show them how to build their own jump systems."

Jon was stunned. "I don't believe it," he said.

"Believe it, Sir. I saw it with my own eyes. He's on the Chaanisar ship in custody."

"Did the Kemmar break him?"

"I don't know who broke him, but he's not all there anymore."

That was bad news. Singh was a genius when it came to the jump system. If anybody could build another one, it was him. They would need him if they hoped to outfit any ship with a jump system. The thought surprised him. An hour ago he didn't know if any of his crew were still alive. He knew nothing of the Chaanisar mutiny. His only thought was keeping everyone safe long enough to try and escape the station. Now he was thinking of building another jump ship. He hadn't even gotten off the station yet and his subconscious was already making plans. Was it his subconscious? Or was it the creature? Were his thoughts his own anymore?

"We rescued Ensigns Petrovic and Yao," continued Kevin.

"Good," said Jon. The Hermes tactical and navigation officers would certainly come in handy if they did build another ship. He would need his bridge crew. Commander Wolfe would have been invaluable in that case, but he knew that wasn't possible. He saw her die on the bridge. A great officer with a promising career. Her death weighed heavily on his conscience.

"We also picked up Tallos and a couple of Diakans."

Jon came to a halt causing a Marine to run into him. He apologized and took off again, but he was no less shaken by what he had heard. His stomach tightened and he boiled over inside. "You have Tallos?" he said, almost in a whisper.

"Yes, Sir."

He had a score to settle with the Diakan. Breeah almost died because of him. He could barely wait to see Tallos. To clench his fingers around that green throat and watch the life drain out of those unblinking fish eyes.

"Lieutenant Jarvi, what is your status," came a voice over Jarvi's communicator.

"Weapon systems are disabled, Sir," said Jarvi. "We have the Captain and his party and are heading for the docks."

"We are in position awaiting your signal."

"Understood, Sir." Jarvi turned to Jon and Kevin. "Our ship is orbiting the station. They are waiting to extract us. We need to move quickly."

Jon nodded his understanding. Soon he would be on board a Juttari warship, surrounded by Chaanisar. He cringed. *Grandfather save me,* he thought

He looked at the rest of his group. Breeah was barely sweating. She was in great shape and wouldn't have a problem making it. Seiben and Darla were another matter. They were both drenched in sweat and out of breath. He was surprised they hadn't asked to take a break yet. Jon looked to Private Burke and said, "Private, carry the child for the rest of the way," pointing at Alina.

"It's okay," said Seiben.

"No it's not," said Jon. "You're going to slow us down. Burke can carry Alina and still keep pace."

Seiben didn't put up much of a fight and handed his daughter over to the younger, fitter Marine.

"Captain," came the AI's voice over Jon's comm.

"Yes, AI," said Jon.

A look of surprise swept over Kevin's face. "You saved the AI?"

"Hello Chief St. Clair," said the AI. "I can assure you I am still very much alive."

"Glad to hear it," said Kevin.

"I am glad that you are alive too," said the AI. "Captain, there is a security contingent gaining on your position."

"How long until they intercept us?"

"Five minutes."

"Understood, "said Jon. "Lieutenant, how long till we reach the extraction point?"

"Ten minutes," said Jarvi.

# Chapter 62

Colonel Bast had no doubt that Lieutenant Jarvi would succeed in his mission. Failure was not in that man's vocabulary. Just as he expected, the station's weapon systems were down, successfully sabotaged by Jarvi's team. He was curious to see how Chief St. Clair's team would perform, however. He didn't think it was right to send a Chaanisar team to rescue their Captain, but he also wanted to test the Chief and his men. He liked and respected the Chief, but wanted to give him an opportunity to prove himself. The Chief didn't need to prove anything to him. Bast recognized that the Chief and his Marines were skilled warriors. Instead, he wanted to give them a victory. In rescuing the Captain they would exorcise any demons that still haunted them from their experience on Kerces. It would revitalize them. Give them renewed purpose.

He hoped they would learn to work with Lieutenant Jarvi's team. He saw the potential conflict building between the Chief and the Lieutenant. He understood Jarvi's attitude. Chaanisar were enhanced soldiers. The Juttari technology in their bodies gave them super human abilities. They had train to be soldiers since childhood. It was difficult to see someone who didn't have these abilities as an equal. He hoped that by succeeding in his mission the Chief would earn more of Jarvi's respect, and the two could work harmoniously.

They were stuck together, after all. They needed to work with each other moving forward. The Hermes was gone. They couldn't continue behaving as two separate crews. They would eventually have to merge. Become one. By doing so they would become stronger and benefit from the other. He would just have to win Captain Pike over to his cause. The Hermes crew was still loyal to him. That was obvious. If Captain Pike agreed to merge the crews, the rest would follow. If he didn't… things might become uncomfortable.

The other thing was Doctor Ellerbeck. If they found her, the Captain's support for their cause would ensure her compliance. They needed to remove the chips once and for all. Otherwise it was like having a gun permanently pointed at their heads. One day someone would come along and pull the trigger.

Under the Juttari, they would have merely sought out the Doctor and captured her. Then they would have used any of a number of methods to force her to comply with their wishes. While that would be the easier course of action, it wasn't who they were anymore. He knew in some ways he was being idealistic, but what else was there? Under the Juttari they never acted of their own free will. They had none. No choice in any action they took. They weren't really monsters. The true monsters were their masters. Now that Juttari control was gone, what would they do? If they still used Juttari methods, then they truly were no different, the brain chips merely a convenient excuse to hide their true nature.

He refused to accept such weakness. Their true nature was human, not Juttari. Their humanity was stolen from them when they were children. But it wasn't lost. When they mutinied they stole it back. He planned to keep it this time. It would not be easy, but they all had to learn to be human again. What better way to start than with the crew of the Hermes?

He knew convincing Captain Pike was not going to be easy. He knew Pike's history. His reputation. He had killed countless Juttari and Chaanisar during his career. No other Space Force soldier came close. That level of success requires more than just ability. It requires zeal. Obsessive commitment. Pure hatred of the enemy. Captain Pike had lost his family during the war. His fury must run deep.

Were they really that different?

Every Chaanisar had lost their families as children. Their hatred of the Juttari was merely suppressed by the brain chips. But would Captain Pike see it that way? Not at first, but maybe over time. How do you win over someone like that? With deeds, that was how. They had rescued his men from the prison planet. They were searching for the escape pods and fighting to retrieve them. Words were meaningless. Their actions would win over Captain Pike in the end. Their actions would reclaim their humanity. They would prevail.

"We are being hailed by the station, Sir."

"Route transmission to my console."

The screen flickered to life and the rather unpleasant looking Mr. Kulberg appeared.

"Colonel Bast, why have you returned?"

"I missed our long conversations," said Bast.

Kulberg frowned, apparently unimpressed by Bast's wit. "I warned you that we would fire on you if you returned, Colonel."

"Yes, I do remember you saying something like that. I think we'll take our chances."

The screen went black and Bast waited, certain that Kulberg was ordering the station's weapon systems to bombard his ship. It didn't worry him. He had full confidence in Lieutenant Jarvi, as he did in all his men. If the Lieutenant said the weapon systems were disabled, then it was so.

Some time passed and nothing happened. No cannons. No missiles. No attack. The screen came alive again and Kulberg's face reappeared, scowling more than before.

"Is there something wrong, Mr. Kulberg?" said Bast.

"I'm sure you think you're very clever," said Kulberg, his eyes all but burning holes through the display.

"Now why would I think something like that?"

"Don't play games, Bast. Somehow you've managed to disable our defenses. I don't know how you did it, but I can assure you we are more than capable of defending ourselves."

"Mr. Kulberg," said Bast, trying hard to sound conciliatory. "We mean your station no harm. We merely want our people. If we can get past this misunderstanding I am willing to establish diplomatic relations."

"Diplomatic relations? Who do you represent?"

"Ourselves."

Kulberg leaned back in his chair, studying Bast. "You want to propose diplomatic relations between this station and your ship?"

"Yes. Why not?"

"You're a fool," said Kulberg, leaning in. "Your people are out of time. As we speak my forces are running them down. They are not going to make it off this station alive. Your ship is not going to fare any better. Two DLC destroyers are coming for you as we speak. Your ship will not make it out of this system. Enjoy what little time you have left."

The display went black again and Kulberg was gone. Bast pulled up a tactical display of the surrounding system. He saw the destroyers racing toward them. They looked to be the same size as his ship.

He pulled up another display analyzing their weaponry. Again they seemed to be evenly matched, with a similar array of weaponry. He felt confident that they could defeat one of the ships, though they would sustain a fair amount of damage in the process. Fighting two, on the other hand, would be far more difficult, and he didn't know if they could win, even with the jump system.

He wasn't sure how much time they had as he didn't know the range of their weapons. He had seen some warships with tremendous energy weapon range. While it was true long distance firing dissipated some of the weapon's power, it could still cause damage. Sustained firing even more so. If the other ship couldn't fire back, well then it turned into a game of target practice. Provided the ship couldn't jump away. But he couldn't just jump away. He had to retrieve his people.

Bast opened a channel with Lieutenant Jarvi. "What is your status, Lieutenant?"

"A sizable force is bearing down on us, Sir," said Jarvi.

"Can you outrun them?"

"No, Sir."

"I am ordering the remaining force guarding the docks to assist you. Transmit your coordinates to them."

"Understood."

"Signal when you've successfully reached the extraction point."

"Yes, Sir."

Bast studied the advancing warships once more. Right now they were spread apart, but as they came closer to his ship they would close the gap between themselves, making them harder to defend against. He didn't know how long it would take for the landing party to reach the extraction point. If the destroyers managed to get within weapons range they could easily shoot down any shuttles sent for extraction. He couldn't allow that.

"Helm, prepare to jump," said Bast. "Plot coordinates to land us directly behind the destroyer on our starboard side."

"Coordinates plotted, Sir."

"Jump."

# Chapter 63

The past twenty four hours had turned Captain Seiben's life upside down. Jon had laughed when he said he should have never picked up the escape pod earlier, thinking he was joking, but he wasn't. He didn't wish for Jon, Breeah and Anki to die, and he knew that if he hadn't picked them up they might very well have died. He just wished someone else rescued them. Someone like Neeman should've found them. Neeman's life should be in tatters.

Seiben worried. The anxiety was almost overwhelming. He worried for his daughters, and for his wife. What if something happened to them? How could he protect them now?

His life had been simple. It was a good life. No matter how much Darla complained, they had all they needed. He had the security of a good job. They had a good apartment. The kids went to a good school. They didn't want for anything. Now it was all gone. They had nothing. All because he listened to his nephew and retrieved that escape pod.

He tightened his grip on the weapon's stock. All that mattered now was that they come out of this alive, and the only way to do that was to escape with Jon and these other men. He looked around at the men. They had stopped running now and took up defensive positions, waiting for the coming DLC attack. Who were they? Where did they come from? They were all clearly soldiers, but from where? He had hauled freight his whole life and had been to all the human worlds, and he knew with certainty that these men came from none of them. How was that possible?

He had listened in on Jon's conversation earlier and from what he understood they weren't all from the same place. He understood they were also enemies at one point, waging war against each other. That certainly hadn't happened in this region of space. Something about it triggered a memory. He remembered the old myths he heard as a child. The stories told of how they came from another part of the galaxy. The birthplace of humanity. They told how a great evil came and destroyed it forever. They were taught in school that they were all that was left of humanity in the universe. Yet these humans were clearly from somewhere else. Could they be from the place the myths spoke of? Perhaps it wasn't destroyed after all? He tried to remember the planet's name. It was so long ago and his memory wasn't what it used to be. It escaped him.

He turned to Darla. She was crouching beside him with the girls. They were hidden behind some trees, with the soldiers in position in front of them and on their flanks. The soldiers had chosen a hill as a good place to mount a defense, and they all spread out along its ridge, their weapons ready. The attackers would have to get past the soldiers to get to his family. If the soldiers couldn't hold them off they were done for anyway.

"Darla," said Seiben. "Do you remember the old myths about how we all originally came from another planet?"

"Yes, my grandmother told me the stories often when I was a child."

"What was the name of the planet?"

Darla thought for a moment, searching her memory for the information. Her eyes suddenly brightened and she said, "Earth."

"That's it," said Seiben, the name awakening more memories.

"Why would you ask me something like-" She looked around at the men surrounding them and said in a whisper, "You think these men are from Earth?"

He thought about it some more and said, "Where else could they be from? They're not from any planet I know."

"But, those stories… they're just myths."

"How do we know that? The stories came from somewhere. What if it wasn't from someone's imagination? What if the stories are true?"

said Seiben, feeling like he had just uncovered some deep, dark secret.

"But they said that Earth was estroyed," said Darla. "If the stories were true, these men can't be from Earth."

"What if that part is wrong?" said Seiben. He felt like he was on the verge of some major discovery, but wasn't qualified to put the pieces together.

"Now you're talking nonsense," said Darla, patronizingly. "You can't just pick and choose only what information suits you. If the stories are true, then they are true. Simple as that. Otherwise they're just myths."

Seiben wasn't convinced. He would have to ask Jon about it. But first they had to survive this encounter.

One of the soldiers yelled, "Incoming!"

Seiben peeked around the tree and saw a line of security craft in the sky, converging on their positions. When they came nearer the soldiers opened fire as one. The sound was deafening and Darla pulled the screaming girls in close. Seiben stayed fixed on the unfolding battle. The initial salvo from the soldiers downed a few vessels. They seemed surprised by the attack and they changed directions, backtracking while returning fire. It seemed like a real passive strategy, almost a retreat, until he realized what they were up to.

They lowered themselves close to the ground and DLC soldiers started to jump out. Soon there was a sizable ground force of black clad DLC troops advancing steadily on their positions. The soldiers stayed low and continued shooting, while the security craft above them fired. They advanced together and the sustained barrage had a noticeable effect on his defenders, forcing them to keep their heads down more than they would prefer.

Seiben got nervous. He wasn't a soldier, but he could see that defending against such a large force was not going to be easy. At this point it even seemed impossible. They were outnumbered and outgunned. The slow, steady DLC advance made it worse. It looked like they had learned their lesson from the last engagement. They respected the soldiers' abilities and were not taking any chances. There were no heroics. Nothing fancy. They moved forward inch by inch like a steamroller. Seemingly unstoppable.

Seiben's mind raced. What could he do? How could he save his family? He couldn't fight. If the men surrounding him couldn't prevail, then what hope did he have? None. He had to surrender. That was his only option. Hopefully they wouldn't kill him anyway. He could plead ignorance. He would be telling the truth. He didn't know why they were after Jon. But he did know that Jon didn't kill Jansen. That was enough. That knowledge made him dangerous to Kulberg. They wouldn't arrest them. They would kill him and Darla to keep them quiet. They could easily justify it after this. How hard would it be to claim that they were killed in battle? That they fired on DLC security?

What about his daughters? They didn't know anything. Could they be that cold? Could they murder innocent children? Could he take that chance? Even if they didn't kill them, what would happen to his lovely girls? How would they be treated? The thought horrified him. He decided he had no choice. If he was going to die anyway, it would be defending his family.

He looked out at the battle and saw that things had changed quickly. The security craft had jumped ahead and the DLC soldiers were charging. The men defending them couldn't fight off both and were focusing their fire on the charging force, in most cases cutting them down before they could reach their positions. The charge didn't make sense until he realized that the hovercraft had sailed over their positions and were now behind the defenders. His heart pounded against his chest as he took quick shallow breaths. The hovercraft were turning. They were going to shoot the soldiers in the back.

Without thinking he raised his weapon and fired on one of the vessels. Terror gripped him when it stopped its turn and swung around to face Seiben. He kept firing to no avail. The vessel pointed its nose downward to get Seiben in its sights.

*Oh no*, he thought. *What have I done?*

# Chapter 64

The Chaanisar ship landed behind the unsuspecting destroyer and opened fire. Energy weapons, missiles and rail guns lit up the void, targeting the warship's propulsion system. It took the enemy's crew some time to figure out what had happened. To comprehend that the ship they were bearing down upon had somehow shown up behind them. In that time the Chaanisar had inflicted a fair bit of damage on the DLC vessel. Not enough to disable it, but enough to get its attention. The destroyer had heavy armor plating that seemed capable of taking a significant pounding. Its deflectors dispersed much of the penetrating power of the energy weapons. The DLC vessel recovered from the attack and returned fire.

Energy weapons hit the Chaanisar ship. While they didn't have deflectors like the destroyer, their armor plating was robust enough to withstand the pounding. Bast monitored the position of the second warship on his tactical screen. It had been notified of the attack and now changed course.

"Helm, prepare to jump behind the destroyer on our port side," said Bast.

"Coordinates plotted, Sir."

"Jump."

The Chaanisar heavy cruiser landed behind the second ship and opened fire once again. This destroyer responded faster than the first, tipped off to the Chaanisar jump capabilities. The Chaanisar were still able to get off the first shot before the DLC ship could respond. When they returned fire it wasn't just with energy weapons, but with a salvo of missiles too.

"Launch counter measures," said Bast. "Rail guns in point defense mode."

Some of the DLC capabilities impressed Bast, especially the deflectors. But their missiles were not sophisticated enough to defeat the Chaanisar defenses. Most of the missiles chased after the decoy drones, and the rest were easily defeated by the point defense shield. Still he had to keep them guessing.

"Helm, prepare to jump directly in front of the other destroyer."

"Yes, Sir."

"Jump."

The Chaanisar landed and fired. Bast hoped to confuse the ship, if only for a split second. Any advantage was useful. The enemy was learning, however, and adapted quicker this time, returning fire from all its weapon systems. The onslaught rocked the Chaanisar ship and Bast's console lit up with alerts reporting damage throughout the ship.

"Sir, second destroyer is firing on us."

Bast saw it on his screen. They used their energy weapons, and while they were quite a distance away, they had enough range to hit the Chaanisar ship. More warnings flashed on his console as the reality of the two on one engagement took hold.

*Now that we have their attention*, thought Bast. *It's time to play a game.*

"Helm, jump us one thousand kilometers behind the destroyers."

"Yes, Sir."

"Jump."

The Chaanisar ship landed a safe distance from the enemy vessels, but close enough that they were clearly visible to the two ships' scanners. He wanted to play chase with the two ships. He wanted them to come after him. To draw them away from the station. He knew it was a simple tactic, but sometimes they were the best. He didn't need both ships to chase. One would do just fine. If he could split them it would be ideal.

Bast sat and waited. The two ships held their positions. Would they fall for it? Staying put could work too. He simply needed to stall them until his team made it to the extraction point. Then the Chaanisar ship could jump back to the station and pick the teams up before the destroyers posed a threat.

Unfortunately the DLC ships were not having any of it. They sat there, like they were going to wait him out. Then they did the last thing he wanted them to do. They resumed course for the station.

# Chapter 65

Seiben had stepped out from behind the cover of the trees and continued firing at the vessel. Darla yelled at him to come back, but he was intent on drawing the vessel away from his family. To his horror his firing didn't do much harm to the craft. He wanted to get it as far away from the trees as he could. He would be dead soon enough. No point getting his family killed as well.

A pair of vicious looking guns came into view and he swore he could see the pilot smiling as he targeted Seiben. He felt like a tiny mouse being toyed with by a sinister cat. He kept firing, not knowing what else to do. Salty beads of sweat stung his eyes. His shirt already wet and clinging to his back, partly from the run, mostly from the fear. Darla was right. He was no soldier. Combat frightened him too much. Yet here he was, playing the military man when he should be with his family.

Any second now the pilot would pull the trigger and it would be over, but if his family was going to see him die, he would make sure it was while putting up a fight. It wouldn't be enough, but it might be something. There are worse ways to die. At least this way his grandchildren might hear stories about how he fought to defend his family. Much better, he thought than dying of some prolonged sickness. He tried to convince himself that his family would get by without him. It didn't work. His actions were foolish. He knew he had let them down. He closed his eyes and braced himself, waiting for the bullets to perforate his body.

*If only I had more time*, he thought. *It's all too short.*

The crash shocked him. He jump back and opened his eyes. It took a moment for his mind to process what just happened. Part of him wondered if he was delusional. Had he been shot already? Was he seeing things before death? When the security craft hit the ground he decided that what he saw was real. A large man, at least he thought it was a man, clad head to toe in metal had leapt over him and onto the floating vessel. The force of the impact pointed the craft's nose downward, so that when the guns fired they narrowly missed Seiben hitting the ground at his feet. The metal man fired his large weapon into the cabin, shattering the glass. The bullets tore through the pilot's body, killing him instantly. With nobody piloting, the craft spun out of control and slammed into the ground. The metal man jumped off just before impact and surged forward with tremendous speed.

All around him the same thing took place. More metal men had appeared and were engaging the DLC security force. First they eliminated the hovercraft. Their incredible agility and power allowed them to leap high enough so as to fire directly at the pilots. Some took advantage of their momentum, and struck the hovercraft with great force, causing them to lose control and hit the ground where they would be finished off.

Then they charged the ground force. They crashed into their line with ferocity and unforgiving strength. The DLC troops wore armor, but still crumbled against the charge. Their line fell into tatters. Some tried to fight off the monsters, but the metal men withstood their weapons. They didn't have enough time to inflict any real damage to the incredible glowing armor. The metal men moved with such speed that each man could only get a few shots off before they were either shot, or seized by a powerful metal glove and thrown across the battlefield. The metal giants streaked through the DLC ranks like demons, dispersing the enemy and gunning them down as they tried to flee. The DLC force had no chance. They couldn't defend, nor could they run. The metal men were merciless.

Seiben was surprised at the soldiers' discipline. When the metal men showed up there were no cheers. No displays of emotion. The soldiers held their positions and kept firing. Even when the metal men charged into the enemy ranks, none of the other soldiers joined the charge. They stayed where they were and continued firing in support.

Not that the metal men needed much help. They towered over their opponents. Their speed and agility was mind boggling. The security craft that had targeted him flew low, but was easily three meters off the ground. Yet the metal man had leapt onto it like it was nothing more than a step stool.

*Who are these people?* He wondered.

Darla's voice pulled him out of his thoughts. She yelled at him to come back behind the trees.

Realizing that there was still fighting and that he was standing out in the open, he rushed back to his family.

Darla punched him several times in the arm. "What were you thinking?" she said, her eyes wide and fearful. "You could've been killed."

"I… I don't know," said Seiben.

"You don't know? You don't know?! Have you finally gone insane?"

"I-"

"I am too young to be a widow. Do you understand me? Too young!" She punched him again, the fear in her eyes replaced by a look he knew well. Rage.

He wanted to say something to justify what he had done, but he knew it would do him no good. He knew that silence was the best approach when she became like this.

"Do you understand that you are not a soldier?" she continued. "You are a father. And a husband. I will not let you commit suicide. Do you understand? You are not getting off that easily."

She whacked him again. He took it all silently. She was right, after all. He had to think of his family. His responsibilities. He couldn't be running around playing soldier. What had come over him? What made him fire on that vessel? That wasn't like him. He was too old to be playing the hero. Still, he couldn't bear to watch those men get shot in the back. Deep down he admired their bravery. Their discipline. In the end they were defending him and his family. How could he just hide while they risked their lives for them?

He looked at Alina and Otka, their cheeks wet with fresh tears, and knew how. They needed their father. He couldn't abandon them. Getting himself killed would be no different than walking out on them. Knowing their father died fighting would not compensate for the fact that he was gone. Nothing would.

He suddenly became aware that the gunfire had ceased. Peeking out from behind the trees he saw the men getting up from their positions. The metal men were returning from the field, their movements accompanied by a distinct whining sound, not much different from some of the machinery on his freighter. A couple jogged by him, each step causing the ground to shudder under their heavy boots. The rest of the group was following and Seiben started to get up as well.

"Is it over?" Darla asked, her face still tense.

"I think so. It looks like we're leaving," said Seiben.

Darla and the girls got up and stepped out from behind the trees. Soon Jon and Breeah appeared, with Burke and Daniels close behind. He noticed that Jon didn't look tired like the others. There was no perspiration. He wasn't out of breath. Nothing. He looked calm and fresh, like he was just starting his day. The other three looked like they were in great shape, but they all showed some signs of fatigue. But not Jon. Seiben wondered if he wasn't a metal man in disguise.

Jon picked up Anki, and the two soldiers picked up Seiben's daughters.

"Time to go," said Jon.

Seiben nodded absentmindedly. He reached out for Darla's hand, and its warm touch allowed him to release some of the stress building in his shoulders. They soon broke into a brisk jog, keeping pace with Jon and Breeah. The soldiers surrounded them, some running in front, while others protected their rear. The metal men created a larger perimeter, with the group at its center.

Seiben looked at Jon and asked, "What now?"

"There's a ship waiting for us," said Jon, without losing a breath. "We just need to get to the docks so they can pick us up. Then we'll be safe."

"Is this your ship?" asked Seiben.

Jon didn't answer right away. The question seemed to trigger some reflection. He took so long in responding that Seiben thought he would ignore the question. When he did answer he simply said, "No, it's not my ship."

Seiben wondered about that. Jon was a captain. If this wasn't his ship then whose ship was it?

"Did all these men come from that ship?"

"Yes."

"Some of these men are your men?"

"Yes."

"But not all of them?"

"No, not all of them."

"The other men, they're on your side?"

Jon looked around at the Chaanisar soldiers surrounding him, "I'm not sure."

The answer stunned Seiben. He wasn't sure why he asked the question, but he didn't expect the answer he got. What were they getting into here? Jon's face didn't give any clues. It showed no emotion. He stared straight ahead, giving no indication of his thoughts.

Seiben took in the landscape surrounding them. All that green. He had always enjoyed taking the girls out of the city to spend a day in the parks. They had some great times out here. He had always enjoyed being around nature. But now he looked at it all differently. For the first time it struck him that none of this was real. Sure the soil and the plants were real, and they grew just like any plant would grow anywhere else. But underneath that soil was metal and machinery. There was nothing natural about it. He had spent his whole life on the station and never thought twice about any of it, yet now it all seemed like a big lie.

Maybe Darla was right after all. She didn't come from the station like he did. She came from a planet. She probably saw this fallacy all along. She would get her wish now. He would ask Jon to arrange for the ship to drop them off on one of the planets and they would start new lives there. He was handy. He could find some work to help get them started. How hard could it be?

He thought about all the people living on the planets, and on the station. He wondered again about where they all came from. He considered the myths again and worked up the courage to ask what was really on his mind. He looked at Jon and said, "Are you from Earth?"

Jon's head snapped around and he looked at Seiben with surprise. The look faded quickly, replaced by a more pensive one. At first he didn't answer and Seiben got the impression that he was trying to decide whether or not to reveal the truth. When he made his decision he locked eyes with Seiben and merely said, "Yes."

# Chapter 66

Bast watched the two destroyers on his tactical display, clenching his fists. They were going to make things difficult for him. They refused to chase him. Refused to play his game. Instead they resumed course toward the station. If they reached it he wouldn't be able to retrieve his men.

There was a sizable distance between the two ships, but they were within each other's energy weapons' range. That made each attack more costly. While his ship was evenly matched with each DLC ship, the fact that both could fire on him changed the odds.

"Helm, prepare to jump beside the ship on our starboard side. Get us close enough that they are within range of our rail guns. Keep them between us and the destroyer on our port side. Prepare to jump us back to this position the second I give the order."

"Yes, Sir."

"Tactical, target the enemy's weapon systems. Rail guns in offensive mode."

"Yes, Sir."

"Jump."

The Chaanisar heavy cruiser landed beside the DLC destroyer and attacked. Rail guns, energy weapons and missiles fired in unison. The enemy deflectors held, dispersing the Chaanisar energy bolts, but the rail guns and missiles found their marks, damaging several DLC gun batteries. That by no means left the warship helpless and it returned fire.

Its energy weapons hammered the Chaanisar armor, but their targeting lacked focus. They didn't hit any major systems. They were trying to adapt quickly to the attacks and that allowed much less time to target effectively. When the DLC ship launched its missiles Bast gave the order to jump. They landed back where they had started a moment before, the DLC missiles streaking off into empty space.

Bast considered the maneuver a success. They had disabled some of the ship's weapon systems and successfully used them to block any energy bolts from the second vessel. The enemy had adapted and so had he. He watched the ships on the display, waiting to see what they would do, but they continued as before, heading straight for the station. They would need more persuading.

He ordered another sortie, same as before. Use the destroyer as a shield to block the second ship's weapon fire, and focus on its weapons. By continually targeting its weapon systems he would seriously degrade their ability to defend themselves. By doing so he hoped to force them out of the fight. He didn't want to destroy the ship. Doing so would require significantly more effort and resources. That type of engagement would result in his ship taking heavy damage. Even if they were successful, they'd be in no position to challenge the second ship. He also hoped that if he could inflict enough damage he would force the destroyers to change tactics.

They landed and the destroyer immediately let loose a volley of missiles, anticipating the Chaanisar assault. Bast had expected this response and had his ship fire missiles before immediately jumping away. The DLC warship launched its own countermeasures which successfully took out half the Chaanisar missiles. The other half, however, found their targets and slammed into the ship's weapon batteries, further degrading its fighting capabilities.

Bast personally didn't like this strategy, but it was working, and it kept his crew safe. None of them were afraid to put their lives at risk in battle, but why do so needlessly? If you had an advantage you used it. Throughout history wars had been won, and empires built, on the back of technological advances. A superior weapon, or strategy, was to be exploited, not squandered in favor of ideology.

So the Chaanisar jumped again and again, tormenting their adversary, confounding their every effort at countering the attacks. The tactic worked. The destroyer's offensive capabilities were diminished to the point that the ship almost helpless.

This created the shift he had been looking for. The second ship changed course and raced to the rescue of their increasingly helpless brethren. The two ships had effectively halted their advance on the station. If Bast kept harassing them he believed he now could keep them from reaching the station in time. Now he just had to wait for word from his men.

# Chapter 67

Earth. Seiben's question surprised Jon. How had he figured it out? He had to give the crusty captain more credit. He didn't expect anyone here to guess where he was from. He had thought Jansen might, but nobody else. There was no point in hiding the truth from Seiben. He too was a fugitive. Besides, what difference did it make out here?

None of the old rules applied anymore. He glanced around. The Chaanisar were fighting together with Space Force. If that wasn't proof enough, he didn't know what was. None of them could go back to Earth either. The Hermes was gone. How would he explain that to Space Force. The Diakans would demand blood, and Space Force would do nothing to stop them from getting it. They would happily hand them all over to Diakus. The Diakans would make a show of some bullshit trial, and they would all be executed.

It didn't look like the Chaanisar could go back home. If what they said was true, the Juttari would revert them into slaves the moment they returned. They were stuck out here too. That made them allies, at least for the time being. How long that alliance would last was anybody's guess. He still didn't trust them, nor did he believe their story. Maybe they did revolt against the Juttari. Maybe that part was true. But a Chaanisar was not a human. Sure they started out that way when they were born, but that changed the moment the Juttari took them. It all changed the moment they turned on their own kind. He didn't care if the Juttari brain chips forced them. They still did it. They still committed horrific atrocities against humanity. The 'how' and 'why' didn't matter. They couldn't be forgiven for their crimes.

He suddenly realized that Darla was speaking to him. "I'm sorry, what did you say?" said Jon.

"They said Earth was destroyed," said Darla.

"Who said?"

"The stories. The myths."

"Earth was conquered, but not destroyed."

Darla looked like she had uncovered some long lost religious artifact. "Who?" she said. "Who conquered Earth?"

Jon looked at Lieutenant Jarvi running up ahead and pointed at him. "They did."

Darla's face blanched and she almost tripped over her feet. "But they're human?"

"Their masters conquered Earth," said Jon.

Jarvi shook his head, obviously listening to the conversation. "Tell her the truth, Captain," said Jarvi. He fell back alongside Seiben and Darla. "The Juttari Empire conquered Earth. We were taken from our parents as children and forced to serve the Juttari."

Darla stared wide eyed at Jarvi. "That's horrible."

"Not as horrible as what they did after they were taken," said Jon.

Jarvi was stone faced. "The Captain is right. The Juttari violated us. Turned us into instruments of war. And then they made us violate our own kind..." said Jarvi, his voice getting softer as he spoke, like he was contemplating the gravity of his crimes.

"You cannot atone for your crimes by blaming the Juttari," said Jon. "The blood is on your hands."

"Perhaps," said Jarvi.

"But you fight together now," said Seiben. "What's changed?"

Jarvi's voice became strong again. "We killed our Juttari masters. We are free to once again be human."

"Killing Juttari doesn't make you human," said Jon.

"It seemed to work for you, Captain," said Jarvi, not visibly angry, but with the faint hint of threat in his tone.

Jon scowled. "I killed lots of Chaanisar too. Don't ever forget that."

"And yet the Chaanisar help you," said Jarvi. "As you can see Mr. Seiben, the Chaanisar do not hold grudges. If only we could say the same about our good friend, the Captain."

"I'm not your good friend."

"No, I suppose you are not."

The two men stared at each other. Jon felt the heat rising inside him. He had to keep it in check. He couldn't lose it now. As much as it grated on him, he needed Jarvi's help. He needed the Chaanisar ship. He needed to get off this station. He would have to be diplomatic, something that was often foreign to him.

"Regardless of our histories and opinions, we need to work together now," said Jon.

Jarvi studied him, as if trying to determine his sincerity, and said, "Agreed." With that he picked up his pace and took his previous position up ahead.

"I still don't understand how you ended up here," said Seiben.

"That is a more complicated story," said Jon. "Let's leave that one for when we're safely off the station."

The AI's voice interrupted the conversation. "Captain, I've found something."

"Yes, AI. What is it?"

"Security footage. They had attempted to delete it, but they missed some of the backup files."

"Security footage of what?"

"Jansen's murder."

"Who killed Jansen?"

"Mr. Kulberg."

"That's great," said Seiben. "That would prove our innocence."

"It would, but do you think Kulberg would give us a fair trial?" said Jon.

"No," said Seiben.

"I don't think so either. We have to get off the station first, and then we can use the footage."

"You're right," said Seiben.

"In the meantime, I have an idea. Let's see how Kulberg likes a taste of his own medicine," said Jon. "AI, do you still have control of all those displays throughout the city? The giant ones on the sides of the buildings?"

"Of course, Captain."

"Excellent. I want you to broadcast that video on those displays."

"Understood."

"And make sure you block all efforts to take the feed down."

"Leave it to me, Captain."

That would keep Kulberg busy, at least long enough for them to make their escape. Up ahead Jon recognized the docks. They were almost there.

They slowed pace and Lieutenant Jarvi accessed his communicator. "We are almost in position, Sir. I will send you the coordinates of our position momentarily."

"Good work, Lieutenant," responded the voice from Jarvi's communicator. "A shuttle is being dispatched."

They identified a free dock and proceeded down its gangway to the docking station. It was a long winding corridor with lighting along the ceiling that lit up as they approached. The hallway was somewhat narrow, allowing no more than four men side by side. Jon didn't like that it forced the group to spread out along the gangway's length. If something happened they might have difficulty getting enough firepower in place. The soldiers with the combat suits stayed back and guarded the entrance to the corridor. They would present a substantial deterrent to any attack. At the very least they could buy the group time till they got out. Jon felt better, but not much. He felt vulnerable.

Once they reached the hatch the only thing they could do was wait for the shuttle. That just made Jon jittery. He felt surrounded. Chaanisar in front of him. Chaanisar behind him. All of them close enough that they could push a blade into his ribs without much effort. He glanced behind, checking out the men there, trying to gauge their intentions. They looked back at him with blank expressions. He turned back around and studied the Chaanisar in front, watching their movements, keeping an eye out for any hint of a threat, no matter how subtle.

He noticed Breeah staring at him with a concerned look on her face. "Is everything alright?" she said, an empathetic look in her eye.

"Everything's fine," he replied. She didn't believe him. He could see it in her face. But she didn't pursue the matter. He liked that about her. She respected his boundaries. If he didn't want to talk about something she left it alone. Still he wondered how she had learned to read him so well? It was uncanny.

The wait was excruciating. Eventually a screen lit up indicating that a vessel was docking. Loud banging reverberated throughout the corridor as the ship locked itself to the dock and established a pressurized seal. The banging was followed by quiet for some time, which was replaced by the sound of metal clanging as the hatch was unlocked. It slid open with a high pitched whine. A man in a Juttari uniform walked out and greeted Lieutenant Jarvi. They exchanged words and the group began boarding. The man stood by the hatch watching as everyone entered. When Jon walked by he eyed the Juttari insignia on his uniform.

*Grandfather save us*, he thought. *We're being herded into the jaws of the wolf*

# Chapter 68

Kulberg stared, dumbfounded, at the report on his display. Dozens dead. Multiple security craft destroyed. How? All his men had to do was eliminate a few people. People on the run with children. How hard could that possibly be? Apparently it was harder than it looked. And now they had help. Real soldiers. Somehow that ship out there was able to get a team onto the station.

That was no ordinary ship. How did it manage to leap from one place to another in the blink of an eye? It confounded the DLC destroyers, and even disabled one of them. Now it was back in orbit around the station, sending a shuttle to retrieve Captain Pike, with the destroyers too far to intervene. He had to stop them. He might be able to send another team to intercept before they boarded. Especially if they left now.

Just then his door opened and a DLC security team rushed into his office, weapons drawn. His guards were surrounded and relieved of their weapons before they could react. Several other soldiers headed for Kulberg, all pointing their weapons squarely at him. Two men flanked him on each side and a few more had spread out in front of him. He considered reaching for his weapon, but thought better of it. He wouldn't have a chance. So he chose to play the outraged leader.

"What is the meaning of this?" Kulberg bellowed.

"Murder," came a voice from the doorway. Kulberg looked to see Dahlen, DLC Head of Security. "That's the meaning of this. You are under arrest for the murder of Mr. Jansen."

"This is outrageous," said Kulberg, sounding properly flabbergasted. "We are hunting the real murderer as we speak. A manhunt that you are recklessly interfering with. This will mean your career. You realize that, don't you? This means all of your careers!"

Dahlen rolled his eyes and started clapping. "Well done. That was quite the performance. Not as good as your last one, but still very good."

"What do you mean, my last one?" said Kulberg.

"You haven't seen it?" Dahlen shook his head and laughed. "You really need to get out more. Turn around and look out your window, please."

What the hell was Dahlen talking about? What performance? He swiveled his chair around and faced his window. He waved his hand and the blinds slid apart revealing the building across from his. He usually kept his blinds closed for precisely that reason. Why would he want to look at yet another building? His eyes followed the structure from the top down and then stopped. On a giant display was his face. *How in the hell?* He was in his office, but he stood with a weapon in his hand. An icy chill raced up his spine. He watched with ever increasing horror as the video showed him firing his weapon at Mr. Jansen.

"I don't know how, but that video is playing on every display throughout the city," said Dahlen.

"It's obviously a fake," said Kulberg, spinning his chair around to face Dahlen. "I'm being framed while the real murderer is getting away."

"I don't think so," said Dahlen.

"What do you mean, you don't think so?" Kulberg snorted. "These videos can easily be faked, and you're falling for it."

"No. You see, whoever is showing this video to the city also sent me the source file. I quickly had its authenticity verified. It's as real as it gets." Dahlen nodded to his men and two of them moved on Kulberg, seizing him by the arms. He tried to resist and his face was unceremoniously slammed against his desk. His arms were painfully wrenched behind his back and warm blood flowed from his broken nose down across his mouth. His vision blurred and he felt something hard in his mouth. Not knowing what it was he spit it out. His tooth. They had knocked out one of his teeth! He was pulled up by the hair, his arms now secured behind his back. His vision cleared and he looked at Dahlen.

"You're going to pay for this," he said.

Dahlen looked at his men and nodded. His face was slammed into the desk again, turning out the lights.

# Chapter 69

The shuttle ride to the ship was uneventful. Jon had watched with concern as his men spoke with the Chaanisar. They had started to form a bond with each other, the way men who have fought together often do. They were beginning to trust each other. How would that affect things if this arrangement didn't work out?

Lieutenant Jarvi didn't join in. He kept quiet and stared mostly at Jon. Was that anger in his eyes? Hatred? Jon played along and stared right back. The Lieutenant was well disciplined. Whatever he felt, he kept it contained. But Jon did feel the silent challenge, and was more than happy to accept.

*Anytime*, he thought.

The shuttle itself had no windows, but there was a display showing their progress. He cringed as the Juttari Heavy Cruiser came into view, the same one he battled months ago. It sat silent and motionless, waiting. Five centuries of terror embodied in that one dreadful ship. It reminded him of childhood anxiety and nightmares. As a child he spent years living with the fear that he would be taken to the Chaanisar, and now he went willingly. Somewhere deep inside him a little boy screamed.

Breeah's hand took hold of his, breaking the spell. She didn't say anything, but he could see that she understood. More importantly, she reminded him that he was no longer alone. He had been given a second chance. He had a family once again. The only reason humanity had persevered during those long, horrific years of occupation was family. Nothing more. What Earth had been before the occupation was largely forgotten amidst generations. There were no idealistic thoughts of resurrecting the old Earth. As much as the desire for vengeance burned inside of every human's belly, it provided little sustenance. The only reason people kept going, and the only reason for the resistance, was family. That ship, with its crew of Chaanisar, was the antithesis of humanity.

The Juttari hangar bay grew larger on the screen as they approached. When the shuttle entered its opening the display went black and the lights inside dimmed. Jon felt himself drowning, like a defeated Ahab. His muscles flexed involuntarily. He fought back a desire to attack the pilot and commandeer the shuttle. There was a thud beneath his feat and he knew they had stopped. The lights inside the shuttle lit up again and the hatch slid open. The Marines and Chaanisar got up and began to exit the shuttle. Jon stood, picked up Anki, then headed for the exit in turn, with Breeah and Seiben's family following close behind.

When they got off the shuttle Jon was somewhat surprised at how different the Chaanisar ship was from the Hermes. They had stolen the Hermes plans from Space Force, but the ship itself didn't look like the Hermes. It was harder. In many ways it looked unfinished. The ship's crew were Chaanisar, after all. He didn't think the Juttari cared much about appeasing the Chaanisar. From what he knew of the Juttari, there would have been a small contingent of them on board. The Masters. They would have overseen the mission, but would have left the running of the vessel to their Chaanisar puppets. It was how the Juttari operated. They ruled, and others did their bidding. He knew that there would be a part of this ship specifically designed as Juttari living quarters. Other than the Chaanisar leader, no other would be permitted to enter that section of the ship. He wondered how it happened when they revolted. Did they storm the Juttari section? How did the Juttari react when they realized they had lost control? Did the green bastards screech like that one did during the war, just before Jon put it down? He thought of the sound, all of them huddled together shrieking as their bastard children passed judgment. If only he had been there.

Lieutenant Jarvi escorted the group out of the hangar bay and through the ship. Kevin followed, but the rest of the Marines had gone off in a different direction. They had been on this ship for a while now and didn't need the guided tour. He looked around as they walked. They were obsessed with their symbols. Every inch of the ship was covered with either the Juttari insignia, or some other scribbles.

"What are all these markings?" said Seiben.

"Symbols, from the Juttari scriptures," said Jon, nauseated by the sight.

"They must be a very religious species," said Darla.

"They're fanatics," said Jon. "They believe it is their divine right to rule."

"To rule who?"

"Everybody. They believe their creator made them superior to all others in the galaxy. Not only is it their divine right to rule, but their divine duty to conquer any species they encounter."

Lieutenant Jarvi joined the conversation, as he liked to. "The Juttari believe their creator gave them power for a reason - to transform the galaxy. Since they believe it is their obligation to serve his will, they wage war and conquer with fervent zeal. They make others fight and die on their behalf. The Juttari rule and the rest bleed. A convenient arrangement if you are Juttari. Not ideal if you are human."

"All these horrors. All because of religion?" said Seiben.

"Yes," said Jarvi. "The Juttari consider themselves the only true believers. All others are inferior and unworthy of their creator's light.

That makes them unworthy of their own lives. The Juttari are here to serve their creator, and the rest of us are here to serve the Juttari."

"Doesn't it bother you?" said Jon.

"I don't understand what you mean," said Jarvi.

"The Juttari took you from your family. Violated you. Turned you on your own people. Yet you show no emotion when you speak of them. Have you completely lost your humanity?"

"Emotions? Is that what you seek, Captain? Will that make us more human in your eyes?"

"It would be a start," said Jon.

"We were not allowed emotions, Captain. Imagine a child of four or five years, taken from his family, and thrown into an alien hell. Imagine the fear. The paralyzing horror. How could such a child serve his Juttari masters?"

"I don't know," said Jon.

"He cannot. By controlling the child's emotions, you can reprogram the child. The brain chips are essential to this. They control the fear. That is why a child is augmented as soon as possible."

"I'm guessing the chips work the same way in combat?"

"That is correct. In battle the brain chips suppress feelings of fear, making for a more efficient soldier."

"So you have no emotions at all?" said Darla.

"We do have emotions," said Jarvi. "I can feel everything that you can feel. The brain chips gave the Juttari the ability to control our emotionns."

"What about now?" said Darla.

"I don't understand."

"The Juttari are gone. They don't control you anymore."

"After years of having our emotions suppressed for us, we have become surprisingly capable of doing the same thing ourselves. In the end, we have been trained as soldiers since childhood. For a soldier, emotions can sometimes be a liability." Jarvi stepped up to a door and said, "We have arrived."

It slid open and he gestured for the group to enter. Inside was a long dark table, also covered with markings. Standing up from the table was a tall man with a more ornate uniform than the Lieutenant's. Jon recognized the man's rank from his uniform. A Colonel. He looked fit and tough, and had an air of quiet authority about him. The man walked around to greet the groups.

"I am Colonel Bast, commander of this ship," the man said. "I trust you are all in good health. Uninjured?"

"We're all fine, Colonel," said Jon.

Bast scrutinized Jon. "You must be the notorious Captain Pike," he said. "It's a pleasure to finally meet you."

"We'll see," said Jon.

Bast looked surprised. "I'm sorry, is there something wrong?"

"Other than the fact that I'm on a Juttari heavy cruiser surrounded by Chaanisar? No. Everything's great. Couldn't be better."

Bast nodded. "I understand how you feel, Captain. This all must be quite a shock for you."

"Not the last, I'm sure." He wondered how shocking it would be for Bast if he knew how many Chaanisar he had killed.

Bast looked at Kevin, "Chief St. Clair, congratulations on a successful mission."

"Thank you, Colonel. It was good to be out in the field again."

"Excuse me," said Seiben, drawing a menacing look from Darla. "I don't mean to interrupt the happy reunion, but what's going to happen to us?"

"This is Captain Seiben and his family. They were with Captain Pike," said Jarvi.

"I see," said Bast. "Am I correct to assume that you cannot return to the station?"

"Yeah, it looks like things might be complicated there for a while."

"You are welcome to stay on board for as long as you like."

"If it's all the same to you, we'd like to be dropped off at one of the other planets," said Seiben.

"Which planets are you referring to?" said Bast.

"The other human planets. We were thinking New Byzantium would work. I can give you the coordinates."

"Certainly. We will be continuing our search, but I'm sure we can find time to drop you off."

"What search?" said Jon.

"For your crew, Captain," said Bast.

"Why are you searching for my crew? Why do you care?" said Jon, his tone accusatory.

"We are actually searching for our humanity, Captain. Rescuing your crew is helping us find it."

"Yeah okay, now do you want to tell me the real reason?"

"We honestly do want to help your crew, Captain. But beyond that, we are also hoping to find your Doctor Ellerbeck."

"Why do you want to find the Doctor?"

"We are hoping she will remove these confounding brain chips," said Bast, pointing to his head. "We do not want to be Juttari slaves anymore."

"I thought you killed all the Juttari on board?"

"We did. But if we ever come across any Juttari the chips will enslave us again. I would prefer to eliminate that possibility."

Jon wondered what would happen to the Hermes crew once those brain chips were gone? What reason would Bast have to keep them around? All the more reason to find another ship for his crew.

"You must all be exhausted after your ordeal," said Bast. "My men can show you to your quarters. I can answer any questions after you have rested."

"They can go rest. I've got some questions I'd like answered now," said Jon.

"As you wish, Captain."

Jon turned to Breeah and said, "Go ahead and get some rest. I'll see you a little later." He bent down and kissed her on the lips. She returned his kiss, causing some tension to dissipate.

Jarvi led the group out of the room and Bast walked back to the table, gesturing for Jon to join him. Jon pulled out the chair opposite Bast and sat down.

"What would you like to discuss, Captain," said Bast. He sat perfectly straight, maintaining strict military professionalism.

"It looks like we're stuck together for a while. I'm not thrilled with that. I mean, I am grateful that you rescued my crew and that you got us off the station, but I just don't trust you."

"We risked our lives to save your crew, Captain. We did the same to save you," said Bast, defensively.

"And I thank you, but I've fought against your kind my whole life."

"I appreciate your honesty, but we are not the same as those you fought against."

"Yes, I know. You mutinied. You killed Juttari. That's what you say. Whether it's true or not is irrelevant. You are the same to me."

"I see. Then what is there to talk about?" said Bast, a slight tone of dejection in his voice.

"Like I said, we're stuck with each other, so I want to establish some ground rules."

"I'm listening."

"My crew. I don't know what's been going on since they came aboard, but they are my crew. Not yours."

"I have no desire to steal your crew, Captain."

"I don't care what your desires are. They're my crew. They don't take orders from you, or any of your officers."

"This can be accommodated, Captain, but we will need to work together toward achieving common goals."

Bast was right, they would need to work together, but the thought made Jon shudder. "You and I can decide what that will look like, and I will issue the necessary orders to my men."

"That is agreeable, Captain. Was there anything else?"

"I understand you have Tallos, and Chief Engineer Singh in custody?"

"Yes, Captain. That is correct."

"They are my prisoners. Not yours."

"I can agree that Chief Engineer Singh is your prisoner. He was part of your crew after all."

"So was Tallos," said Jon, his tone adversarial.

410

"Not exactly, Captain. While he may have been assigned to the Hermes, I would hesitate to call a Diakan General a member of your crew."

"General?"

"That is correct, Captain. That makes him a high value intelligence source."

Everything about Tallos made more sense now. Why hadn't he seen it before? "Tallos was already in my custody for crimes he committed on the Hermes," said Jon.

"Perhaps, but he escaped the Hermes. Look, I don't want this to cause a rift between us, but I believe Tallos has some important information that we require. I propose we share this prisoner."

"Unacceptable," said Jon.

"Captain, I believe I am being more than fair. We captured Tallos and he is in our custody. I could simply keep him to myself. Instead, I am offering to share. Can we agree to a compromise?"

Jon didn't want to agree, but Bast was right, he had no reason to compromise. He had to be more diplomatic. Might as well start now. "Agreed," said Jon.

"Excellent," said Bast. "There is just one small condition, however."

"What's that?"

"You agree not to kill the Diakan."

"You ask a lot," said Jon, still craving Tallos's death.

"Believe me, Captain, I know, but I must insist."

"Okay, I won't kill him."

Bast smiled. "See, Captain, we are already working together."

"Let's not get ahead of ourselves," said Jon, sarcastically. "There is one more thing. I was told you rescued some Reivers from the prison planet."

"We did."

"After Breeah is rested, I'll need to take her to see them."

"I will provide you with an escort, Captain, but don't expect too many escorts in the future."

"What do you mean?" said Jon, the temperature inside him beginning to rise.

Bast smiled. "What I mean, Captain, is that your crew will have free access to our ship. You will no longer need escorts once you know your way around."

Jon thought he was hearing things. "Why would you do that?" he said.

"Because, Captain, I want this to work."

# Chapter 70

Breeah held Anki's hand as they walked through the strange ship. It was odd to see all these humans living and working on this alien vessel. Jon had told her about the Chaanisar, but she never expected to actually meet one, let alone be on board one of their warships. It was difficult to get used to. Everything was so dark and depressing. Then there were those bizarre symbols that covered the walls, ceilings, and floors. They were all over their quarters, and had unsettled her so much that she didn't get any rest at all. At least Anki managed to get some sleep.

Now they were being taken to see her people, who had also been rescued from the prison planet by the Chaanisar. She thought she would never see any of them again, and part of her didn't want to. She was happy with Jon. For the first time in her life she felt free. She knew her people wouldn't understand. They were ruled by their traditions. While they learned to be adaptable in combat, they remained inflexible in societal structure. It was stifling. It wasn't that she wished her people ill. She was genuinely happy they had been rescued. But she had a new life now, and didn't want that to change.

"You okay?" said Jon, looking at her with concern.

"Yes. I didn't get much rest."

He didn't seem to believe her, but he let it go and said nothing else. He made so few demands of her. Nor did he treat her like his property. He loved her. She knew that. What was more surprising was that she loved him. After her marriage, she didn't think that love would be part of her life. Her marriage had been practical, like everything the Reivers did. It had been arranged since she was a child. A union of families, rather than a union of lovers. She didn't hate her husband. She actually liked him and considered him a good friend. But she didn't love him. At least not in the way a woman should love her husband. They had known each other since they were children, and they knew then that they would be wed one day. But romantic love had never blossomed between them.

It wasn't for lack of trying, either. Both families worked hard to create a bond between the two. They were encouraged to spend time with one another. She was constantly told that it was her responsibility to make her marriage work. That it was up to her to make it a happy union. And she did try. Her feelings, however, wouldn't budge. She thought that Anki's birth might change things. In some ways it did make her care more for him. He was the father of her child after all. The spark, however, never came. The emptiness inside her was filled with the joy of motherhood instead. That joy sustained her, and she continued doing her duty as a wife, and as a daughter. Nobody could point a finger and accuse her of bringing shame to her family. That life was all she knew, and then it was gone.

The Hermes came along and blew up her husband's ship, and just like that it was over. Once the shock wore off she realized she was free. She could sail away on the Hermes, with all its wondrous technology, and start a new life. More importantly, she could ensure a new life for Anki. One where she was free to be whoever she wanted. She clung to that hope, but the Kemmar came and Jon wouldn't let the colony go. At first she thought him a fool, another man incapable of backing down from a fight.

Her opinion quickly changed, as she got to know him better. He turned out to be an honorable man. A man with ideals and the courage to stand by them. He cared for her and Anki when he didn't have to. He saved their lives at great risk to his own. But there was more. There was a spark. An attraction. The more she saw him, the more she wanted to see him. Despite his scars, he was a ruggedly handsome man. He was also a kind man, and she had fallen for him.

They had lost everything when the Hermes was destroyed. She had almost died herself. But he saved her, yet again. In that tiny escape pod, adrift in the endless emptiness of space, she was happy. They were together and that was all that mattered. She knew they would survive, somehow. The loss of the Hermes didn't matter. Whatever hardships came next didn't matter. It was a new beginning for her, and for Jon.

The past, however, is an unforgiving enemy. It pursues with relentless ferocity, and superior endurance. It was naive of her to think they could be freed so easily. Here they were, on a ship from Jon's past. A ship that tormented him by nature of its very existence. On their way to see people whom she never expected to see again. She wondered who had survived the ordeal on Kerces. Did she have any relatives left?

The Chaanisar had explained that the Reivers had been given quarters near each other, and that there was a common area on their level for them to congregate. That was where her reunion was to take place.

Their escort pointed to a door, indicating that they had arrived. She looked up at Jon and he gave her a reassuring smile, but couldn't hide the concern in his eyes. She hadn't told him much about how she felt, but he saw it nonetheless. She smiled in return and for a moment thought herself ridiculous. She was a grown woman. A warrior. A Reiver. Yet here she was behaving like a nervous little girl. Chastising herself for her weakness she gave Anki's hand a motherly squeeze and strode up to the door.

It slid open and they walked into the large room. She was immediately surprised at how many people were there. Did they all know she was coming? And if this was all of them, how many had died? The horror of the thought seized her. This was all that was left of her people, in this one room. The Kemmar had murdered, or enslaved the rest. An overwhelming feeling of guilt smothered her and she struggled to breathe. She had run while they died. What kind of person was she? Powerful feelings of duty returned and she struggled to contain her grief.

She recognized the faces of the first Reivers she saw, but didn't know them very well. They bowed their heads to her in customary greeting, and she did the same. It was a simple gesture, yet it caused tears to fill her eyes and run down her cheeks. A few more noticed her and bowed. Then Anki let go of her hand and ran into the crowd shouting the last word she expected to hear. Grandfather.

She wheeled around and craned her head to see. Could it be true? Could he still be alive? She saw Anki run up to a tall, gray haired man, but she couldn't see his face. He picked her up and turned towards Breeah. Anki had wrapped her arms around his neck, partially obscuring her view of his face, but it was enough. There could be no mistake. Her father lived.

He turned the rest of the way and his eyes locked with hers. Those hard, unmistakable eyes. She felt her knees go weak in the same way they did when she had gotten in trouble as a little girl. He held Anki with one hand and stretched out the other to Breeah, beckoning her. She rushed to him, sobbing, the gravity of her emotions surprising her. He pulled her in with his free hand and she cried into his chest.

"Come now, child. I would think you would be happy to see me," he said.

Breeah laughed and wiped the tears away with her hand. "I am happy to see you, father," she said.

"Tears of joy then. Come, let me look at you." He gently pulled her back a step and gazed down at her. "You look strong, as does your daughter. I am pleased." He then looked past her and said, "I see you've brought a friend. You must introduce us."

Breeah realized he was talking about Jon. She had been so overcome with the emotions of the reunion that she forgot he still stood there. "Of course, father," she said. She stepped back and waved Jon over. Jon smiled as he approached. "Father, this is Captain Jon Pike. Jon, this is Jonas Viken, my father."

"A pleasure to meet you, Sir," said Jon, extending his hand.

Jonas looked at the hand with some measure of confusion, unfamiliar with the custom. He set Anki down and extended his own hand, which Jon gripped into a handshake.

Jonas withdrew his hand, "You are the Captain of the ship that fought the Kemmar?"

"Yes," said Jon.

"The one that destroyed Breeah's ship?"

"I'm afraid so," said Jon, a hint of regret in his voice.

"We watched the encounter, Captain. You defended yourself. There is no shame in that."

"Thank you, Sir," said Jon.

Jonas looked at Breeah, "Am I correct in assuming your husband died in the battle?"

"Yes, father."

"I'm sorry, child," said Jonas. "Fear not. You are with your people again. Many strong men survived our encounter with the Kemmar. I will find you a suitable husband."

Worry spread across Jon's face and Breeah gave him a reassuring shake of her head. The gesture was not lost on Jonas, who said, "Is there something you want to tell me, child?"

"I do not want you to find me a husband, father," said Breeah, timidly.

She saw the anger flash in her father's eyes. She could count on one hand how many times in her life she had refused to follow her father's wishes. He looked at her sternly and said, "Explain yourself."

"I am together with Jon now."

"He is not a Reiver. What does he know of our ways?" said Jonas, pointing a finger at Jon.

"It does not matter. He makes me happy and I love him," said Breeah, more defiantly now, regaining her courage.

"He is not our kind. You must marry a Reiver," said Jonas, raising his voice.

"Our kind?" said Breeah. "How many of our kind are left?"

"We must stay united now, most of all. Otherwise our way of life will be lost."

"Our way of life is lost, father. The Kemmar saw to that. But there is hope for a new life here. There are humans. Billions of them. There is no need to isolate ourselves."

"Enough! I will not have my own daughter argue with me." Jonas looked at Jon and said, "You are responsible for this. You turned my daughter against me."

"With all due respect, Sir, your daughter is a grown woman, not a child."

Jonas's face turned red and Breeah saw him subtly shift his weight into a fighting posture. Jon saw it too and took a step back, raising his open hands, palms out, showing he did not want trouble. Breeah stepped in between them and said, "Father, please."

"Step away," said Jonas.

She noticed that the mood of the room had changed and several of the men were stepping closer. She knew they would fight for her father. She also knew if that happened people would die, and as skilled as the Reiver men were, she didn't think Jon would end up among the dead. She had to do something. She could not allow anymore of her people to die.

"Father!" she yelled, surprising herself. "I warn you, father. If you do anything to harm him you will never see me or your granddaughter again."

Jonas looked like an asteroid hit him. In her whole life, she had never raised her voice to him. She felt just as stunned as he looked.

"You dare raise your voice to me? You dare to take my granddaughter away from me? My own flesh and blood?"

"I mean it father. You will not harm him," said Breeah, feeling strangely liberated.

"Jon is my friend," said Anki, to everyone's surprise. "He is a nice man, and he saved my life."

"What did you say?" said Jonas, surprised by Anki's outspokenness.

"He saved my life. He fought against five Kemmar and killed them all to save me."

Jonas stared at the little girl, speechless. He then looked up at Jon and said, "Is this true?"

"It is," said Jon.

Jonas relaxed his posture. "You saved my granddaughter's life. I am in your debt." He bowed his head to Jon showing his gratitude and respect.

With that gesture the men who were advancing on Jon stepped back and the room went back to a more relaxed state. Breeah had forgotten how quickly a perceived slight could turn bloody among her people. She looked at her father and spoke with a more respectful tone, "He is a good man, father. He saved both our lives, more than once."

Jonas's eyes hadn't left Jon's, but thankfully his posture remained relaxed. "It appears I am doubly in your debt, Captain," said Jonas, begrudgingly.

"Forget it," said Jon.

Breeah looked down at Anki and put her arm around her.

Anki looked up, smiled and said, "I think Jon and Grandfather are going to like each other."

# Chapter 71

High Lord Toth surveyed his forces on his tactical display. His fleet was now fully mobilized along the edges of Otan space. The military movements hadn't gone unnoticed and the Otan responded by mobilizing their own forces in response. Now the two fleets were squared off against each other with just empty space between them. Of course that empty space consisted of the border between the two, as defined by treaty. It was that treaty in particular that High Lord Toth intended to break.

With his forces in position it was time to act. As a customary diplomatic gesture he established communication with the Otan fleet commander, Admiral Gurzail. A communication display flickered on and Gurzail's face appeared. The Otan were hideous creatures with no hair on their bodies and only a handful of teeth in their mouths. Their heads were obscenely small for their bodies with disproportionately large eyes. Toth could barely stomach looking at the thing and wondered why a treaty was ever established with such repulsive looking lifeforms.

"This is Admiral Gurzail, of the Otan Fleet Commander. Why have you mobilized your forces along our border?"

"Admiral, I am High Lord Toth, of the Kemmar Empire. I am here to offer you a gift."

"What kind of gift?" said Gurzail, cautiously.

"The gift of life. Recent developments have made it necessary for the Kemmar Empire to annex Otan space. I give you one opportunity to withdraw and save the lives of your men."

"This is outrageous. The Kemmar and Otan have a treaty, which you will be violating if you cross into Otan space."

"You are correct, Admiral. It is out of respect for that treaty that I am giving you the opportunity to withdraw peacefully. What is your answer?"

"You want my answer?" shouted Gurzail. "Cross our border and I will bathe in your blood. That is my answer you Kemmar scum."

Toth bared his teeth at the display. "I was hoping you would say that," said Toth, and turned off the display. He opened a communication with his fleet officers, "This is High Lord Toth. Begin operations."

He watched on his tactical display as his fleet lurched forward, crossing the border into Otan space. In response, the Otan fleet moved to engage the invaders. Each side's carriers spit out hundreds of fighters which raced forward to attack each other. The darkness was lit up with energy bolts and explosions as innumerable celestial dog fights took place. The squadrons met each other in a no man's land where they were out of the range of the other side's heavy guns. Here, the first important victory in this battle would be decided.

The fighters streaked back and forth across the sky. Toth watched with interest as the Kemmar pilots displayed their fighting prowess. The Kemmar were a warrior race. They lived for battle. Admiral Gurzail was foolish not to take his offer. The Otan were simply outclassed. As the battle progressed it started to show. It became clear that the Kemmar possessed the more advanced fighters. The Kemmar kills were adding up and the Otan fighters were slowly finding themselves losing ground. With the Kemmar fighters starting to dominate the engagement, Toth ordered a squadron of destroyers to move in. The Otan countered with their own squadron, blocking the Kemmar advance. The two destroyer groups engaged each other with energy weapons and missiles. While they weren't as fast and agile as the fighters, they still had some maneuverability, but moved together in tight battle formations.

Toth sent in the remaining destroyer squadrons, trying to overwhelm the Otan. Gurzail impressed him by keeping up and countering his moves with his own squadrons. A broad line of battle took shape between to two groups of destroyers. Whenever one side tried to gain an advantage, the other countered the move. The back and forth between the two continued, while the Kemmar fighters easily outclassed and destroyed the Otan fighters.

A squadron of Kemmar heavy cruisers entered the fray to support the destroyers. They tried to outflank the Otan squadrons, but the Otan Admiral was still up to the task and moved a squadron of his own cruisers to intercept. The Admiral's abilities continued to impress Toth. He fought defensively, which compensated somewhat for the weaker nature of his force, but it would not be enough. The Kemmar fleet was superior in ability, and in numbers. The outcome of the battle was never in doubt.

As the battle wore on the Kemmar fighters really started to show their superiority, enjoying a two to one advantage against the Otan fighters. That advantage allowed some of the fighters to support the larger cruisers and destroyers. In an attempt to even things out the Otan deployed their battleships. Toth bared his teeth and ordered his own battleships to engage. The battle would now be fought in earnest as the hulking warships squared off against each other and traded blows. The battleships on each side were evenly matched and both sides took damage as the giant vessels pounded each other.

The earlier fighter battle proved to be the deciding factor, as Toth had expected. The Otan fighters had now been virtually wiped out which freed up all the Kemmar fighters to assist the heavier Kemmar squadrons. One by one the Otan destroyers and cruisers were destroyed. With each lost ship the Kemmar advantage grew greater and the Otan became increasingly outnumbered. As the battle wore on destroyers and heavy cruisers were able to offer their assistance against the Otan battleships. With the Otan battleships weakening under the weight of the Kemmar attack, the Kemmar fighters hastened their demise with suicide attacks. Each fighter that got through the Otan defenses punched a hole in their target's hull. The hull breaches compounded, crippling the Otan battleships until one by one each ship fell off the battlefield in blinding explosions.

With the battle all but over Toth opened a communication with the Grand Sovereign.

"It is done, Eminence. The Otan fleet has been defeated."

"Excellent, High Lord Toth. You will take your force to the capitol and remove the Otan rulers. You will then secure Otan space," said Grand Sovereign Tsogt.

"Yes, Eminence."

"While you are doing so, you will dispatch scout ships to their far border and amass as much intelligence as you can on their neighbors. These humans. I want to know everything about them, their worlds, and their defenses."

"Understood, Eminence. May I ask the goal of this information?"

"Invasion."

# Thanks for Reading!

If you enjoyed the book please consider leaving a review at Amazon

To join my email list and be notified of new releases go to **http://gphudson.com**

# Also By G.P. Hudson

**Sol Shall Rise – Book 1 of The Pike Chronicles**

**Prevail – Book 2 of The Pike Chronicles**

**Ronin – Book 3 of The Pike Chronicles**

**Ghost Fleet – Book 4 of The Pike Chronicles**

**Interstellar War – Book 5 of The Pike Chronicles**

**Vanquish – Book 6 of The Pike Chronicles**

**Galactic Empire – Book 7 of The Pike Chronicles**

Printed in Great Britain
by Amazon